C000150315

Sleepless in Saunton Paperback Edition
Copyright © 2023 by Nina Jarrett. All rights reserved.
Published by Rogue Press
Editing by Katie Jackson

All rights reserved. No part of this book may be used or reproduced in any form by any means—except in the case of brief quotations embodied in critical articles or reviews—without written permission.

This is a work of fiction. Names, characters, places, and incidents are products of the author's imagination or are used fictitiously and are not to be construed as real. Any resemblance to actual events, locales, organizations, or persons, living or dead, is entirely coincidental.

This e-book is licensed for your personal enjoyment only. This e-book may not be re-sold or given away to other people. If you would like to share this book with another person, please purchase an additional copy for each reader. If you are reading this book and did not purchase it, or it was not purchased for your use only, please return to your favorite retailer and purchase your own copy. Thank you for respecting the hard work of the author.

For more information, contact author Nina Jarrett. www.ninajarrett.com

SLEEPLESS IN SAUNTON

INCONVENIENT BRIDES
BOOK FOUR

NINA JARRETT

ROGUE
PRESS

To my family.

For being able to count on you, no matter how dark or late the hour.

I love you all.

PROLOGUE

*B*arclay descended the stairs, sliding his hand over the banister, the muscles in his back protesting his movement. It had been a long journey from one of their minor Yorkshire building sites, and even a night stretched out in his own bed had not eased the stiffness brought on by too many hours in the carriage over the past days.

As his foot hit the bottom stair, he looked up to find an unknown gentleman staring at him from the doorway of his grandfather's study. His grandfather, Tsar, stood behind the man's shoulder.

Noticing his descent, Tsar called out, "Barclay, there you are! I just sent Robins to find you. Join us for coffee?"

Barclay frowned. Was the gentleman a prospective client? He certainly looked moneyed in his black Hessians, expensive buckskins, snowy cravat, and perfectly tailored wool tailcoat. His sable curls were artfully cut and his face clean-shaven.

But they rarely met clients in the family home. And something about how the visitor's emerald green eyes followed him was unnerving. Barclay sensed this was not a typical client meeting.

He entered the study in their wake and took a seat in a leather armchair beside their unknown guest, who fidgeted nervously with his cravat. Barclay's unease mounted.

"Allow me to make introductions. This is Lord Richard Balfour, the Earl of Saunton."

Barclay was startled. He made to rise to his feet to bow. "My lord—"

"Please, it is unnecessary, Mr. Thompson. I am quite embarrassed about this situation, so we shall not observe formalities."

Barclay raised a hand to run it through his hair, puzzled about what was happening. He shot a glance at his grandfather, who looked away. Barclay's own anxiety increased.

Thomas Thompson, better known as Tsar, was a renowned architect now in his mid-seventies. He had apprenticed and worked with Robert Adams himself in his youth, before being discharged along with three thousand other workers because of the failing *Adelphi* project in 1772. With a young Italian wife, whom he had met on his Grand Tour, and a two-year-old daughter to provide for, Tsar had risked everything to begin his own firm.

He had quickly built his name and reputation with grand Palladian designs, designing country homes for the wealthy over the subsequent decades.

Known as Tsar because of his commitment to purchasing quality timber and supplies from the Baltics and St. Petersburg, he was famous for his relationships with merchants from that region. Timber had become highly priced over the past decade or two because of heavy taxation during the troubles with France, but everyone knew that timber from

2

Northern America was inferior due to the extended sea journey, often arriving with dry rot set in. Tsar was unwilling to compromise.

If one wanted to conduct business in St. Petersburg, one called upon Tsar, well known to be a determined man of ideals and fierce loyalties. A man of integrity. He had taken part in thousands of negotiations with clients and suppliers over the decades, and he never looked nervous.

Of course, today proved that the observation was inaccurate. Tsar fiddled nervously with papers on his desk while no one spoke. Eventually, the gentleman to Barclay's left broke the awkward silence by clearing his throat.

"If I may explain?"

His grandfather grunted a bashful consent, his cheeks growing suspiciously red.

What on earth is going on?

"This is a rather indelicate subject to discuss, so I shall be blunt." Despite the announcement, Lord Saunton hesitated. He stared down at his hands folded on his lap.

Barclay did not like to express emotion in public. He was a man of restraint, except with his close family, whom he adored, but even he could not maintain his patience any longer. He frowned, then demanded, "What is this?"

His lordship took a deep breath. "I have recently discovered through extensive investigation that you and I are brothers ... well ... half-brothers. A fact that your grandfather has just confirmed this morning."

Barclay's jaw dropped. After several heart-pounding moments, he turned to Tsar. "The late Earl of Saunton was my father?"

Tsar kept his eyes lowered, dropping his head in a curt nod.

"You and Mother informed me my father was an officer in the Royal Navy, lost at sea before they wed!"

3

"It was … easier. It was what your mother desired," he mumbled.

Aurora Thompson! He was going to have words with his mother when he saw her next. She and Tsar had lied to him. He was a man in his early thirties, discovering his parentage for the first time. He felt like a callow youth discussing this subject in front of a stranger, with his shock and outrage on display.

Nay, not a stranger, but a brother!

He attempted to gather his wits, but could not make sense of what was unfolding. "Grandfather, I have always appreciated that you did the right thing by my mother and me—standing by her when she … but this is … Why did you lie about who my father was?"

Lord Saunton coughed quietly into his fist. "I believe, if you think on it, that the idea of an officer lost at sea with a wedding planned was a more romantic notion for a young lad than …" The earl pulled at the knot of his cravat in agitation before finishing. "Than … the Earl of Satan seduced the young daughter of his architect and abandoned her to her fate."

"Satan?"

Wincing, Lord Saunton's face gradually turned red while he struggled to respond. "Rest assured, your ignorance of my —our—hedonistic father is a blessing. Now that I am the head of the Balfour family, it is my responsibility to acknowledge our connection and ensure you receive the benefits of our relationship … brother."

Barclay's thoughts were swimming, and his customary composure was nowhere to be found. He straightened, ready to spring to his feet. "I do not want it!"

"Barclay." His grandfather spoke quietly, but firmly. Barclay had always trusted and respected Tsar, so, despite his struggle, he could not rise and stride away.

Reluctantly, Barclay paused before settling back into his chair, his hands resting on his knees while he drew a calming breath. "Yes, Grandfather?"

"Barclay, these many years your mother has struggled with the burden of being unwed. My reputation has assisted her to maintain some relationships, but she is not accepted in general society. One day, my great-granddaughter ... Tatiana will struggle with the burden that her father is a by-blow. When I am gone in the not-too-distant future, none of you will enjoy the benefit of my protection any longer. Lord Saunton's offer to acknowledge the connection will elevate you from a by-blow to the son and brother of an earl. It will open doors for you, as well as for your daughter and mother ... All this will provide me with the solace I sorely need." Tsar ran his fingers through his short, curling gray hair in a gesture reminiscent of Barclay's own a few moments earlier. His rounded face was creased in concern when he continued. "I ... often worry about what will happen to my family when my reputation and relationships from fifty years of professional excellence are no longer available to all of you to facilitate your social and professional interactions."

Barclay hung his head, closing his eyes while he thought. "I am an excellent architect in my own right. My awards attest to that."

"I will not deny that, but you have yet a decade of work, which simply does not compare to my five decades. You must acknowledge that, as a by-blow of an unknown officer, you will encounter difficulty when I am no longer here to lend you my support. Lord Saunton can make that difficulty disappear, which will benefit our womenfolk. Society is much harder on them than it is on men."

Barclay leaned his head back in the chair to stare at the ceiling, swallowing hard while his thoughts raced.

The earl sat forward on the edge of his chair to speak in

earnest. "Mr. Thompson, it would be my great pleasure to acknowledge you publicly and unite our families. You will gain two brothers, along with extended family, for your mother and daughter. My—our—cousin is the Duke of Halmesbury. He and his duchess are certain to sponsor Tatiana in society when that time comes. Even now, we can open doors for your mother."

Barclay wanted to walk out of the room, but reflecting on the advantages to both his mother and Tatiana, he realized that would be the immature act of an excessively proud man. *A duke?* And not just any duke, but the much-lauded Duke of Halmesbury? Only a fool would reject such a prestigious connection.

He might tolerate the challenges he faced as a bastard, but if that burden could be lifted for Tatiana … If his late wife were still with them, she would place her much smaller hand gently over his and counsel him to accept this offer.

His heart squeezed at the thought of Natalya and the words she would have said if she had been here to say them, but it had been two lonely years since she had died. Tatiana no longer had a mother, and he no longer had a wife, yet now his young daughter would gain uncles, aunts, and cousins in the peerage.

He swept a trembling hand through his hair, leaning forward to place his elbows on his knees before mumbling to his boots, "What does this entail, Lord Saunton?"

"Please … Barclay … we are brothers—blood. If our father had done right by your mother, even now you would be the earl, instead of myself. My family address me as Richard."

Barclay sighed. "What does this entail … Richard?"

CHAPTER 1

*J*ane Davis stood at the window, watching the guests arriving. The Earl of Saunton was hosting a grand house party at his Somerset country seat, and many of the guests were young gentlemen earmarked to meet Jane. Despite the impending festivities, she was feeling rather melancholy as she observed the hive of servants, guests, carriages, and trunks.

"I cannot believe you are married and leaving us."

Her older sister, Emma, came to stand next to her by the window. "You encouraged me to accept him."

Jane sniffed. "I merely informed you that Peregrine Balfour was your Darcy."

"How strange that I am now married to the brother of the earl. You should have been there when Perry and his friends serenaded me. I shall never forget his proposal as long as I live."

"Perry truly sings that poorly?"

Emma smiled lovingly, looking down on her groom who was assisting the earl to greet his guests. Perry and Emma had been married a few days earlier and were eager to leave for their new home. Shepton Abbey was a fine country estate, and her sister was elated to assist with managing it. "He promised to never sing again."

Jane huffed a quick laugh. "To think our entire family was there to witness it except for me."

"And Ethan."

Jane nodded. "And Ethan."

The Davis family was connected to the earl in an unusual manner. A few years earlier, during the time the earl had been a notorious rake, he had dallied with their cousin, Kitty, who had been in service.

Kitty, being with child as a consequence, had retreated to the Davises' tenant farm where she had died in childbirth and left Ethan in their care. No one had known who his father was until the earl had begun a crusade to make amends for his past earlier this year and unexpectedly learned about Ethan. Lord Richard Balfour had claimed his four-year-old son, gifting their father with a small country estate in gratitude for taking care of his first child.

A few weeks earlier, wanting Emma's assistance with settling Ethan into his new household, the earl had invited Emma and Jane for a Season in London. Perry had acted as their tutor to prepare them for entry into high society, but Emma and he had quickly fallen in love.

Both of their families had just gathered at Saunton Park for the wedding in the chapel a few days earlier, before bidding the Davis family farewell when they had returned to nearby Rose Ash to make room for arriving guests.

Perry and Emma had delayed their own departure for Shepton Abbey because Perry was to meet a very important guest who was arriving today—a brother who had just been discovered by the earl.

Jane was grateful for the additional time with Emma. Her sister was one year older than her own eighteen years, but infinitely wiser. A bluestocking who had raised Ethan. And now she was leaving. Embarking on a new adventure while Jane tried to sort through her thoughts of what she wanted from her own life.

"Have you thought about what we talked about?" It was as if Emma was reading her thoughts out loud.

Jane drew a deep breath. "I do not know what I want my future to hold. If you were anyone else, you would accept my first answer. That a young landowner would likely suffice."

"The husband you choose will greatly influence your future. Please assure me you will not follow society's dictates on what a successful match consists of and that you will think on what your own desires are."

"How will I know when I meet the right man?"

Emma sighed. "You must know your own heart, your own dreams. Then you will know if the gentleman will make the appropriate partner."

"I have no dreams beyond a happy family with lots of children."

Emma snorted. "One moment I am impressed with your maturity and the next you sound like a silly child once more."

"Why?"

"You answer my question as if you have no thoughts of your own. You like to write. Your prospective husband should support that. Not so many years ago you spoke of traveling, of seeing the length and breadth of our fine kingdom, and perhaps voyaging to parts of the Continent. You appreciate fashion plates, and family, and you wish to have children. And you plan to spend time with your children and not relegate them to a nursery as some of those fops plan to do." Emma waved her hand at the arriving guests below.

"Hmm … you make it sound as if I have a mind of my own."

Emma tilted her head back to look up at her with thoughtful coal-black eyes. Jane's sister might be older than her, but she was diminutive in stature. "You do! I have seen many gentlemen gravitate towards you, but you have not yet shown interest in any of them."

"They seem so dull. I am looking for a gent who engages my mind, as you have with your Perry."

Her sister beamed. "Excellent. Keep that in mind and you should be fine."

Jane yawned, shaking her head to invigorate her thoughts.

"You still do not sleep?"

"I am just too excited. Just think, the next time we meet, it could be for my own wedding. How can one sleep with so much to consider?"

Emma frowned. "I wish you would see the earl's physician to discuss what might be causing you to stay awake all night."

Jane shrugged. "I am young and in good health. It is the excitement of this unexpected Season."

"If it persists, will you at least consult a herbalist? There should be one nearby."

Jane bent forward to embrace her sister. "I shall be lost without you. You are my dearest friend."

"I shall miss you so much, Jane!"

"Nonsense! You have a handsome husband and a new estate to manage. You will barely think of me while I am left bereft to meet all these strangers."

They both turned to the window once more. Another carriage had arrived, and Jane watched as an intriguing man descended from its depths.

He was tall, the same height as the earl, who hurried over

to greet him, but he appeared taller because he was so slim. There was not an ounce of extra flesh anywhere on his form. A very fine form at that, with shining black Hessians covering his lower legs, buckskins stretched over long, muscular thighs, and a black tailcoat draped over wide shoulders and a lean torso. The coat was in an unusual choice of color but suited his black waves of hair, which he wore a little too long. He had a close-cropped beard and a strong, narrow face.

Jane found her attention riveted by the sense of energy and purpose he exuded, wondering who he was as he thrust out a large hand to greet the earl. Was this one of the gents whom Richard intended for her to meet?

A pang of disappointment followed when the man turned to assist an elegant woman from the carriage. Her jet-black hair and olive skin suggested an Italian or Spanish heritage. This must be his wife. As if to confirm her assumption, he reached into the carriage and turned back with a little girl in his arms. The only oddity was that the child had thick, silver-blonde hair. Perhaps this was a child from an earlier marriage?

Jane yawned again and turned away from the window. Walking across the room, she leaned over and breathed deeply of the coffee aroma wafting from the tray. Taking a seat, she poured a cup, adding cream and sugar before settling back to drink.

Emma came over and joined her, pouring a cup of tea. "I cannot believe that you have taken up drinking that foul beverage, Jane. I do not know why Perry agreed to let you try it."

"It awakens me, especially when I have not slept until the early hours."

Emma rolled her eyes. "I still think it is a mistake. Not least because it is noxious."

Jane did not comment. Draining her cup, she put it down and crossed the room to pick up the gift she had made for her sister. "I wanted to give you this ... for your new life at Shepton Abbey."

"What is it?"

"Some needlework to celebrate your nuptials."

Emma came over, and Jane handed her the embroidered cloth. Her sister stretched it out, gasping in surprise. "Jane! It is beautiful. I swear you are a veritable artiste with the floss! When did you find time to do it?"

Jane smiled. "I am not sleeping, Emma. I have plenty of time on my hands."

They both gazed at the embroidered scene. It depicted a towering oak tree surrounded by a field of colorful wild-flowers—wildflower was a private sobriquet she had over-heard Perry calling her sister since their wedding ceremony. "May your marriage grow strong while allowing you the freedom to follow your own way, sister."

Emma reached over to embrace her sister once more. "Thank you."

* * *

Barclay tilted his head back to view the grand Palladian manor that Tsar had completed building in early 1787, glimpsing two women standing at a window in what would be the family block to the left of the main house.

The house had been completed the year Barclay was conceived, when a seventeen-year-old Aurora Thompson had been seduced by the then-owner, the late Earl of Saunton.

Or Satan, as the current earl had referred to our sire.

A rusticated lower level was crowned by a towering upper level which was perfectly cut, symmetrical planes soaring up into the deep blue vaults of the Somerset sky. The many windowpanes reflected the bucolic lawns and oak trees spreading out to where the earth and firmament met, a marriage of the solid and the ethereal.

High above them, classically inspired statues stood as silent sentinels, while twin majestic staircases converged on a landing in front of the Corinthian columns beneath their feet. It was one of Tsar's finest works, a testament to his talent, but until this day Barclay had only seen it in his grandfather's architectural plans.

His newly discovered brother, Richard, had walked away to fetch someone for Barclay to meet while he gazed up with fascination at the monumental facade. This building was the legacy Tsar would leave behind, and his grandfather's creation impressed Barclay.

Tatiana gazed up with him. "Grandpapa built this?"

"He did. Or rather he designed it, and then supervised the master builder who built it over the next fifteen years."

"It is beautiful," she said reverently.

Barclay smiled down at his daughter, her small hand clasped in his. "As are you."

At that moment, a servant approached them. Barclay assumed it was the butler, based on his rigid decorum and immaculate attire.

"Mr. Thompson, one of the maids will escort your daughter to the nursery."

Barclay narrowed his eyes. "Nursery?"

The ginger-haired servant straightened up, looking down his hawkish nose with the utmost dignity. "Indeed, sir. The nursery."

Barclay's lips thinned as he thought. The Thompson family was inseparable, and Tatiana had never been sequestered on a different floor, with only servants to interact with. Not only that, but his nine-year-old child had struggled with night terrors since her mother died and he frequently attended her at night. When he was traveling, his mother took his place in comforting her.

Barclay shot a perturbed look at Aurora, who held up her hands in question. They had failed to think about what the arrangements for his young daughter would be at such a country house, but Barclay should have predicted these circumstances as a man who drew plans of these homes for the wealthy. However, he personally had never subscribed to the notion that children should be kept separate from the family.

He frowned. Agreeing to attend the house party was a mistake. He should have insisted he remain in London. Now Tsar was handling his work for him, which was more than the old man should deal with, and his daughter was peering up in fright at the servant.

"Papa?" Her voice quavered.

"It will not do."

The butler tensed, clearly uncertain how to respond. "Sir, I assure you that the nursery is well-attended and there are several children already arrived. We set aside a place of honor for your daughter—"

"It will not do." Barclay ensured his voice was firm but low. He did not want to alarm Tatiana any more than she was already. "Do not worry, Tatiana. We will return home if we must."

From the corner of his eye, he saw the earl rushing over. His new brother must have noticed the stiffness of the inter-action, as he appeared mildly alarmed.

"Is there an issue?"

"Your butler wishes to remove my daughter to the attics, like some sort of prisoner. I know how the peerage treat their children, and it will not be tolerated in the Thompson family."

Richard bit his lip. "Barclay, I assure you we are not a traditional family. My son, Ethan, joins me for breakfast each morning before we ride together. Then he goes to the lovely and well-equipped nursery for lessons and whatnot before coming back downstairs for family time."

Barclay straightened to his full height, satisfied to discover he was a good inch taller than his younger brother. "I thought you married earlier this year?"

"Yes, that is correct."

"You are a young man. The countess must be your first wife?"

Richard's expression reflected strain. "Yes."

His new brother was turning out to be no better than his debauched sire, who had ruined his mother. Barclay struck without sympathy. "How do you have a son old enough to breakfast with you?"

"An astute question," a velvet voice drawled from behind his shoulder, but Barclay did not react. He merely listened while firming his jaw to glare at the earl. "I thought the entire kingdom knew my brother had sired a son on the wrong side of the blanket."

Barclay narrowed his eyes into an accusing stare. The earl fidgeted uncomfortably with his cravat, a telling gesture. "It is not what you think. I did not know about Ethan … I mean …"

"Calm yourself, brother." The voice moved as a man stepped around into Barclay's view to reveal the earl's apparent twin, who bowed. "Good afternoon, Barclay. I am Peregrine Balfour. Your younger brother." The gentleman's sable locks, square jaw, and emerald eyes were a mirror of his older brother's. "I assure you that my brother claimed Ethan as his own the moment he learned of him. Subsequently, he posed that perhaps our father had sired children we did not know of and set his men to finding you. There is little resemblance between him and the late Earl of Satan."

Barclay sized up the newcomer carefully. "You just married?"

Peregrine inclined his head in acknowledgment. "I did. I married Ethan's cousin, Emma Davis. The entire Davis family has just departed for their estate, which my brother gifted them. As I said—no resemblance. My brother is a good man with a notorious past, which he has taken pains to set right."

Richard closed his eyes. When he reopened them, he appeared more composed, his cravat only slightly crumpled. "I apologize for not explaining the circumstances before your visit. It was difficult to inform you, considering your circumstances. I had hoped to discuss it in my study before Ethan came down to play chess with the family this afternoon."

Barclay sighed in capitulation, relaxing his stance. "I appreciate that this is an awkward situation we find ourselves in. However, my daughter is accustomed to being close to her family."

The men turned to acknowledge Aurora, who had joined them and appeared disconcerted by the two brothers, her eyes darting from one to the other. Barclay wondered if they resembled the late Earl of Satan in their coloring, their features and height being similar to his own. Was it a strain for her to return to the site of her social ruin after these many years?

Stepping forward, the earl took up her hand, bowing solemnly. "Miss Thompson, it is our great pleasure to host you. Please allow me to introduce my brother, Peregrine Balfour." Perry stepped forward, bowing deeply.

Barclay's mother responded with a dignified curtsy. "My lord. The pleasure is mine, I assure you." Then she moved her head to the side to pout at Tatiana, who giggled in response, hiding behind Barclay.

"I am afraid both the family wing and the guest wing are fully occupied. There are no rooms left for Tatiana."

She smiled graciously. "Then Tatiana will sleep in my room. In the guest wing."

Richard's tension visibly eased. "If that is acceptable ..." He glanced at Barclay for confirmation, who inclined his head. "... then we shall have a cot brought to your room. But, Miss Thompson, we have situated you and Barclay in the family wing."

Barclay's mother was a woman well accustomed to keeping her composure under trying circumstances. She had been forced to acquire the skill when she had kept her natural-born son despite society's censure of her as an unwed mother. At the news she was to stay in the family wing of Saunton Park as an honored relation of the earl, Aurora threw a hand over her mouth in consternation. "My lord ... that is not necessary."

To Barclay's ear, it sounded like his mother might be overcome with emotion, her words quavering and tight. Was she fighting back tears?

The earl bowed deeply. "I assure you ... it is long over-due." Then he turned to drop a bow to Tatiana, who was peeking around Barclay's elbow at the scene. "Welcome, Miss Tatiana. It will be the great honor of the Balfour family to host you in our family rooms."

Tatiana blinked her big blue eyes, then stepped forward to curtsy, craning her neck up to address the tall nobleman. "Thank you, milord."

Richard delivered an exaggerated wink. "I am your Uncle Richard." The earl glanced over to Barclay, as if seeking permission to continue. Barclay gave a brief nod, and

Richard turned back to Tatiana. "Here, come meet your Uncle Perry."

As Barclay observed the introductions, he wondered what more surprises lay in store for him on this unanticipated jaunt to the country.

CHAPTER 2

*E*mma and Jane spent their final hours together while Perry and Richard were somewhere in the manor acquainting themselves with their new brother. Finally, Jane bid her sister and Perry a tearful farewell, before watching their carriages depart for Shepton Abbey. It was late afternoon, and the manor cast long shadows across the drive as the carriages disappeared around a corner.

Turning back to the house, Jane addressed the earl's wife. "Sophia, I think I shall retire to my room to eat dinner. I did not sleep, and I rose early to spend these last hours with Emma."

The countess walked over to clasp her hands with concern. "Of course, Jane. There is no pressing need to attend dinner this evening. Our guests are still arriving, so I believe it will be an informal gathering and you can meet Mr. Thompson and his family in the morning. Should we send for the physician?"

Jane shook her head. "It is nothing that a nap will not set right."

Sophia's stormy blue eyes displayed her worry. "Please do not hesitate to have us summon him."

Jane smiled in acknowledgment before departing for the family wing. Soon she was undressed and attired in her nightclothes, settling her weary head to the pillow.

Some hours later, she awoke. Night had fallen, and the room was dark. Rising from the bed, she lit a beeswax candle before walking over to the dressing table. She uncapped her dental elixir to pour into a glass before adding water from a pitcher. Then she raised it to her lips to take a mouthful, which she swished around before leaning over to spit it into an empty pitcher.

"What are you doing?"

Jane jumped in fright, spilling several drops of the watered-down elixir over the table, but managing to hold on to the remainder of the contents. Her hand came up to clutch her chest, where her heart beat like that of a panicked rabbit while she gasped for breath. Turning around, she saw a tiny form in the corner of her room. The figure stood up to move into the light, and Jane saw the little girl from earlier, her silver-blonde hair shining like rays of moonlight in the dimly lit room.

"Hallo?"

The girl's cherubic face broke into a smile. "Hallo."

"Are you lost?"

Her little face grew thoughtful. "No, but I am a little bored. I am not accustomed to traveling anymore, and I believe I should have brought more books with me."

Jane fumbled mentally. She was familiar with dealing with children, and this girl appeared to be about the same age as her youngest sister, little Maddie, but she was groggy from her nap and not sure how the child had come to be in her room.

"What were you doing?" The girl pointed a slender finger

at the bottle of elixir and the water glass standing on the table. "Why did you spit that out? Did it not taste good?"

Jane gathered her wits about her. "It is a dental elixir that the countess's French maid prepared for me. It is not intended for drinking."

"What is it for?"

"It cleans the mouth. I had sensitive gums recently, so Miss Toussaint made the elixir for me. You swirl it around in your mouth, then spit it out."

"Curious." The waif wandered closer to inspect the glass, diminutive compared to the height of the dressing table. "What is in it?"

"Pyrethrum, some rosemary essence, nutmeg, a little bergamot, and some very strong brandy. Which is why I water it down before I use it."

"What is pyrethrum?"

"It is a daisy."

The girl reached out and took up the glass, raising it to her nose to sniff it. "It smells good and foul at the same time."

Jane grinned. "Indeed."

The girl tilted her head back, her deep blue gaze so intense that Jane unintentionally stepped back. "May I try it? My gums have been bothering me." She stretched her mouth open to reveal pearly white teeth. The front two were missing to give her a gap-toothed smile.

Jane found herself rather charmed by the child. She gave a nod. "If you promise not to swallow any?"

Raising the glass to her mouth, the girl took a mouthful to swirl it around for several seconds exactly as Jane had done, then turned to spit it into the empty pitcher. She straightened back up, smacking her lips. "It does taste foul!"

Laughing, Jane took the glass from her. "How are your gums?"

"They feel clean."

"Excellent." Putting the glass down, Jane dropped a little curtsy. "I am Miss Jane Davis. Who might you be?"

"Tatiana Thompson. The earl is my uncle." The last was said with reverent pride. Jane realized that the gentleman she had seen disembark from the carriage earlier that day must be the new brother of the earl.

Well, not new, per se. Just newly discovered.

"Then we are related … distantly. The earl's son is my cousin."

"Ethan?"

"That is correct."

"My papa grew quite stern when he heard about Ethan."

"Did he?"

"He did. I think he had an issue with how long the earl had been married."

Jane rubbed her face, not sure how to respond. "Um …"

"Is it because Ethan is a bastard? Like my papa?"

Jane could not prevent a grimace from flickering across her face. How did she wind up being the unfortunate party to address this question?

"I think it best you ask your papa about that."

"Is Ethan a bastard?"

Jane shook her head. "Ethan is a very nice boy. A true gentleman. It is true his mother and the earl were not wed, so he is natural born. But it is not polite to call someone a bastard."

"Why?"

Tucking a curl behind her ear, Jane dropped into the chair so she might be more of a height with the little girl. "Bastard is an impolite word. Ethan cannot help the circumstances of his birth. It is more polite to say natural born."

Tatiana contemplated her for several seconds. "Then the person who called Papa a bastard was being rude?"

"Yes, it is rude."

"I did not like the man. He was complaining to his companion the entire time he waited in the drawing room, and I thought he was not very nice. Or correct about his complaints."

"How did you know what a bastard is?"

"The man sort of explained it during his complaining. He did not know I was hiding behind the sofa. It was enlightening."

Jane chuckled. "It is not polite to eavesdrop."

"What is that?"

"It means to listen to another's conversation."

Tatiana shrugged. "What they do not know cannot offend them."

At this, Jane could not hold back a laugh. *From the mouth of babes.*

Tatiana stepped forward, placing a hand on Jane's cheek as she stared deep into her eyes. "I like you."

She smiled in response. "Thank you. I like you, too."

"You treat me like a person."

"Thank you. I have several younger brothers and a sister who just went home, so it is pleasant to talk with you in their stead."

"Will you marry my papa?"

Jane sputtered, turning her head to cough into her hand in her surprise. After several moments, she responded in a dry, hoarse voice, "Does your papa not have a wife?"

"No." Tatiana leaned closer so her face was just inches away from Jane's. "Mama died. I am sad, but I think it is worse for him. Papa is very lonely, and he does not smile like he did before. I think he needs a new wife."

"Well … that is a choice your father must make."

Tatiana's cherubic face fell in disappointment, her little lip quivering as she bit it. "You will not marry him?"

"Your father must decide when he is ready. And he must choose his own wife."

The little girl turned and walked away, standing in the shadows with her back turned. "I am worried about him."

Jane felt her eyes prickle with threatening tears. The child was so sweet, and her heart went out to the little one who had lost her mother so young. "How long has it been?"

The blonde hair bobbed as she inclined her head. Jane thought she might be counting on her fingers. "It is two years."

"That is a long time to be without a mama."

"I miss her."

Jane could not help it. A tear of sympathy escaped the corner of her eye at the little girl's plight. Reaching up, she brushed it away, and when she was ready, she spoke in a steady voice. "I am sorry, Tatiana. I cannot imagine how that must be."

"I miss Papa, too. We used to go with him to see his buildings, but since Mama died, he leaves me at home with Grandmama. I want to go with him, and have a mother to read me stories at night … and I want … I want to see him smile." The little girl's voice was thick as she stated the last. Jane hurried across the room. Dropping to her haunches, she embraced the little girl, burying her face in her sweet-smelling silver hair.

"I am sure when he is ready, your papa will find a wife."

Tatiana hugged her back. "I hope so."

They spoke for several more minutes before Jane escorted the girl back to her room down the hall. Knocking on the door quietly, she waited hand in hand with Tatiana until the door opened to reveal the black-haired beauty she had observed earlier that day. "Miss Thompson? I believe I have something of yours."

The woman was lively, and although she must have been

close to fifty to have a nine-year-old granddaughter, her olive face was barely lined. Her high cheekbones and flawless skin spoke to a Mediterranean heritage, while her thick black hair fell to her waist in a gleaming plait. She had risen from bed, her brown eyes bleary and unfocused until she caught sight of her granddaughter peeking from behind the skirts of Jane's wrap. She looked back in the room to the cot near the bed, as if expecting to see a replica of the girl lying there. Turning back, she wailed, "Tatiana! What are you doing out of bed?"

Jane noted a slight Mediterranean lilt to the older woman's voice. "She came to find me in my room."

Over the next few moments, they made their introductions. Jane led the child into the room, and then, with a nod of her head, gestured that she needed to speak out in the hall with the grandmother.

Miss Thompson understood her. After tucking Tatiana back into the cot, she followed Jane from the room and closed the door behind her. Jane told her of the conversation that they had had. When they parted ways, the grandmother had a look of worry on her face, but Jane felt better for meeting the woman, who appeared genuinely concerned about Tatiana's request. She was certain that the woman would address the matter.

Walking away as the door clicked shut behind her, Jane visited the library in search of a new book. She was wide awake in the middle of the night, and recent evenings had taught her it would be some hours before she fell asleep once more. With no sister left in residence, a good book was needed to keep her company.

* * *

BARCLAY SAT on the ledge of his bedroom window, staring up at the moon which cast a silver light across the landscape. He pondered what Natalya would say about this recent turn of events.

They had acquired a whole new family. An important earl, his various relations, and tonight, at dinner, he had met the Duke of Halmesbury and his duchess. The man had been imposing in stature, several inches taller than Barclay, who was himself six feet. But the big, blond Viking had a steady manner and calm gray eyes, and appeared genuinely honored to meet him.

After dinner, the earl and the duke had met with him in the study to converse—the younger brother with the smooth manners and even smoother tongue had departed earlier in the day with his new bride.

Once in the study, the duke had taken the time to explain their connection. The late earl, whom no one seemed to remember with any relish, was the younger brother of the duke's late mother. As Richard had stated, Barclay was indeed a first cousin to the duke, which was still a fact he was having difficulty assimilating.

If Natalya had been by his side tonight, she would have been so pleased on his behalf. His late wife had never been tolerant of anyone who socially snubbed the Thompsons because of Barclay's parentage and would have heartily approved of the earl's decision to find him and acknowledge him as kin. With that thought, his memories turned to his young wife.

When Barclay had been a much younger man, Tsar had sent him to negotiate new contracts with suppliers in St. Petersburg. He had stayed in one of the merchant's homes, an old friend of his grandfather, where he had met the merchant's youngest daughter, recently returned home from completing her schooling.

Natalya had immediately caught his attention, acting as an interpreter for him at social events around the city. Her silver hair, deep blue eyes, and pleasing manner had been fascinating to him, and his dishonorable parentage had been inconsequential to her. She only cared for him, and her father had approved of the match, considering it to be a great honor to unite families with Tsar despite the shadow cast by Aurora's unwed status.

Barclay's initial trip of one month had turned into three, and by the time he set foot on the ship that would take him home, his Russian beauty had been on his arm as his bride.

When Natalya had accepted his proposal and embarked on a new life in England, they had both known that their days together were numbered. She suffered from a weak heart, but she had refused to allow her condition to hold her back. She was determined to live life to its fullest, and Barclay was grateful for every moment he had shared with her on this earth.

When she had decided to have a child, which the doctors had cautioned her against, his wife could not be dissuaded. She wanted to leave a piece of herself behind.

"You must allow this, Barclay. One day I will no longer be here, and then you will be grateful to have our child to remember me by."

He had reluctantly agreed, and Natalya had bravely taken the journey of motherhood, taking every precaution to protect herself during that time. And she was proved right in her quest. She had survived the ordeal to bring Tatiana into the world and lived another six years as her mother. Long enough to see their daughter walk for the first time, learn to laugh, and grow from a tiny babe into a young girl.

Barclay could regret none of their time together, even more sweet because his beloved had fulfilled her dream of motherhood and been there to witness their daughter grow into a beautiful, tiny version of herself before Natalya's heart had taken its last beat and she had slipped away from them for the final time.

His wife would have been so pleased for him this evening. So happy that Aurora and Tatiana would gain a new level of social status with this recent development. She had believed in family, and honor, and would have admired the earl for searching him out and elevating their family.

He wished she were here to view this beautiful moonlit night with him. To discuss the events of the day and their arrival at this magnificent country home. To enjoy a story with Tatiana in the room next to his.

"Barclay, you did well, bringing our family here."

As he had so often done since her death, Barclay had summoned Natalya from his memories to stand at his side. "I knew it was what you would want."

She smiled, resting her delicate head against his shoulder. "You were right."

Barclay's heart squeezed tight. He knew this fantasy could only survive so much—he could not attempt to touch her, or his imagination would fail and his grief would return. He missed his wife so much, it was a physical pain. "Anything for you."

"But, my love, you promised me you would find a new wife. A new mother for Tatiana."

Barclay grimaced. Recently, every time he called Natalya from the recesses of his mind, she admonished him for not fulfilling his last promise to her. "I am not ready, Talie."

"It is ... *vremya* ..."—she searched for the English word, as she often had in the past—"time. It is time, Barclay. I have been gone two years now, and Tatiana needs a mother."

"I cannot, my love. I still hear your voice. I still turn to find you when I wake. I cannot ... replace you."

She smiled, tears dampening her silver lashes. "Not replace. Someone new. Someone different to provide you comfort. An English girl, perhaps, who does not care about your lack of a father. Who cares for you."

"Please, Natalya. I cannot."

Natalya frowned lightly, turning to place a hand on his chest as she always had when imparting advice. "You must let me go, Barclay. My child needs a mother. And you need a new partner."

"Talie—"

A knock at the door interrupted his thoughts. Shaking his head, he returned to the moment to cross the room as the memory of Natalya departed as quietly as it had arrived.

* * *

JANE SAT in a wingback chair in the far corner of the library, reading the book of poetry she had found on the shelves. Since arriving in the Balfour household, she had been struggling with insomnia, but had grown to enjoy the late hours when the household had retired to bed. It allowed her to read in peace.

She turned the page to her favorite sonnet, tracing a finger over the familiar words from the bard as she mouthed the words to herself.

In the distance, she heard footsteps approaching. Not sure who might be entering the library so late at night, she pulled her long legs onto the seat, adjusting her wrap to hide herself until she knew who interrupted her solitude.

"Why is it we need to converse in the library at this hour, Mother?" Jane shivered at the husky quality of the man's voice, her skin tingling in response to the pleasurable sound. Leaning around the wing of her chair, she stole a peek. It was him! Tatiana's father.

Jane realized she should announce her presence, but she found herself reluctant to do so. She wanted to enjoy listening to him for a few minutes more, but if she made herself known, they would have to make polite introductions. And, if she revealed herself, their first meeting would be in their nightclothes which did not seem an auspicious beginning.

"Barclay, it is important that Tatiana not overhear us. You know how she is. I thought if we talk here in the library, we will leave her undisturbed. The poor mite only just fell asleep." The honeyed, accented voice confirmed his mother was the companion who had followed him into the room.

The son gave a dry laugh, which skidded over Jane's scalp like warm honey. His tone had such a dark and unique timbre, which was thrilling to listen to. "Are you certain she was not faking?"

Miss Thompson responded pertly, "Quite certain. She already snuck out for the evening while I was asleep, but a charming young woman returned her to me."

It sounded like the pair had taken the seats near the entrance of the library. Jane considered rising to inform them of her presence, but she held back. Once again, she found her romantic nature stirred by the presence of the gentleman, and this was her chance to gain insight into him.

"What was so urgent we needed to meet at this late hour?"

"We need to discuss your future, Barclay. This house party represents an opportunity for you to move forward. Natalya has been gone for two years now, and you need to think about the future."

Barclay was quiet for several seconds before making a sound of dissension. "I do not wish to talk about Natalya. Or the future, for that matter."

"Barclay, I just want to help. You are not aware that Tatiana approached a stranger this evening and asked the young lady to be her new mother?"

"What?"

"You heard me correctly. She found a young woman in the family wing. Miss Davis is a distant relation to the earl, and Tatiana was quite taken with her because she proposed that Miss Davis marry you."

The gentleman paused before replying, "Why would she do that?"

"Tatiana is worried about you. Which is why I insist we need to discuss this situation ... for Tatiana's sake. It has been a long time since Natalya left us. It is time for you to pursue a new relationship. To start again."

The gentleman sighed, while Jane held her breath, awaiting his response. The daughter and the melancholy father captivated her attention. If only she knew how to help them.

"We will be fine."

Miss Thompson snorted. "Barclay, something must be missing from your lives if your daughter is proposing on your behalf to strangers. We must deal with this, son. Are you sleeping?"

"No, but who can sleep when the most beautiful woman in the world was stolen to the heavens by greedy angels, leaving us mere mortals behind to grieve?"

It was poignant, his love for his lost wife. Jane wished to comfort him in his sadness, and wished ... that a man could one day love her in that way.

"Son, your child needs a mother. And you need a wife. It is time to consider the future."

"How can I consider the future?"

There was silence. Then, "Do you think you could love again?"

Jane rested her chin on her knees, scarcely breathing in her anticipation of what he might say.

"That seems an impossibility."

"Then what will you do?"

"I will … continue. I will rise in the morning and go about my day. I will spend time with Tatiana and then return to bed in the evening and remember my dear wife until …"

"Until?"

"Until one day I wake up and this terrible sense of loss has faded, and I can forget how wonderful it was when we were a family. When my silver faerie was at my side … and my child had a mother."

In the silence that followed, Jane could swear she could hear the gentleman's heart cracking in two. The discussion had become so intimate, she knew there was no possibility of informing the two that she was in the room with them. She had the urge to hold her breath lest they hear her taking air in the deep silence. It would be mortifying to be discovered now.

If she were older, more worldly, had something to offer him … she would … do something about it. Offer him solace?

But what could a young girl such as her, with no life experience, offer a single father in his thirties with a dead wife haunting his steps? Jane had never felt so helpless. She would be an immature flibbertigibbet compared to this weary gentleman.

His mother interrupted the gloom that had descended on the conversation. "I appreciate you loved Natalya with all your heart, but you understand this cannot continue?"

There was a long pause. Finally, he responded, "I … know."

"So you will make an effort to meet some women at this house party? Ask the earl and his countess to make introductions to eligible women?"

"I … suppose … I must … for Tatiana's sake."

CHAPTER 3

*B*arclay had grown weary of the house party, and it was only the second day. Tatiana and Aurora were having tea with the countess in the family drawing room, but he was unaccustomed to idle days. Idle house-guests made it even worse, drawing him into annoying discussions.

After escaping an inane conversation with a spoilt young beau who had introduced himself as Lord Julius Trafford, Barclay sought the library. Surely anyone he encountered in that venerated room would be inclined to be more intelligent than the pontificating fool, along with his insipid poetry, whom he had just left behind in the billiard room?

Barclay relaxed as he entered the room of shelves and books, even considering shutting the door behind him when … when he saw her.

The earl's son, Ethan, was playing chess. Barclay had met the lad the afternoon before when he had been bullied into his own match with the boy, whose current companion distracted Barclay.

She was utterly glorious. A mane of ebony curls poised on

her elegant head, smooth creamy skin to draw his eye, and long limbs. Long, long limbs.

The young woman finished her move and then sat back in her chair, her ice-blue eyes flickering over to notice him standing at the door. She blinked in surprise, gazing at Barclay intently as she nervously tucked a lock of silky hair behind her ear. It was a magical moment, intensity sparking between them in visceral awareness. Something he had not experienced since the first time he had laid eyes on Natalya upon his arrival in St. Petersburg.

The profound connection was abruptly severed when Ethan spoke to her from across the table. Barclay resumed his breathing, blinking several times as the room came back into focus.

"Uncle *Bar-clee*!" The little boy had just noticed his presence, hopping off his chair, careful not to disturb the board, before racing over. He lifted his arms, and Barclay realized the boy wanted him to lift him. He bent over to scoop the boy up, who embraced him in a hug. "Are you here to play chess with me? I am in the middle of a game at the moment, so you will have to wait a bit."

Barclay chuckled. The boy was unbearably sweet, only four or five years old, but Richard had informed him that the lad had grown up with a large, exuberant family, so he was in his element to have new relations in residence. "I suppose I might wait my turn. Who is your lovely opponent?"

Ethan wriggled out of his arms as Barclay gently lowered him, racing back across the room. "Miss Jane Davis, may I present my Uncle *Bar-clee* Tom … Tom's son …" The boy's face fell at his failed attempt to formally introduce him.

"Thompson."

Ethan tried again. "May I present my Uncle *Bar-clee Tom-son*?"

The lovely creature he addressed stood up and politely

curtsied. "Good afternoon, Mr. Thompson. I am glad we finally meet."

This was the woman his daughter had proposed to? She was heavenly. Barclay bowed deeply, deeper than he intended. Blazes, was he nervous about meeting the young woman?

"The pleasure is mine, Miss Davis."

She laughed, the sound harmonious, like the ringing of one of the perfectly pitched bells his firm had recently arranged to be hung in a church tower up in Yorkshire.

"Please, we are all extended family of a sort, so there is no need for formalities." She frowned slightly, as if that statement made her uncomfortable, before elucidating. "That is, you are Ethan's uncle on his father's side of the family, and I am his cousin on his mother's side."

Barclay quirked an eyebrow. Was Miss Davis elaborating that they were not blood relations? "Of course, we are more directly related because my sister married your half-brother, Perry." Her face fell at this announcement before she finished her thoughts in defeat. "You may call me Jane."

Barclay was having trouble focusing on her words, fascinated by her glowing countenance. He managed to bob his head in a brief bow. "Please call me Barclay ... Jane."

They stared at each other, wordless, until Ethan broke the crackling tension. "Will you wait for me to finish my game, Uncle *Bar-clee*?"

He nodded, following them back to the game they had set up. He took a seat to observe them play, using the opportunity to run his eyes over the fascinating woman. She was beautiful. Her eyes were framed by sooty black lashes, and she was taller than most women, a mere hand shorter than him. Willowy and graceful, she fueled his overpowering desire to sweep her into his arms in a waltz. His eyes fell to her bow-shaped mouth, which was when he realized he was in trouble. He might not have noticed a single woman other than his own wife in ten years, but now he found himself entranced by a young girl who could be no more than eighteen, considering she had not the faintest line on her flawless skin.

She is too young, Barclay. You cannot possibly be thinking there is a possibility of courtship!

He closed his eyes as Jane moved a piece across the board, collecting his wits. When he opened them once more, he focused on the board and the strategy his young nephew was employing. He looked up to find Jane watching him, but her eyes quickly skittered away. It would appear she was just as aware of him, of the frisson of excitement that her presence evoked.

This is horribly inappropriate, Barclay. You need a mature woman who can be a mother for your daughter. Are you your father's son to have your head turned by a woman who has not yet reached her majority?

He shivered in repulsion. Jane could not be more than a year or two older than his own mother when she had been seduced by his lecherous sire. He needed to seek an appropriate woman of … appropriate years, not have his head turned by a young girl.

Yet … there was something about her. A spark of magic.

It is not magic; it is lust! Latent hereditary impulses.

On the other hand, she seemed just as enamored as he was.

Fantastic! It is certain that is precisely what the Earl of Satan said to himself just before he seduced Aurora in this very house more than three decades ago.

His chest tightened, and Barclay wished he was back in London to discuss all the events of the past day with his grandfather. Tsar was a pragmatic man who could assist Barclay to make sense of all this confusion with Tatiana and now … this … surprising fascination for this radiant new relation who had just made a point of their lack of shared blood.

A few minutes later, Ethan announced his triumph. "Checkmate!"

"You won," she replied in her tinkling voice.

Then the boy frowned. "That was too easy. Did you allow me to win?"

Barclay watched as a delicate blush rose over her neck to color her creamy cheeks while her lashes fluttered down to accentuate the high cheekbones in her embarrassment. "Nay, little cousin. I am distracted. We shall play again tomorrow when I shall challenge you more fiercely than today."

Ethan dropped onto his feet and walked over to peer up at her face. "Did you not sleep, Jane?"

Jane flicked a glance at Barclay, looking decidedly uncomfortable at the personal question. "I slept fine."

"At what time?"

"I fell asleep at dawn." Barclay noticed the dark smudges under her eyes, visible evidence of the nocturnal habits his nephew was questioning her about, which did nothing to mar her graceful splendor.

The boy shook his head in admonishment, his arms akimbo on his chubby waist. "You are no country lass anymore, Jane!"

Jane lifted her hand to cover a smile. Barclay himself pressed his lips together to restrain a chuckle at the boy's antics. "I shall attempt to do better."

Ethan gave a quick nod of approval, setting his sable locks bouncing about his little head. "You will stay and drink your *cough-ee* while I play Uncle *Bar-clee*?"

She dropped her hand, inclining her head graciously. "Of course."

Rising, Jane took the seat near to Barclay, who now

noticed the tray laid out on the table between them as he rose to his feet. She poured out a cup of coffee, just as the boy had suggested. As Barclay took his seat to play with his nephew, he noted her pour cream and stir sugar into the cup.

He had never seen a woman drink the beverage before, especially not a refined young woman. He wondered if she knew of the potential troubles related to drinking coffee before being distracted by his nephew's instructions to prepare the chessboard for their game.

* * *

JANE WAS FINISHING her last sip of coffee, for all appearances watching the chess match between Ethan and his uncle. Surreptitiously, she was using it as an opportunity to observe the gentleman up close.

He was a splendid specimen of manhood. Slim, long-limbed, with olive skin inherited from his mother. His hair was a mane of black waves that brushed his broad shoulders. A close-cropped beard suited his strong but narrow face. Once again, he wore a black tailcoat, which Jane had come to realize was probably a sign of his extended mourning and the deep regard he held for his departed love.

The man needed a wife, which was clear from both the conversation of the night before and his hair, just a little too long. She yearned to brush it back from his cheek.

And he did everything with sincere attention. Even now, matched against the four-year-old Ethan, he paid every attention to the game, deliberating his moves while his nephew squirmed in his chair.

"There you are, Ethan!" The earl walked in and made his way to the board. "I see you started chess early today?"

The boy tilted his head back quite far to look up at his father. "I found Jane, and she wanted to play."

Richard chuckled. "She wanted to play, or you made her?"

The lad's face broke into a huge grin. "I made her."

"Well, all I can say is it is a pity you are busy, because I was going to teach you to play cricket this afternoon."

Ethan stood up in riveted surprise. "Cricket?"

"Have you played?"

"No! Oliver and Max play with the local boys, and Jane and Emma have played with them." Jane smiled at Ethan's mention of her younger brothers, who would wheedle her into playing when they were short of boys for their teams. In a dejected voice, he lamented, "But I was too small to hold a bat."

"Hmm ... if only there was a bat small enough for a little boy to learn cricket at Saunton Park?" The earl lifted his arm to reveal what he had carried behind his back. It was a miniature bat—a shortened blade of wood, with a cloth-wrapped cylindrical handle and a thick edge. The earl pulled a leather-seamed ball from his pocket with the other hand.

Her cousin almost launched into the air with his excitement. "Where did you get that? I have never seen one so small before!"

"I had it made for you in London."

Ethan had reddened in his excitement, scrambling to join his father and take it reverently in his hands. "We are to play cricket? Together?"

"I will have to help you when it is your turn at the wicket."

"Do you mind, Uncle *Bar-clee*? Can we play chess later?"

Barclay inclined his head. "Of course, we shall leave the board set up for later."

Jane stood up and walked over. "Shall I place the board on that table? The servants know to leave it alone if it is resting there."

Ethan nodded vigorously, not able to take his eyes from

the specially commissioned club. "Are you playing with us, Uncle *Bar-clee?*"

"Say yes, Barclay, and I promise a full-length bat for you," Richard joked, his emerald eyes as bright with enthusiasm as his son's. Jane had never seen the sophisticated earl so eager and boyish.

The gentleman chuckled. "It has been some time since I played, but I suppose I might rack my memory to recall the rules. Will you play with us, Jane?"

Her breath caught in delight at the invitation. His brown eyes were studying her as he waited for her reply, and Jane had difficulty finding her voice as she became lost in his warm gaze. For all the reasons that made no sense for a match between them, something inexplicably drew her to the man.

"Yes! Do join us, Jane?" Richard spoke from behind Barclay's shoulder, oblivious to the heat between his brother and his houseguest. Jane reluctantly turned her gaze to him as he continued. "Sophia is coming to watch, and a few ladies have expressed an interest in joining in. One of them attended that women's match at Ball's Pond nearly ten years ago. She claims she is one of the spectators depicted in the drawing by Thomas Rowlandson. We are short players to make a proper match of it."

Jane was taken aback by the earl's zeal. It was clear he had a love of the bat and ball that hitherto she had been unaware of. Her family, who had just left to go home after Emma's wedding, would have happily taken part in a match had they been aware of his fondness for it.

Realizing that Barclay would be there, she inclined her head in assent. "Of course, it has been a year or two, but I am sure I can manage. I shall go change into my boots. Where are we playing?"

"We have created a playing field on the west lawn to take full advantage of the afternoon sun."

Ethan grasped his white willow bat, tugging on his father's sleeve. "How long will we play? For three days? Must I tell Miss Lovell we will not be doing lessons in the morning?"

Richard and Barclay both burst out laughing. Jane herself held her palm against her mouth to keep a giggle back at Ethan's transparent attempt to evade his governess.

"We are all amateurs," his father replied. "We shall see if we can even make it last the afternoon."

Ethan's face fell. "Oh. We were going to practice Latin tomorrow morning. I was hoping to tell her I was busy."

The earl pursed his lips as if giving the matter serious consideration. "If you learn Latin, we can practice talking to each other. Latin is important, is it not, Barclay?"

"Without my Latin lessons, I would not have been able to visit Florence and Rome and learn to draw plans for important buildings," agreed the gentleman with a sage expression for his nephew's benefit.

Ethan grumbled but appeared mollified as they departed the library. Jane was too distracted to pay him any mind. She headed to her room to change her shoes, with nervous excitement that Barclay had personally invited her quickening her steps as if a tail wind pushed her down the hall.

It means nothing, you silly chit! He was just being polite.

Nevertheless, she was excited to be seeing him again so soon.

* * *

WHEN JANE REACHED the western lawns, it was to find that most of the houseguests had gathered. Because the countess was increasing, she sat on a bench in the shade of a tree to watch while lamenting that she also wanted to play. She looked lovely in her blue day gown with her red-blonde hair in a coif, having removed her bonnet to take advantage of a breeze that rustled the verdant leaves above her.

The Duchess of Halmesbury elected to sit with her, although there was envy in her brandy eyes as the teams assembled and Jane thought she might have wanted to play, but felt obligated to keep the countess company. "I suppose it is only fair I sit out if my husband is one of the umpires," she remarked to Jane before making her way to join Sophia.

Tatiana was standing by to join a team, looking exuberant. She raced over to Jane when she spotted her, grabbing her hand. "Are you playing, Jane?"

Jane agreed she was, and Tatiana asked if they could be on the same team, so Jane might instruct her on how to play. The little girl had never attended a game, but was caught up in the ebullience of the other guests.

When Jane reached the crowd of gathered players, she was disappointed to discover that Barclay had already been assigned to a team that was now full. They had assigned the players to put an even number of men, women, and children on each team, which was only fair, and Barclay, Richard, and Ethan were teamed together.

She was to play against him.

Jane could not deny her drop in spirits at this news. It would have been much easier to spend time in his company if they were on the same team, but she could hardly make a fuss without rousing suspicions.

Instead, she found herself grouped with Peregrine Balfour's friend, Lord Julius Trafford. The foppish heir to the Earl of Stirling had a bizarre thatch of wheat-colored hair at the crown of his head, but the rest of his hair was a deep chocolate color. She was suspicious that the gentleman's valet was using lemon juice or vinegar to lighten the nobleman's hair in some sort of style choice, but she considered it to be a silly affectation. Lord Trafford and the duchess's brother, Mr. Brendan Ridley, were both friends of Perry's who had remained for the house party after attending his wedding a few days earlier.

Jane preferred Mr. Ridley over the spoilt young lord. Despite his involvement with widows, Mr. Ridley was an affable young man who had spent a great deal of time cavorting with his infant nephew, Jasper, who was the duke's heir and had the same rich, chestnut hair as his uncle and mother.

Additional members of her team included a Mr. Adam Dunsford, Mr. Ridley, Tatiana, another child, and several men and women she had not become acquainted with yet.

Mr. Ridley was elected team captain. The duke oversaw the coin toss, and Jane's team won. Two batters went to the pitch, while Tatiana and Jane hurried off the field along with the other batters to await their turn.

The earl's team scattered over the field to prepare for play.

Jane found a bat suitable for Tatiana's height from the collection that had been laid out. She showed her how to grasp and swing it, being mindful of their skirts. Then she explained how to score a run, including how to scarper to the other wicket so their skirts did not trip them up.

The little girl was brimming with excitement, chattering questions at Jane as they went through the rules. It gladdened her to see the child so animated after their first encounter when Tatiana had been so sad about her mother, and she could not help reaching out a hand to smooth the girl's hair affectionately.

* * *

BARCLAY TOOK his place on the field, bemused, while he observed Tatiana interacting with Jane across the field. When he had agreed to play, he had not realized Tatiana was participating, or he would have made sure they were on the same team in order to help her learn the game.

By the time he had realized she was there, she had already latched onto the intriguing young woman from the library and he had been loath to interrupt the bonhomie he had seen forming between the two. It had been some time since Tatiana had laughed or chattered as much as she was now, her face lit up as Jane demonstrated how to swing the bat and run while wearing skirts, then smoothed his daughter's silver-blonde hair with affection.

Jane truly was a unique young woman in how she took such an interest in children, playing with Ethan in the library and now with his daughter. Natalya would have approved of such engagement. His eyes ran over her willowy form with appreciation as his thoughts returned to the notion of courting her.

She is still a child herself! There are no more than ten years between her and your daughter, you degenerate lech!

Barclay grimaced. His thoughts were only on courtship because of his conversation with his mother the night before. He needed to find a woman more suitable and forget about the vivacious woman who was far too young for a man at his stage of life.

Looking about the field, he noticed a blonde woman glancing his way in admiration.

Mrs. Agnes Gordon.

He searched the archives of his mind and remembered she was the widow of the vicar from the local village. The earl had provided her with a cottage at Saunton Park when her husband had unexpectedly died three years earlier.

Mrs. Gordon flickered a flirtatious smile from under the

brim of her bonnet before approaching him while Barclay contemplated her. A woman closer to his own age. A more mature woman who was of Natalya's age, if she had still been here with them.

Mrs. Gordon had experience running a household and assisting a vicar—certainly she would make a good wife to a professional man like him.

"Mr. Thompson, I hope I might impose on you to explain the rules of the game?"

Barclay smiled, bowing in acknowledgment. With an appreciative eye, he noted she had a lively manner and was quite comely in her striped muslin dress.

Mr. Adam Dunsford, the sole heir to a local Somerset landowner, had just been bowled out. Rambling over, he took a seat by Jane under the oak tree while Tatiana held her bat aloft proudly as she walked away to take his place at the crease.

He was a handsome young man, with a mop of curling brown waves that must have taken his valet endless time each morning to perfect into looking effortlessly unaffected.

"You played rather well for a woman, Miss Davis. Twenty runs, was it?"

Jane smiled in return, while wishing she had had more sleep the night before because all the sunshine and activity was making her drowsy. It was not the most effusive compliment—*For a woman?*—but it was well intended and the gentleman had such a warm manner, it was difficult to take offense. "Yes. Thank you, Mr. Dunsford."

"I am afraid I batted rather poorly. Barely made twelve runs before a child bowled me out. They are getting more and more talented each year. It has nothing to do with my deplorable talents, I assure you."

She chuckled in response. His self-deprecation was endearing as he threaded his fingers together and pulled a slight face, leaning forward on his elbows to observe the game. Jane had been watching Barclay with Mrs. Gordon across the field, but now she averted her eyes to watch the bowling. "Have you known the earl for long, Mr. Dunsford?"

"Yes, but I must admit, not very well. It is his brother, Peregrine Balfour, whom I went to Oxford with."

"Oh? Perry just wed my sister a few days ago!"

"I heard he had just wed. Your sister must be a lovely woman if she is related to you."

Jane warmed at the compliment. The attentions of a charming young man were almost enough to take her attention off the intriguing architect across the field who was currently demonstrating how to bowl to the lovely Mrs. Gordon before she took her turn at the pitch.

Almost.

Jane had the sinking feeling that she had lost an opportunity when she left his side to find her boots. Now he and Mrs. Gordon were making a connection. All the times she had encountered Barclay, he had been so serious. Now he was laughing while Mrs. Gordon attempted to mimic his bowling demonstration, and the widow was laughing with him.

You are too young for him. He could never take you seriously when he has achieved so much and you have done so little.

It was disappointing. It was the first time she felt a genuine attraction for a man, and he would have to be someone unattainable. If only she had anything to offer a man who had been through so much, but she was merely a country lass who was away from her immediate family for the first time in her brief life. What could she possibly offer such a gentleman? She could play the pianoforte. She was excellent with a needle and thread. But, despite her fascination for the handsome widower, she had no experience with the kind of loss the Thompsons were recovering from.

Are you going to embroider his heart back together?

Jane sighed and turned her attentions to Mr. Dunsford, sitting up straight to force some energy into her tired limbs. She wished … she could sleep a full night and consider her future with a fresh mind.

Failing that, the architect was beyond her reach and she needed to set her sights on a gentleman interested in pursuing her. What had she said to Emma last week? A landowner who was young and fun? Mr. Dunsford fit the bill rather well.

Emma's advice to pursue a gentleman with whom she shared a connection of the minds seemed a poor option in the bright sunlight when a young man was at her side to exhibit his regard, and the object of her desire flirted with an eminently suitable widow who had all the right qualifications to be a wife and mother to his daughter.

Jane was well disposed to be the wife of a young gentleman of the gentry, such as Mr. Dunsford, and she need never feel gauche or awkward with such a safe choice.

Perhaps she should discover how deep the young man's interest ran?

CHAPTER 4

*J*t was late morning when Jane woke up. She had not fallen asleep until dawn yet again. Perhaps she should visit a herbalist in Saunton to discuss the matter as Emma had suggested because she was wearing down from so little sleep.

The evening before had been wonderful. She had been seated with Adam Dunsford for dinner. The gentleman had a quirky sense of humor and had kept her laughing the entire evening. After dinner they had paired up for parlor games, which Jane had enjoyed all the more for his charming company.

Then she had retired to bed, where she had been unable to fall asleep. Eventually, she had found a captivating book from the library and stayed up reading until the first threads of dawn had stolen into her room.

Stretching her limbs out, Jane yawned widely before sitting up. Then she remembered her plans for this morning, and with a burst of vigor, she scampered from her bed to pull on a wrap before loping over to her door. Opening it wide, she found the cart she had requested.

Her breakfast tray was still warm, and a fat, silver pot of tea was speckled with drops of condensation which promised a piping hot drink to pour.

In addition, the extra supplies she had requested were heaped on a tray of their own. Jane clapped her hands in excitement. She had been looking forward to trying this ever since she had read about it in a women's periodical.

"What are you doing?"

Jane shrieked and jumped in surprise. Clutching a hand to her pounding heart, she found Tatiana staring at her from the door of her and her grandmother's bedroom.

"My goodness, you startled the wits from me, Tatiana!"

"You are very twitchy. I noticed it the other night."

"I ... have had trouble sleeping. It has me on edge."

"Why all the strawberries? And what are those nuts for?"

Jane beamed in delight as she recalled this morning's task. "Do you wish to join me? I can show you what I am about?"

The girl nodded her head enthusiastically, skipping over to follow Jane into her room with a broad smile on her little face. "Shall I close the door?"

"No, leave it ajar in case your family wishes to find you."

Jane wheeled the cart over to the table and chairs at the end of the room. Sitting down, she poured out a cup of tea. Adding cream and sugar, she sat back and breathed in the floral flavor with a radiant smile. "You may eat one of the strawberries, if you like. Just not too many because we will need them."

Tatiana's face lit up. She inspected the bowl and then delicately took hold of the largest strawberry she could find, pulling it up by its cap and holding it in front of her face to sniff it. With a deep breath, she took a bite, smiling in pleasure while she chewed.

"Have you thought more about courting my father?"

Jane choked, quickly putting the cup down while she

coughed into her hand. "I thought we agreed your papa needed to find his own wife?"

"I went around meeting all the women since then. You are the only one who is right for Papa."

"Perhaps this house party is not the right place to find his wife? If you did not like any of the women here, there will be more women in London for him to meet."

"No, I did not mean you are the best woman at the house party." Tatiana shook her head, clearly exasperated with Jane's simpleness. "You *are* the right woman for him. I know it! Did you meet him yet?"

"I did, and your papa is a gracious gentleman. But I must confess there is a difference in our ages, and he might prefer someone with more maturity than me. He seemed quite taken with Mrs. Gordon."

Tatiana's blue eyes narrowed. "The blonde woman? She is awful!"

"Your papa seemed to like her. He played cricket with her and sat with her at dinner."

Tatiana stood up, outrage quivering in every line of her body. "Not Mrs. Gordon. She does not like children!"

Jane frowned. "What do you mean?"

"I could tell when I met her. She smiled, but it did not reach her eyes, and she asked me if I had a doll to go play with like I was a simpleton."

Jane bit her lip, uncertain how to respond. "I am sure if you give her time, she will grow accustomed to you."

Tatiana clenched her jaw. "Promise me you will think about it. I know you are perfect for Papa. You must spend more time with him and then you will see what I mean."

Jane did not want to encourage the girl's hope of a match, but she would distract her and then search out the grandmother to discuss the matter. The older woman seemed sensible, and she had a warm manner. Perhaps they could meet for tea to work out how to address Tatiana's surprising desires. "Do you want to see what the strawberries are for?"

Tatiana's little face lit up, her appreciation of the aromatic fruit obvious as her eyes darted back to the bowl.

"I recently read directions for preparing strawberry water. It softens and lightens the skin."

Tatiana grinned. "We are going to smell like strawberries?"

"That is the plan." Reaching out her hand, Jane took hold of one of the plumpest fruits and brought it to her lips. Breathing in deeply, she took a bite, tasting the sweetness of its flesh, and finished it quickly. "Pass me that empty bowl."

Tatiana solemnly handed over the extra bowl, along with the pestle resting in it. Jane selected several well-ripened strawberries, dropping them into the empty bowl and offering the girl one of the remaining fruits to eat.

Then she crushed the strawberries, pulling the caps out to discard them. Once she had the fruit reduced to a pulp, she requested a second empty bowl which she placed on the table before picking up the white muslin. Pouring the pulp onto the muslin, she diligently pressed it through until she had the juice of strawberries in the vessel. She discarded the muslin and its pulpy mess onto the tray before popping one of the remaining strawberries into her mouth, biting it off at the cap to place it back onto the tray as she ate the fruit.

Walking over to the washstand, she used the pitcher of water to rinse her hands before returning to take her seat.

Tatiana leaned over the bowl of juice to breathe in the fragrance which was permeating the air. "Now what happens?"

"Now I mix it with milk and a little water, and then we can dab it on our faces. After our long afternoon in the sun yesterday, it should be quite soothing."

"And what about the almonds?"

"That is for afterwards."

"I want to do things like this with you every day."

Jane smiled. The girl was sweet, and she enjoyed her company. Tatiana had a calm presence unless she was excited, as she had been to play cricket the day before. "I enjoy spending time with you, too."

"If you were my mama ..."

* * *

BARCLAY HAD SEARCHED for Tatiana throughout the splendid home of Saunton Park. When he had drawn his first plans for a similar large and extravagant building, it had been the greatest of honors, but now that he searched for one small, nine-year-old girl who liked to hide, he could curse the wasteful spending that created such long halls with so many ridiculous rooms sprawling in every direction.

How the peerage lived in such vast spaces was something he could not comprehend. If he, Tsar, Aurora, and Tatiana lived in such a home, they would not see each other for days on end. Their London townhouse was quite sufficient for a family of means.

Stopping in the great hall, he glanced up at the richly colored, oversized oil paintings of Balfour ancestors in ornate gilded frames and tried to think where else he might look for his child. He had been certain she was with her grandmother, but when he had found Aurora sitting with the ladies for tea in a large drawing room of blue and gold, she had not seen Tatiana since breakfast when she thought the child had left with him.

Barclay encouraged her to continue her tea, mindful that his mother was making important connections with well-placed women of high society, which would elevate her status when they returned to London.

Aurora had mentioned Jane in parting, but Barclay had not found her in his search for Tatiana. Was it possible they were together somewhere? Tatiana seemed quite taken with the young woman, so she might have sought her out.

Ethan had mentioned during the chess match the day before that Jane had trouble sleeping. Could she be in the family wing still?

He turned and began the long walk to the family wing, where he heard his daughter's voice echoing down the hall. Following the sound, he reached a door that stood ajar.

This had to be the young lady's room. He noted it was right next to his mother's as he raised his hand to knock and then lowered it to listen to the conversation floating out into the corridor.

"Mama used to read to me every night."

"Every night!" exclaimed Jane. "That is an admirable mother. What did she read to you?"

"My favorite were the ones she read from *Abian Nights*."

"Do you mean *Arabian Nights' Entertainments*?"

"Yes! That is it!"

"I was just reading *Aladdin* last evening. See, it is there next to my bed."

"Oooh! It has been so long since I heard that one."

Tatiana sounded both excited and disappointed at the same time, leaving Barclay feeling guilty. Had he not paid sufficient attention to his child since Natalya had left them? He ensured he spent time with her and took her to the park regularly, but somehow he had not realized that she might miss the simple joy of a story at bedtime. Perhaps he had been too consumed by his own grief and failed to notice how his daughter was suffering.

"I can read it to you, if you wish?"

The young woman's offer surprised him. She had no obligation to his daughter, but she freely offered her time. It was a generous gesture. Surely a young woman like her had more absorbing ways to pass her time than in the company of a child. What of the fidgety young gentleman she had been spending time with since the cricket match the day before?

Realizing he was shamelessly eavesdropping, Barclay raised his hand to knock. He heard a chair shifting and then Tatiana's light footsteps as she raced across the room to peer around the corner of the door, which was only open by a few inches.

"Papa!"

"There you are, young lady. I have been searching everywhere for you." He noticed the fragrance of strawberries and almonds wafting in the air.

"Jane and I were using strawberry water and almond oil for our faces."

Barclay tilted his head in confusion. What on earth did that entail?

At that moment, Jane swung the door open to appear in her night rail and wrap, looking a little embarrassed by her attire as she crossed her arms. The motion plumped her rounded breasts, and Barclay found his mouth had gone dry while he did his best to keep his eyes on her face—which only highlighted the glorious ebony hair plaited to drape over one of those same generous mounds.

Every base instinct he had ever possessed screamed at him to glance down, and he firmed his jaw to prevent himself from acting on the impulse.

"I hope you do not mind? Tatiana joined me when I awoke, but I left my door open in the event you came looking for her."

The young lady was decidedly nervous, lowering a hand to fidget with the edge of the wrap and drawing his eye to where he vowed not to look. Barclay found himself ill-equipped for the situation, taking several moments to respond because of his scrambled wits. He would not usually be making contact with a young woman in her nightclothes, but as they were both considered family of the earl, they were without a chaperone, staying in the same wing with only his daughter as a buffer between them.

He found his tongue. "Not at all. I hope she is not bothering you?"

She smiled; the curving of her pink bow lips drew his wayward eye. Good Lord, she was lovely.

"Tatiana is good company. She could never bother me."

"Papa, Jane said she would read me Ladin, and the Lamp. Can she put me to bed tonight?"

"Tatiana, I would not want to impose on the young lady. During your bedtime, she should attend the games in the parlor."

"I can come up and read to her. No one will miss me if I leave for a short time after dinner."

"I would not wish to interrupt your entertainment."

Jane shook her head. "It is no bother. I miss my younger brothers and sister, so this will be fun for me ... unless I am imposing?" Her face fell, and she appeared genuinely disappointed. "Would you prefer to do it? I can lend you my book."

Barclay was thankful for the reminder of their age disparity. He had just caught a whiff of the strawberries, cream, and almonds clinging to her skin and was battling an overwhelming urge to lean over and lick her. Would she taste as sweet as she smelled?

Clearing his throat, he struggled to recall her question as his breathing grew shallow and the heat rose. Tearing his gaze away from those surreal ice-blue eyes that put him in mind of a frozen lake in the winter, he lifted his head to peer at the ceiling for a long moment before replying, "Tatiana does not like my reading. She says I do the voices wrong. If you are sure it is not an imposition ..." He looked back at her, and she shook her head once more. "... then we would be honored if you would join her at bedtime ... for a short time, mind you. I do not wish to take you away from your leisure."

Both girls clapped their hands at the news. This woman was so lovely. And sweet.

And far too young, you lech.

Had visiting his father's home somehow triggered his own roguish impulses? His thoughts had grown decidedly lewd in the past few moments. Fighting down his inexplicable desire, steeling his nerve in the manner he would when entering a tough negotiation, Barclay took Tatiana's little hand in his. "Come, little one. I wish to play some chess with you in the library."

Tatiana beamed. "Good. Ethan made me play after cricket yesterday, and he beat me. It was most embarrassing. I should have paid more attention when you were teaching me to play."

"We will improve your skills." He gave a brief bow. "We shall see you later, Jane?"

Jane inclined her head in agreement, then gently closed the door as they walked away.

While Tatiana chattered about the beauty treatment that she and Jane had partaken in, Barclay scolded himself mentally. No matter how alluring or kind the young woman was, it bore remembering that she was not for him. She could make a much better match than a man born on the wrong side of the blanket who also happened to be at least fourteen years her senior.

This attraction was ... so inconvenient.

He really needed to find someone more suitable if he was to hunt for a new wife. When he was finished with his chess game, he would seek Mrs. Gordon. She was good company and pleasing to the eye, not to mention mature enough to mother a nine-year-old girl.

CHAPTER 5

*J*ane was a keen observer of people, thus she wondered what she had done to anger the widower. One moment, he had been gazing at her with admiration, so that she had swayed toward him. The next, he had been staring at the ceiling, his jaw tight and his husky voice tighter when he next spoke.

Closing the door on the retreating pair, she turned and leaned against it. Brushing her fingertips over her lips, she wondered what it might be like to kiss such a man. He smelled of leather, ink, and some sort of spice she could not quite place, and she wanted—with every ounce of her being—to reach out a hand and feel the shape of his broad chest. To lean in and feel the stubble of his beard against her skin as their lips met in a moment of intense passion.

She had been kissed a couple of times, as a girl back in Derby, when she had been the daughter of a tenant farmer. It had been pleasant, but nothing momentous.

When her sister and Perry had met, Jane had seen the sparks flying. Their passion for each other, despite their constant confrontations, had been unmistakable, and Jane had lamented in the recesses of her mind that she had never felt such intensity for a man before.

Gentlemen had pursued her, especially now that she was a member of the gentry. Jane knew well that she was a woman of fine looks. She had excellent prospects. Yet she wanted to find what Emma had—a deep connection with a gentleman that transcended society's expectations. She wanted to find her Darcy, no matter how much Emma teased her for her whimsy.

Jane had been right in her prediction that Perry would turn out to be Emma's Darcy, even when her sister had been adamant that the earl's brother could not possibly want her. Perry had proven himself worthy, giving up his carefree life as an indolent spare to pursue a life in the country with Emma and manage the fine estate of Shepton Abbey, both for Emma's passion for estate management and for his own sake to pursue a purpose greater than idle pleasure.

Jane perceived that Barclay Thompson was aware of their visceral connection but, inexplicably, it angered him. She supposed that, like her family was inclined to do, he saw her as an immature young girl who could not offer a worldly man much in the way of useful skills.

It was a pity because Jane had never felt such a connection to any gentleman before him.

Did his parentage pose some sort of problem? She was well aware of the challenges he must have faced, what cousin Ethan would face in his future as the son of an unwed mother.

She hoped the gentleman did not think she minded such things. A man's worth was displayed by his actions, not those of his father. Neither her nor her family would ever turn away from someone for something they had no control over.

Whatever the problem was, whatever was causing Barclay to grow stiff in her presence despite their mutual attraction, she knew when a gentleman was interested in her, and it was clear he was not. It caused such a sense of disappointment to see him harden himself against her.

If only Emma was still in residence, so she could discuss this unexpected attraction, but Jane was alone at Saunton Park and dealing with a decidedly adult situation for the first time.

For a moment, Barclay had appeared to be admiring her, but then the flash in his eyes had disappeared so quickly, she had been left to wonder if she had imagined it because of her own desire to spend more time in his company.

Regardless of his reasoning, he and his daughter were recovering from a great loss, and it was not Jane's place to assert herself into their lives. Only Barclay could know what was best for his little family in the wake of his wife's death.

Jane turned to wash up and get dressed. She had assured the countess that she could manage without a lady's maid until they hired a new one. Their last one had left with Emma, but Jane was accustomed to preparing herself, despite enjoying the luxury of assistance, and Sophia's abigail was occupied with other tasks with so many guests in residence.

Later that afternoon, Jane arrived for her match with Ethan in the library. Richard was there, showing his son a strategy with a reference book at hand. Ethan's face lit up when Jane arrived. "Jane! I just finished playing with Papa. Are you here to play?"

"Of course. You asked me to come at this time."

The earl rose. "I am happy you are here. I am to meet the duke and Barclay in my study, but I thought I would have to find Daisy to take care of Ethan."

"That is unnecessary. I can return him to the nursery when we are done playing."

Richard smiled in gratitude, heading for the door. "You are an excellent houseguest, Jane."

A maid arrived with her tray of coffee, leaving it on the side table as Jane took a seat across from Ethan. Soon they were absorbed by their game, so that Jane barely noticed when Mr. Dunsford entered the room.

"Miss Davis! I am so glad to find you. I was hoping we could take a walk on the front lawn? Lady Saunton and Her Grace are seated on the terrace, so several couples are taking a turn around the garden under their watchful eyes."

Jane smiled politely. "Certainly, Mr. Dunsford. I will join you once I finish this match with Ethan."

The young man glanced at her cousin as if noticing him for the first time. Ethan shot him a glance of irritation, dissatisfied at the interruption to their game, before turning back to contemplate the pieces on the board.

"I shall wait for you." With that, the lanky gentleman sat on a chair. "Oh my! The servants here are so attentive. They must have placed this coffeepot here for the guests. I wonder how frequently they replace it?"

He picked up the tall, tapered coffeepot and poured it into the single cup provided. Ethan swung his head to scowl at the man in outrage. "Hey! That *cough-ee* is for J—"

Jane shot out a hand to caution Ethan. Her little cousin stopped, shooting her a look of inquiry. She shook her head, which he understood. He closed his mouth abruptly, but his expression was irritated as he resumed play. Opportunely, Emma had taught the boy how to hold his tongue in public, but Jane would be required to explain it to him once they were alone again.

Fortunately, Mr. Dunsford barely noticed the boy had exclaimed at him, too engaged in drinking the coffee he had poured.

When Jane had tried coffee for the first time weeks ago, Perry had warned her it would be frowned upon socially because it was considered a drink for men alone. She had not been concerned about revealing the habit in Barclay's presence. Not only were they relations, but intuitively Jane knew that no one in the Thompson family would disdain a woman for something so frivolous.

Mr. Dunsford was a prospective suitor, and she was yet uncertain of his character. She had no desire to reveal something so intimate to the gentleman until she knew him better. Jane had hopes that the charming young man might become a match, a matter which had become more pressing now that Emma had left her on her own. Jane did not wish to spoil their potential relationship early on with something so trivial.

* * *

WHEN BARCLAY ENTERED the earl's study at the designated time, he was surprised to find both the duke and the earl with cups of tea in their hands. The dainty china cup looked especially fragile in the duke's large, bronzed hand.

Barclay rubbed his cheek in perplexment. "When you said I should join you for a drink in the study, I did not understand that to mean tea?"

"Barclay, there you are. Please help yourself." The earl gestured to the sideboard where a tray of decanters stood. "Halmesbury does not like spirits, and I suppose I might reveal to my own brother that Sophia's father drank himself into an early grave. She asked me to not partake in liquor, and I find my mind is much clearer since I switched to tea."

Barclay lifted a hand to stroke his beard while he thought, looking between the sideboard and the tray. "I suppose a cup of tea would be a pleasure. I have always had a preference for it."

He took his seat, leaning forward to pour a cup before settling back.

"Thank you for joining us, Barclay. Halmesbury and I were ..." His brother stopped, fidgeting with his cravat. Barclay frowned with suspicion. He had noted that his brother would toy with his cravat when he was anxious.

The duke set down his cup and leaned forward. "My cousin and I are thinking about the future. Ethan's future. I know it is impudent to ask, but ... how has it been for you?"

Barclay exhaled, his worry eased. His brother merely sought insight on a delicate matter. "To be a bastard, you mean?"

The duke blinked, his gray eyes clouding. "Please be assured I have never used that word ... not in that context."

Contemplating His Grace, Barclay toyed with the cuff of his sleeve. The duke was widely regarded for his philanthropic works and had been polite and welcoming since they had met the first day of the house party. He believed the venerated nobleman differed from many of the peerage that Barclay had dealt with. Even his brother continued to surprise him, taking care to include the Thompsons as valued family members and contrite for his—their—sire's actions. This conversation was decidedly uncomfortable, yet they did not broach the topic out of vindictive intent.

"I understand. You wish to anticipate the troubles that the child might face in the future. To predict and take measures to prepare the boy for the challenges he will face."

The duke's face relaxed. "I understand it is an imposition, but you are uniquely experienced to deliver insight. You are a lauded professional in your field despite your mother's unwed status, so we felt that your situation would have some parity to Ethan's as the acknowledged son of a peer, yet with similar parental circumstances."

"It will not be easy for him. Some will accept him for his connections and his own merit. Others will mock him, or turn from him without explanation. Unwarranted antago-

62

nism is assured. I would prepare him for school. Take measures to teach him how to defend himself in the event of a physical scuffle, but instruct him on how to ignore taunting and follow his own path when he can. Some battles are unavoidable, but diplomacy is always best to pursue."

Richard shook his head in disgust. "I cannot believe I have created this situation for my son."

Barclay tilted his head back to study the painted ceiling. His own grandfather had overseen the beauty of the patterns depicted there. When he was prepared to speak, he leaned forward to peer directly into his brother's eyes. "Richard, you are here for him now, and that is worth something. Tsar could have had me raised by strangers, but he did not. I owe everything to the old man for standing by me. Ethan is fortunate to have a father who feels responsible for the situation and who takes care to pave the way for his future."

His brother's hand came up to fidget with his cravat once more. "How did you handle it? All those issues you referred to?"

"Tsar is a man skilled in negotiation. From a young age, he taught me how to handle men. How to make self-important lords pay their bills in a timely manner, how to manipulate suppliers when they attempt to raise prices or delay deliveries, how to contend with competitors and maintain good relationships with all of these men while refusing to be taken advantage of. You will do the same for Ethan. The boy is intelligent, and he will turn this situation to his advantage."

The duke cleared his throat. "The question that really lingers is … are you accepted socially?"

"No. I am tolerated for my professional prowess, but I am not invited into their homes. Tsar assures me that will change now that Richard has acknowledged me as his brother, but I have to say I am not excited by such a prospect. If I was not acceptable in my own right, I cannot respect these people for changing their minds because of my new connection to the wealthy Earl of Saunton. However, if it will ease the path for Tatiana, or allow my mother entry to places she wishes to be, then I will ignore the slights of the past. I will grin and bear it, so to speak."

Richard's face displayed his alarm. "You are not accepted socially? Not anywhere?"

"I have good relationships with tradesmen and suppliers. Some clients. They are more accepting of my situation, especially given my talents, but my mother has struggled. She has been attempting to join a lady's society for some time, but she has been rejected on several occasions. Now she has re-applied on the strength of our change in circumstances. I prefer to not pursue unworthy connections, but it is important to her because my grandmother was a member and she wishes to follow in her footsteps. I have yet to discover how my own situation will be altered once word of this ... our new relationship gets around."

"What of your wife? Was she affected by the situation?"

"Natalya was a private woman who valued her time on this earth. Her days were numbered, and she had no patience to pursue relationships with English families that were hostile. She made friends where she could easily do so, despite being wed to a by-blow, and ignored the rest to spend her time with Tatiana and myself."

His brother slumped back in his chair, his cravat now askew from his compulsive fidgeting. "I am sorry I did not learn of you sooner."

Barclay smiled. "It is not your cross to bear, brother. The blame is squarely at the feet of the man who is not here to answer for his actions. I respect what you have done for Ethan, and I hope his path will be easier than mine. After all, he has the advantage of your support."

The three men sipped on tea, each lost in the privacy of

their respective thoughts, while Barclay thought of how Natalya's fierce loyalty had meant so much to him.

Eventually, Richard broke the silence. "On another matter, I could do with some advice."

The duke chuckled. "Is that not what we have been doing here? Advising you?"

"I meant on a less strenuous subject. This matter involves Jane Davis."

Barclay nearly choked on his tea. He carefully placed his cup and saucer back on the tray and drew a fortifying breath. "Should I leave you to it?"

Richard frowned. "No, you are family now. I would appreciate your thoughts."

Halmesbury finished his tea and put his own cup down. "What of the young lady?"

Barclay leaned back and found his head tilting so he might stare at the ceiling once more. The discussion about his situation had been uncomfortable, but he had seen the value in sharing his knowledge. Being in the room while Richard discussed the young woman he was so enamored with was bloody awkward.

"I received a letter from London. Lord Lawson has written to me to pose the possibility of his courting her. He states he was quite taken with her at the ball we held for Emma and Jane earlier this month."

Halmesbury frowned. "The man is forty years of age! He has daughters of an age as Jane."

Richard rose to his feet to pace. "Precisely. I know that the man is yet to have an heir, but his wife has been gone only two years and now he wishes to pursue a young woman under my protection."

The duke sighed. "Unfortunately, it is common amongst the peerage for such disparate ages to exist between a husband and wife."

"Not in our particular set. The man is a good friend, but I find myself quite repelled by the notion and I do not know how to reply to his letter. Jane is lovely and young. She could marry a gentleman with far more in common with her. There is no hurry to marry her off, and I know from Sophia that she is a romantic who wishes to marry for love."

Guilt twisted and churned in Barclay's gut. He was in his thirties. He had a daughter only nine or ten years younger than Jane, and he was coveting the young lady like a degenerate old man. Not dissimilar to the late Earl of Satan, in fact. How had he arrived in this situation, where he sat beside the earl repressing his shameful secret? He restrained himself from reacting as he concentrated his attention on the ceiling and reminded himself that a young Aurora had been robbed of her virtue in this very building, which was why he needed to stay away from Jane Davis, despite his daughter's encouragement to pursue her.

"Perhaps Jane will find a gentleman at this house party and it will not be necessary to dissuade Lord Lawson's inquiry?" the duke mused.

"Blazes, I hope so. This is deuced awkward!"

Barclay nearly flinched as his own thoughts from moments ago were echoed out loud. There were so many issues, he did not know which to focus on—setting a young woman up to be rejected by society because she was married to a bastard, or that she was far too young to foist a nine-year-old child onto. And if he had had any thoughts of approaching his brother about the possibility of courting Jane, they had been soundly put to rest. All he knew was that he needed to stay away from her before he gave in to his base desires.

If Tatiana needed a new mother, he would need to look elsewhere than the lovely Jane Davis.

CHAPTER 6

*A*fter dinner, Barclay discreetly signaled Jane from across the parlor where the guests gathered for games. Making her excuses, she rose and followed him out of the room to find him waiting for her in the hall. He held out his arm, and she accepted. A warm, roiling feeling of awareness unraveled from her fingertips, through her forearm, and up to her shoulder to ignite a flame of yearning in her heart as her fingers grazed over his powerful forearm. She could not deny her fascination for the gentleman, no matter how unattainable he might be.

He walked along, solemn while they made their way down the connecting corridor to the family wing. Jane soaked up every moment of their silent journey, wishing it could last longer but, alas, they reached the door of his mother's room. Barclay raised his hand to knock while Jane wistfully imagined what it might be like to be his wife. To tuck Tatiana into bed each night. To travel to towns across the realm, as Tatiana had reminisced about.

It was lowering to be envious of a dead woman, but she

could not deny that the late Mrs. Thompson had lived her ideal life.

Tatiana's grandmother answered the door and smiled warmly. "Miss Davis, this is so generous of you. Tatiana is so excited!"

"Please, Miss Thompson, you must call me Jane."

The older woman smiled in delight. "I would love to! You must do me the pleasure of calling me by my own name. Aurora."

"Aurora? That is lovely."

"My mother was Italian," explained Barclay's mother.

Barclay, Aurora, and Jane discussed the bedtime story she was to read to Tatiana. It was decided that Aurora would return to the guests in the main house, and Barclay accompanied Jane into the room, where Tatiana sat in her cot. The little girl clapped her hands with such excitement, settling down as Jane came over to sit beside her. The book had been delivered earlier that night, so she picked up *Aladdin* and began to read out loud.

With four younger brothers and sisters, Jane was confident of her storytelling abilities. Oliver and Max, the rambunctious twins, were not shy to criticize, so she had long since learned how children preferred their stories read to them.

Tatiana was in raptures, listening with an intent expression on her sweet little face, while her father sat in an armchair across the room, observing but not reacting in any way as Jane told the little girl about the treasures in the cave. Soon the little girl's eyes drooped, and when she finally let out a gentle snore to inform them she slept, Jane gently closed the book and placed it back on the table.

Nodding to Barclay, they both rose and quietly left the room. Closing the door behind him, Barclay turned to look down at her. "Thank you … Jane. It is a long time since I have seen Tatiana so content. What you did tonight was exceedingly kind."

Jane looked up at his solemn face, noting the faint lines at the corners of his eyes and the close-cropped beard that made him seem more guarded than the other men in the manor, and smiled wistfully. "It was my great honor, Barclay."

He escorted her back to the main house, and Jane rejoined the countess on a sofa, musing to herself that it had been a surreal way to have spent the past hour. A moment in time, she suspected, she would always cherish.

Bringing succor to both the child and, hopefully, her father had been immensely fulfilling, which highlighted that it was high time she sought a suitable match so she might start her own family and know the joy of tucking her child in with a bedtime story.

Since Emma had left to embark on her new life as a married woman, Jane was feeling the pangs of loneliness quite desperately. She had no wish to return home to Rose Ash Manor. She needed to secure a husband and start the next chapter of her life, as her sister had done.

You are all grown up, and you need to find yourself a match!

* * *

BARCLAY SAT on his window ledge, watching the fog roll in over the park. Eventually, it blocked out the stars and moon and he was left staring into the abyss of midnight. It was … unpleasant.

He could no longer summon Natalya to his side as he had done the first night at Saunton Park, and he supposed he must have made a decision to move forward after the revelation that Tatiana wanted a new mother in her life.

It was what Natalya had wanted, and her continued absence suggested that it was too late to turn back.

He considered the widow, Mrs. Gordon, who seemed to be quite taken with him. She was pleasant company and clearly did not mind his family situation. Barclay shifted to lean his back on the chilly window, inspecting the ceiling with an expert eye, and wondered how he was going to sleep. Or what he was to do if he remained awake now that his recollection of Natalya obstinately refused to join him in this quiet hour as she had always done before.

Eventually, he rose and left the room to roam the halls. The manor was quiet, all guests and family having retired for the evening. It was surreal to walk the corridors of this grand home his grandfather had built. So much history there. Tsar had made his reputation with the design. Aurora had been seduced. Barclay had been conceived. And now, whimsically, it was the place where memories of Natalya had finally been released from the living, so she might pursue her own journey while Barclay attempted to plan for a new future without her at his side.

Contemplating all these issues in the middle of the night did nothing to settle his mind. He needed to find a distraction until he could finally relax enough to fall asleep.

Entering the main block of the manor, he walked along a corridor until he noticed that the library was still lit. Who would make use of the room so late in the evening? Deciding he could do with some company, he headed in that direction to learn whom his fellow insomniac might be.

Entering the library, he came to a panicked halt. Jane was bent over a library table, scratching over a page with a quill. He should leave. Turn around and return to his room.

But the hour was late and his soul was weary and he could not command his feet to walk away. He wanted to enjoy this quiet hour alone with her. In the morning, he would do the right thing. The honorable thing. He would stay away from her then, but tonight ... tonight he was so damned lonely, and this captivating creature was the only solace he had found in two long years.

"What are you writing?" He moved to take a seat by the fireplace.

Jane flinched, startled by his presence. Her hand moved reflexively to cover the page as if she hid the words from him. His curiosity was piqued.

"It is nothing."

"Jane ... it is midnight and evidently neither of us can sleep. Share your thoughts with me." He was unsure why he cajoled the young woman, but she looked utterly lovely in the candlelight and he wanted to hear her melodic voice.

She contorted her face, twin spots of color appearing high on her cheeks. "It is poetry," she mumbled.

"You write verse?"

She nodded, seemingly unable to meet his eyes.

"Tell me about it."

She chewed her lip before she replied. "I wrote it in the style of Shakespeare—each line is five feet of two syllables to create the ten syllables of the iambic pentameter. But I used variations of the iambs, so not all my lines are the traditional *duh-DUH* rhythm. Some of the stresses are reversed—*DUH-duh*—while others are not stressed—*duh-duh*—in order to punch up other feet in the line ... I am a bumbling amateur at best."

Barclay hid a smile. The endearing young woman was babbling, clearly nervous to be caught with her poetry. "Read me a verse."

Jane straightened in her seat. "Oh, no! I never share my work. Even Emma has never heard my verses."

"Poetry is food for the soul. It is to be shared, and I wish to hear what you have written."

71

"No. I cannot—"

"I will not judge. I know the challenges of creating something and showing it to another for the first time. My first design, I was certain Tsar would hate it. I had to find the courage to display it. Now I have won awards and am paid to design monumental buildings."

His gaze was drawn to where she nibbled on her luscious pink lip while she thought on his words. Barclay averted his face, a stirring of desire heating his blood.

"What if it is terrible?"

"Just look down on that page of yours, and wherever your gaze happens to fall, read me that verse."

She gazed at him, then finally nodded. Closing her eyes, Jane drew a deep breath. When she opened them, she found a place on the page and read it to him in a rush.

> *"Old eyes, cold eyes, eyes that have seen too much.*
> *Aware of what it is to love and lose.*
> *How my heart cries out to ease his burden.*
> *To banish the dark shadows from those depths,*
> *And bring back a sure smile to his firmed lips."*

Barclay went still.

Were the lines about him?

Was that how she perceived him?

Was his grief so evident?

Staring at the flames in the hearth, he found himself spellbound by their flicker while he tried to sort through his reeling thoughts. The silence in the room thickened, growing heavy with indolent meaning, until he turned his head to look at the girl.

Jane was blushing so fiercely, staring at the page in front of her, that he was afraid she would singe her glorious mane of ebony locks with the emanating heat.

"That was"—Barclay hesitated while he sought the right description—"evocative."

"Uh ... thank you?" Jane mumbled in reply, clearly too embarrassed to look at him.

"Truly, Miss Davis. You should share your verses more often. I think you could write a volume and seek a publisher."

She gasped in reaction. "What? Why would the poems of a country lass be worth publishing? You are funning me!"

"Women are the jewels of our civilization. She is grace and kindness. She is the beauty of our world. Without her, men would be mere barbarians in the mud. We could all dare to hear more from the feminine perspective."

"My sister is the one with something to declare. I am not."

"I beg to differ. Your words contain profound insight."

She glanced at him. "I observe people. Most of my verses are regarding what I think I see."

Barclay swallowed. "You see much, if that verse is anything to judge by."

"You are most encouraging."

He shrugged nonchalantly, but internally, he was still recovering from the words she had read aloud. "There are plenty of people who could criticize you for your effort. I prefer to be a man who encourages worthy individuals to pursue their dreams. I owe my grandfather for taking a chance on me, so I feel obligated to create opportunities for others. In that vein, I have publisher acquaintances if you ever wish to submit your work for consideration."

Jane sat back in her chair and stared at him intently across the width of the room. "You are an unusual man, Barclay Thompson."

Barclay drowned in the ice-blue depths of her gaze, his breath quickening along with his pulse. He imagined lifting her in his arms, without breaking that intent gaze, and walking her down the hall to place her in his bed. To lower his mouth and taste her creamy skin. To sip the gentle grace of her soul. To hold her in his arms while he brought her to the heights of new passion. To fall asleep with her cradled in his arms and wake in the morning to begin his day with her. All the while, comforted by the knowledge that she was young and strong. That her days were not numbered, and that she could stay at his side long into the future. That they could grow old together, and he would not know the forbidding shadow of imminent loss as he had done with Natalya every day of their lives together.

He blinked, and that idyllic future disappeared as the room came back into focus.

She is not for you, Barclay.

But he wished she was. His entire being yearned to spend more time with the graceful woman who treated his child with such kindness and allowed him to forget the pain of loss for the first time.

They spoke for a little while, discovering a mutual love of Shakespeare and Wordsworth, and he was impressed with the quickness of her mind and the depth of her understanding regarding their verses. Eventually, Barclay returned to the family wing. He walked along the dark hall, musing over the interlude with Jane, who had remained in the library.

The corridor was dark, the fog blocking all moonlight from weaving its way in. Barclay could barely see his way because the sconces cast little light. He assumed that the large sash windows allowed plenty of moonlight in and that the sconces were sufficient under most circumstances, but the fog had been unexpected so the servants had not taken pains to increase the light for the gloomy conditions.

Just then, a flash of lightning lit the hall. A clap of thunder masked Barclay's yelp of surprise when a small ghostly figure was revealed several feet in front of him.

"Papa?"

Barclay caught his breath, realizing that it was Tatiana who had startled him out of his wits. "What are you doing out of bed, little one?"

"I miss Mama." She broke into tears when she responded, causing Barclay to hurry over to her side.

Dropping to his haunches, he folded her into his arms. "Oh, Tatiana. I promise wherever your mama is right now, she misses you dreadfully, too."

Tatiana's little shoulders shook as she cried into his shoulder, breaking Barclay's heart as he swept her up against him and carried her to his room. Walking over to a sofa by the fireplace, he settled her down next to him. "What is it?"

"I woke from a dream. Mama was in my dream, but I couldn't see her face. When I awoke, I realized I have forgotten what she looked like." Barclay's heart fractured as he stared down at the tear-streaked face of his little girl and thought about what he should say.

He reached out a finger to wipe away her tears. "That is ridiculous, little one. Of course you remember how she looks. Why, you look just like her!"

Tatiana's tears stopped. "I do?"

"All you need to do is look in the mirror. Come, see here."

Barclay ushered his daughter over to a mirror on the wall. Holding her up with one arm, he raised his hand to finger her hair. "She had silken hair woven from moonbeams ..."

"Like mine?"

"That is correct. And, see, she had eyes as blue as the Baltic Sea."

Tatiana gazed at her reflection. "Like mine?"

Barclay bobbed his head. "And her skin was as smooth as fresh cream."

Tatiana stared intently into the mirror, raising a hand to touch her cheek. "Like mine?"

75

"Just like you, little one. Just like you."

"She will always be here with us?"

"Always." Barclay's voice was hoarse when he responded, and he accepted the truth. Their mutual grieving must come to an end. He could not live in the past any longer, and he must help his child to find joy once more, as she had during the reading of *Aladdin* earlier that evening.

Somehow, this visit to Saunton Park had unlocked a door, and Barclay could see clearly that he had been keeping them trapped in the past with his lingering state of mourning. Natalya had instructed him to find a new wife once she was gone. Barclay had failed to pay her heed, and it would disappoint his late wife that her child suffered for his neglect in fulfilling his promise to her.

He must accept that Natalya was gone. Come morning, he needed to make a serious attempt to find a new mother for Tatiana. No more mourning. No more mooning over the beautiful young woman he had met a couple of days ago, but a genuine effort to find a suitable mother.

CHAPTER 7

*J*ane woke up late the following morning, staying awake until dawn before falling asleep as first light appeared on the horizon. This inability to slumber was becoming so frustrating. She had never had trouble in the past, but ever since she had joined the Balfour household in London, and now Saunton Park, she slept fewer and fewer hours.

Before her visit, she could slumber anytime and anywhere. That was now a distant memory. Insomnia had been a fact of life for many weeks.

Jane prepared for the day, eating her breakfast from a tray that a maid had brought in. Fortunately, her strange schedule was not widely known outside of her relations. What kind of country lass kept such late hours? Her twin brothers, Oliver and Max, had teased her relentlessly for the few days they had been in residence for Emma's wedding the week before.

She left the family wing to read in the library, excited but nervous to encounter Barclay after the intimate words she had shared with him the night before. When she reached the library, she found a tray of coffee waiting for her—the servants had grown accustomed to her unusual habits.

Just as she was reaching over to lift the coffeepot to pour a cup, Mr. Dunsford walked in.

"Miss Davis, there you are. Did you hear me coming?" The young gentleman was dressed in a fine wool coat of burgundy that fitted him to perfection. His waves of curls were at once wild and perfection. Jane envied the man his valet, who made it look so effortless.

She frowned in confusion.

"You were pouring me a cup of coffee?"

Jane pasted a smile on her face. Her head pounded from her lack of sleep, and she had really been looking forward to sipping her coffee as she fully roused herself before seeking any company for the day. Now that Mr. Dunsford had seen her pouring *the gentlemen's beverage*, she would have to forsake her cup. "Of course." She poured, breathing in the aroma with envy, before putting the pot down. Reluctantly, she picked up the cup and offered it to the young buck.

"One wonders why the servants are providing cream and sugar?" he mused, gesturing at the tray.

Because that is how I prefer to drink it!

Jane shrugged. "Perhaps some guests prefer to add it."

"Fie! That is something a lady might do. What type of man would drink it in such a feminine manner?"

It was time to change the subject, lest she reach over to grab the cup back out of his hand. She had noticed a propensity to be a little grumpy before she had her first coffee of the day, and she was liable to say something unladylike when she so desperately wanted to take it back and swallow it down herself.

Mr. Dunsford was not to know that he was irritating her, so it was hardly fair to take it out on him. "Were you looking for me, Mr. Dunsford?"

"I was. I was hoping you were available to play lawn bowls? Several guests have gathered on the east lawn. Do you play? I can teach you!"

Jane really needed that cup of coffee. She had grown up in the country, one of six children. They played bowls every Sunday, and Jane was the best player of all of them. Again, it was not Mr. Dunsford's fault that she found his comments so irritating. She simply loved drinking her coffee as part of her waking-up ritual. Perhaps she should call for some tea in its place?

"I have played it before." She thought about refusing in order to find a new cup, but then recalled her decision after reading to Tatiana. She was to be seeking a husband, so she might start her life's next chapter. "I would love to play."

Mr. Dunsford's boyish face lit up. "Excellent!" He stood up and put the cup down.

Jane glanced at the untouched coffee with yearning, her mouth watering at the thought of picking it up and downing it. She smiled at the gentleman, before her eyes once more flickered to the coffee. "I shall need to collect my bonnet, Mr. Dunsford. How about I meet you on the lawn?"

"Of course! A lady as fair as you must take care of her complexion. I shall wait for you by the terrace." He bowed politely, his face hopeful, and Jane realized that if she encouraged it, she could obtain a proposal from Mr. Dunsford. He was quite keen on her. She simply needed to spend some time with him and decide if he was a suitable match—the man at her side whom she could tolerate for the rest of her days.

The moment he left the room, Jane quickly prepared her coffee before anyone else could interrupt her. Lifting the cup to her lips, she breathed deeply before downing it. She dabbed her lips to ensure there was no evidence—it was not the relaxing reprieve she had hoped for, but at least the pounding in her head dissipated.

Feeling invigorated once more, Jane went to collect her bonnet from her room and wash her mouth with dental elixir before walking through the manor to exit from the terrace. Several guests were gathered and tables were laden with lawn bowls.

Mr. Dunsford spotted her arrival and came racing over. Taking up her hand, he bowed deeply. "Miss Davis, I am looking forward to demonstrating the nuances of play to you."

"That would be delightful."

"We are playing in teams of two. Mr. Ridley and his sister will play against us."

Jane looked out over the bowling green that had been created. She waved at the duchess, who walked over with a jaunty bonnet bedecked with elegant feathers, her brandy eyes luminescent in the sunlight. "Jane, we finally play a game together. I grow weary of sitting as a spectator."

"Which rink is ours, Your Grace?"

"We are playing on the first one."

They strolled over to where Mr. Dunsford and Mr. Ridley were waiting for them. Mr. Dunsford tipped his beaver with a little bow. "Your Grace, I am honored to play against you."

The duchess beamed. "And I, you, Mr. Dunsford. I must warn you that my brother and I have played together many times."

"If you win, I shall be able to say the Duchess of Halmesbury beat me," he responded with a polite grin.

"Excellent. Let the best team win."

Mr. Dunsford and Mr. Ridley proceeded with the coin toss, the duchess winning the right to toss the jack. Her brother ran out to center the jack on the pitch after it came to rest.

Jane walked over to the table where the bowls had been laid out, and Mr. Dunsford joined her. "I shall bowl last because it will be more difficult. You should do your best to place your bowl near the jack."

She smiled amiably in response. They had not discussed who was to play first or last on their team, but she had no wish to quibble over it. Jane turned to watch as the duchess approached the mat, dropping to roll her bowl, which curved out before arcing back and coming to rest just four inches from the jack. Jane was impressed. The duchess must be quite strong to have bowled so far up the pitch. She must have played as much as she had claimed.

"Well done, Annabel." Mr. Ridley leaned down to peck his sister on the cheek, holding the brim of his hat to prevent it from slipping.

Mr. Dunsford rubbed a hand over his jaw. "Her Grace has done very well. Please do not be alarmed if you cannot place closer than her, Miss Davis. Just do the best you can."

Jane smiled enigmatically. Taking her place at the mat, she studied the placement of the bowl and jack. Then, kneeling down, she bowled a slow arc which came to rest just two inches from the jack.

Mr. Dunsford walked forward, viewing the placement with his jaw agape.

Mr. Ridley, too, inspected, then called out an instruction to his sister. The duchess picked up another bowl. Returning to the mat, she bowled once more, getting the shot a smidge closer to the jack than Jane had to take the winning position.

As the game continued, the duchess formed a head with her remaining bowls, blocking any direct route. Jane studied her options, then went to the mat. She bowled a fast run shot, which sped down the pitch, knocking into two of the bowls obstructing the jack. They skidded out, one dropping into the ditch and out of play while Jane's own bowl knocked into the jack. They quivered and then dropped apart.

Jane quelled a victorious grin from crossing her face. Her run shot had been fast and precise.

Mr. Dunsford shook his head in disbelief, his beaver teetering for a second before settling back down. "Miss Davis, I believe you should have been last to play! I hope Mr. Ridley is a poor player, because I cannot do better than you."

"Not at all, Mr. Dunsford. I am sure you could have thrown a run shot more impressive than mine. You are stronger, after all." Nevertheless, Jane was pleased. Mr. Dunsford should know she was a sensible young woman in her own right. She would forgo drinking coffee in front of the gentleman until she knew his sensibilities, but she would not curb her talents.

The game progressed slowly until eventually the duchess and Mr. Ridley won by just one shot. It had been exhilarating, no one certain which team would win until the very last end was played. Mr. Dunsford was an adequate player, but not quite good enough to knock apart the head that Mr. Ridley had formed, which won the last point for the opposing team.

They congratulated each other on a fine game, with a number of notable shots, before returning to the terrace, which was now shaded. The afternoon sun had moved behind the manor sufficiently to escape the heat of its rays. They found tea and biscuits laid out, which Jane was delighted to see.

Walking over to take a seat next to the duchess, the two of them watched the game on the third pitch, the only remaining in play.

"I must say, Jane, I was happy to observe that you did not restrain your skill to pander to the gentleman." The duchess spoke in a low voice to not be overheard, indicating Mr.

Dunsford with a nod of her head. "Many young ladies would have done so."

Jane sipped her tea and grinned. "I think there should be some honesty during courtship. I would not want the gentleman to get the wrong idea of who I am."

"You seem quite a competitive young woman."

"Not really. I love feminine pursuits. I embroider well. I am adequate at pianoforte. But I do not wish to be controlled when I marry. I would like a partnership such as the one my sister and Perry share."

The duchess chuckled in response. "I see. It was a demonstration for the young buck that you have a mind of your own."

"Precisely."

"I appreciate that. When my husband and I met, there could be no doubt that I was an independent hoyden. I am still uncertain if the duke was impressed with my audacious behavior, or if he married me to protect me from my wild spirit."

Jane tilted her head. "You were audacious?"

The duchess shook her head in remonstration. "My goodness, I hope I am still. Perhaps more refined, but under this regal exterior beats the heart of a rebel."

Jane giggled. "I would not say that I am a rebel. However, I would like a husband who respects my needs as I respect his. I wanted to ensure the gentleman noted me as an individual and not just a pretty face."

"That is well advised. He will have to acknowledge that you are a person in your own right after the way you played today."

"Then I have succeeded in making my point. All that remains is to discover if his pursuit continues now that he has been informed of my skills."

Mr. Ridley and Mr. Dunsford chose that moment to join them, their own cups of tea in hand.

"My word, Miss Davis. You play exceptionally well!" She found the admiration on his youthful face to be quite validating.

"I come from a large family who like to play. We have competed on many a Sunday afternoon."

"I am most impressed with your run shot. You must have quite a bit of steel running through you to bowl so fast and hard."

Jane smiled in reply, satisfied that Mr. Dunsford had, indeed, seen she was a capable young woman and still wanted to spend time in her company. Woolgathering over Barclay Thompson be damned. This burgeoning relationship was showing promise, and perhaps she could be betrothed to a suitable young man, who deigned to exhibit an interest in her, before the summer ended.

Behind them, the terrace door swung open. "Jane!"

Mr. Dunsford flinched in surprise. She swung around in time to see Tatiana's face lit with joy before the girl raced over to throw her little arms about Jane's neck. She smiled, raising her own to embrace the child while noting that Mr. Dunsford had leapt out of the way with an appalled expression.

"Jane, have you been playing bowls with Papa? I cannot find him anywhere."

"I am afraid not. I have not seen your papa today, Tatiana."

"Oh." Her little face fell in disappointment, tugging at Jane's heartstrings. She lifted a hand to tuck a silver-blonde lock behind the child's ear.

Mr. Ridley cleared his throat. "Some guests are playing nine-pins beyond the rose garden. Perhaps Mr. Thompson is there?"

"Where is that?" asked Tatiana.

"I can take you, if you wish. I was going to join a friend."

"Yes, do that," exclaimed Mr. Dunsford quickly, his relief evident.

"Yes, please, Mr. *Riddee*." The gentleman grinned at the mispronunciation of his name, his brandy eyes reflecting warmth as he held out a bronzed hand. Tatiana took it and they walked away, the young girl asking him what were nine-pins. Jane watched their departure, inexplicably wistful to join them in their search for Barclay.

* * *

BARCLAY HAD BEEN DISAPPOINTED in meeting with Mrs. Gordon when she had elected to play nine-pins. He had hoped they might play bowls, a game of precision and skill, but she had claimed the game made her head hurt to think so hard.

Considering he was making a sincere effort to determine whether the woman would be a suitable wife and mother, not to mention the only gentlemanly thing to do was to agree, he had wound up playing nine-pins.

There were very few gentlemen present, predominantly women in lavish bonnets engaged in the so-called sport.

His mother was there, and knowing full well how he would feel about playing, she pressed her lips together in an effort not to laugh at his discomfort on his arrival.

Bowls might make Mrs. Gordon's head hurt from the *excess* of challenge, but nine-pins made his own head hurt for the *lack* of challenge. As a man who dealt with mathematical formulas and angles, bowls was a game he could appreciate.

He would wager coin that the brilliant Jane was partaking in bowls right at that moment, but he quickly pushed those thoughts aside.

When the widow had eventually lamented the strength of the sun, Barclay had quickly suggested that they sit and converse in the shade of a nearby tree, assuring her he would not mind with barely disguised relief. They had ended their game to take a seat on the bench that curved around the base of the majestic oak.

Barclay had smoothed his hands over his buckskins and regretted he had not brought any tailcoats of a different hue. With his decision to come out of mourning, he had realized that very morning that he could not continue to wear the black tailcoats, which had become something of a uniform.

If he were on a work site, he might loosen his cravat to breathe easier, but it would be scandalous among the house-guests to do so, which meant he had to suffer through the rigid dress standards throughout the day and night while he engaged in trivial pastimes.

Nevertheless, he was to try to find a new wife and a mother for Tatiana, so inhaling, he told himself he would need to prevail. How simple his courtship with Natalya had been as a young man. When had life become so complicated?

For the next half hour, he made small talk with the woman, fetching lemonade and biscuits from a nearby table the earl's staff had set up for the guests.

Eventually, Mrs. Gordon sighed. "Would you mind terribly if we no longer partook in small talk? Perhaps we could share more entertaining tales if we relax the proprieties a little?"

Barclay straightened in his eagerness. He needed to learn about the attractive woman at his side, and polite chitchat revealed little of a person's character. "Indeed. It can become dull. Did you have a subject in mind?"

"Tell me, Mr. Thompson, do you ever have difficulty with a client? Does anyone refuse their plans, or whatnot?"

Barclay laughed. "It is the constant dread of an architect

when an important client changes their mind midway. Just recently I planned a Neo-classical folly for a client up north. Building had begun, and I traveled to visit the building site, where he met with me. The foundations were already dug and construction had begun, which we inspected together."

Mrs. Gordon leaned forward. "What did he do?"

"The client mentioned he had recently visited Stourhead near to here in Wiltshire, and could we adjust the foundations to make the building round, such as the Temple of Apollo at that grand home designed by Colen Campbell."

Mrs. Gordon giggled. "My word! How far along were the foundations?"

"We had already constructed them and had begun on the first level."

"That is a ridiculous request to have made! What did the gentleman think you were to do?"

"He asked me if we could simply leave what we had constructed, but knock out the corners of the square to form a circle."

The widow broke out laughing, holding up her hands to cover her mouth in her mirth. Barclay could not deny that her absorption in his story, not to mention her response, was flattering. It had been some time since he had enjoyed the company of a woman in a leisurely manner, and Mrs. Gordon evidently found him amusing. Gasping for breath, she responded, "How did you address his request?"

"I told him, certainly we could do precisely as he requested. I would simply prepare an estimate for the change in specifications and bring it to him that evening."

"And did you do so?"

"I did. When he saw the cost, he appeared to be in the grip of an apoplexy. I asked him if I could commence work on the changes, and he sputtered he would sleep on it and inform me in the morning."

Mrs. Gordon's shoulders shook with glee as she laughed even harder. "And then?"

"Come morning, the gentleman had left me a note that he was needed elsewhere, and that he had decided that the Hoares of Stourhead were pretentious tradesmen who knew not their place, and that Colen Campbell was naught but an upstart from *louse land*. My master builder informed me that the contemptible denigration referred to Scotland, being himself a Scot from Edinburgh. The note directed that I was to proceed with the original design of taste and distinguishment that *he* had designed."

Mrs. Gordon clutched her stomach, practically doubling over in her mirth. "What a rude man!" She gasped for breath. "Well played, Mr. Thompson."

He grinned back at her. "One does not get far as an architect if one does not learn how to manage one's clients."

She leaned forward and asked in a conspiratorial whisper, "Who was the gentleman in question? Was it someone I would have heard of?"

Chuckling, Barclay shook his head. "I am afraid I cannot speak out of turn. Suffice it to say that he was not as distinguished as he claimed."

The afternoon had become unexpectedly entertaining, and Barclay was pleased to find the widow was more fun than he had initially thought. Perhaps they could form a comfortable companionship? She was attractive, amiable company, and she had a sense of humor.

Not to mention that she is of an appropriate age.

Barclay exhaled in contentment. This might actually lead to something. He had to admit he was enjoying himself for the first time since Natalya had died. It was as if he had been asleep these past two years and this visit to Saunton Park had suddenly awoken him from his slumber. He still did not sleep at night, but mayhap once he had a wife in his bed once more, he would recover his ability to relax.

Certainly, he felt relaxed at this moment.

He had not realized how much tension he had had coiled throughout his body until this week. Since arriving here, it had been releasing in tiny increments. Perhaps by the time he left for London, he might be engaged in a serious courtship with the handsome widow.

It was at that moment when he noticed a gentleman approaching, with his little girl in tow. Mr. Ridley, spotting him under the tree, headed over hand in hand with Tatiana.

"Here is your papa."

Tatiana pulled her hand away to cross her arms, belligerence etched in every line of her body as she took in Barclay's proximity to Mrs. Gordon. "What are you doing?"

"I am enjoying a conversation with Mrs. Gordon. What are you doing?"

"I was playing with the children in the nursery when I came to find you. I thought you would be with Jane, but—" Tatiana turned her glare on Mrs. Gordon, who started, then giggled nervously.

Ridley raised his eyebrow as he observed the awkward interaction. He shot a sympathetic look to Barclay before bowing, with a tilt of his hat to the widow, and striding away to join Lord Trafford, who was the only other gentleman playing nine-pins.

"Mind your manners, little one." Barclay firmed his jaw, shooting a look of remonstration. "Mrs. Gordon, may I present my daughter, Tatiana Thompson?"

Tatiana did not move.

"Please curtsy, Tatiana."

With great resentment, she dropped into a slight curtsy as her grandmother had taught her. "Can we go play chess now?"

"I am not done playing nine-pins with Mrs. Gordon." He spoke with a firm voice. It would not do to allow his daughter to control him, especially in front of an audience. He could not believe she was being so rude.

Damnation! Had he just defended nine-pins? Repressing a groan, Barclay accepted he was now committed to playing the game. Standing up, he held out an arm. Mrs. Gordon rose, and they fell in step back to where the players were assembled. Nine-pins, it was.

From the corner of his eye, he saw Tatiana racing past, back to the manor. Her face was scrunched, and he thought she might have been on the verge of tears, but he could not allow his child to dictate his actions. Guilt assailed him. She had spoken of wanting a new mother, and he was taking steps to fulfill the request. So why did he feel such a scoundrel now?

With a sense of resignation, he went to place their pins once more to resume play, wondering how long was an appropriate length to play to make his point that he was the adult in their family.

He wanted to chase after Tatiana and discover why she was so upset, why she had been rude to Mrs. Gordon, which was out of character, and restore their affinity, but first he needed to make this point. He could not allow his daughter to run rough-shod over him, especially not in front of veritable strangers. It was disrespectful.

Fortunately, the game passed by quickly, and it was less than an hour later that he accompanied Mrs. Gordon back to the manor where she joined the other guests on the terrace. He noticed Jane talking with the countess, quelled a surge of interest, and left quickly to search for Tatiana, whom he could find nowhere.

Sighing, he realized she was hiding. Hopefully she would reappear to eat her dinner.

He returned to his room with a book and took up a seat in the armchair to wait for his daughter to make an appearance, his door left ajar to welcome her in.

When he awoke, the sun was setting, pink and red light staining the sky. Barclay stretched his arms and yawned, realizing his lack of sleep had caught up with him and amazed to have dozed off. He certainly was becoming more at ease since he had arrived at Saunton Park, not usually being the type of person who could take a nap while the sun was up and there was an endless list of things to do.

As he gazed at the majesty of the Somerset sunset over the park, he heard the door creak open behind him and close as Tatiana made her way into his room.

"Papa?"

"Tatiana."

"I am sorry I was rude."

"I thank you for your apology. Will you come sit with me?"

She approached, the patter of her feet as light as the treading of angels. When she stopped by his side, he reached over and picked her up to plonk her onto his knee. She was getting heavier, growing before his eyes, but somehow, in his grief, he had failed to notice the changes in his young daughter. Tatiana leaned back to rest her head against his chest as they both contemplated the dramatic colors painted upon the firmament.

"Why were you so upset, little one?"

"I want Jane to be my new mother. I do not understand why she was with the Mr. Dunsford fellow and you were with that Mrs. Gordon."

"Jane is too young to be your mother. I have to find a suitable woman to marry, and I am spending time with Mrs. Gordon so I can get to know her."

"Mrs. Gordon is the wrong woman. You must court Jane."

"You understand that I am the parent? I am the one who must decide about what is best for us. For you."

"But if Mama were here, she would tell you that Jane is the one who is to be my mother."

Barclay froze, his heart twinging in his chest with the pain of it. "If your mother were here, we would not be discussing who should be your new mother."

Tatiana fell silent. She pushed away, dropping to her feet to go stand at the window, where she toyed with the drapes. "I do not wish to have Mrs. Gordon as my mother."

"If matters progress with Mrs. Gordon, you will grow to like her."

Tatiana turned back, her delicate face hardened with her outrage. "If Mama were here, she would say to look into my heart. I looked into my heart, and Mrs. Gordon is nowhere to be found!"

"What are you saying? That Jane is?"

She came forward, grabbing hold of his hand as if to implore him. "Yes. Jane likes to spend time with me. She reads me Ladin! That is what Mama used to do. It is a sign, Papa!"

Barclay shook his head. "How old are you, Tatiana?"

"Nine."

"And how old is Jane?"

"I don't know."

"I think she is eighteen."

"Why does that matter?"

"How many years older is she than you?"

Tatiana counted on her fingers. "Nine?"

"And how much older am I than Jane?"

Tatiana's little face screwed in concentration as she counted.

"Aaah! One, two, three, four"—pulling his hand back, Barclay smacked it rhythmically against the other in time with his counting before flinging them both up in frustration —"there is something like thirteen or fourteen years between us! She is closer in age to you than she is to me!"

He stood up and, taking hold of her hand, he stalked out of the room with her back to her room, where he settled her in a chair near the supper tray that had been brought for her. "So there you are. It is a sign! I must pursue Mrs. Gordon. She is the same age as your mother!"

Tatiana scowled up at him, clearly at a loss for words.

He bussed a kiss to her mulish face and brushed her hair back. He could not remain in her company at the moment. Too many thoughts about this complication with Jane. Too many memories of Natalya. His mind was flooding.

He needed to get some distance so he might calm down. "I love you, little one. Your grandmama will be here shortly."

With that, he rose to stride across the room. Yanking the door open, he found Aurora on the other side, her arm still extended to open the door. She swiftly pulled her hand back.

"Mother," Barclay acknowledged politely before stalking past her.

CHAPTER 8

*T*he clock announced the last few minutes of the midnight hour. Jane's quill hovered over the page of her journal, but she had no words to write. All she could think was that the midnight hour was ending. Their time. Would he make an appearance?

She had barely caught a glimpse of him all day, but now the manor was sleeping. Last night, he had startled her when he appeared while she sat in this same chair in this very room, encouraging her to speak her thoughts in a way that no man ever had.

Barclay appreciated her mind, and it was invigorating. No one had ever heard her verses before, but she knew he had been the right person to share her inner secrets with.

And he was right. She needed to take bigger risks. Put herself out there. Even if the gentleman was not interested in her, and even if she needed to pursue a courtship elsewhere, she would steal this interlude and use it to build her confidence in herself as a woman with a mind of her own, who had something to contribute to the world at large.

It was such a pity that their courtship was not meant to

be because she was very much afraid that she had found the man Emma had spoken of. The one with whom she shared a meeting of the minds. If only he could look at her as a woman. As a potential wife.

Her mind had connected with the wrong gentleman, and she was afraid she would never meet another like Barclay Thompson.

As she stared at the hands of the clock, she realized he was not coming. Disappointed, she put the quill down and gazed at the empty page in front of her. She had no muse tonight. No lines to write.

Pushing her chair back, she gathered her things. A book waited for her in her room, and it would have to be what kept her company in her sleeplessness. Turning toward the library door, she jumped in fright.

Barclay! And he was staring at her with the strangest expression as he leaned with his hand on the doorframe. "I knew you would be here."

"I hoped you might join me."

Silence followed her statement.

"I tried to stay away," he eventually admitted, his husky voice gruffer than she recalled. He had no tailcoat, just his white linen shirt which was agape at the neck to reveal the long column of his sun-bronzed throat.

"Why?"

"Because this does not make sense." Barclay waved a hand between them.

"What does not make sense?"

"This attraction."

Jane's breath caught. He was admitting he felt it, too? Her breath quickened and a tingle raced across the surface of her skin as if she had caught a sudden chill. She turned back to the desk, placing her things down while she tried to gather her thoughts. She must have taken too long because the next thing she knew, Barclay had come up behind her, the heat of his body warming her from behind.

"Since I met you, it is as if I awoke from a deep slumber. The slumber of mourning. And you were the first face I saw when I finally opened my eyes." The pace of her breathing quickened further until she was panting, barely daring to move in case she broke the magic of this moment. Or awoke to find herself in her bed while this delicious dream evaporated to leave her in solitude with only her yearning for company.

Barclay waited in silence, as if to observe her response. She did not move, frozen in fascination, while her stomach sparked with anticipation. He stepped closer, and she felt the warmth of his breath on her nape, teasing the tendrils of her hair. She heard him inhale deeply near her ear. "You smell of strawberries and almonds again. I have a craving to …"

She felt his lips touch fleetingly where her neck met her shoulder. Melting with delight, she moaned when she felt the velvet tip of his tongue brush over the same spot. Hot sensation cascaded down into her breasts, where her nipples puckered in startling response, before continuing its path down through her belly to heat the juncture of her thighs.

Jane tilted her head back, raising her lips toward him, and he accepted the invitation to fleetingly brush his mouth against hers. For the first time in her young life, passion burst into flames, threatening to consume her as his long, muscular arms came up, and he slowly turned her to face him.

She looked up at him and nearly swooned at the ardent desire shining in his brown eyes. Raising her hand, she brushed the long hair back from his face and gazed up at him with longing.

"Jane—" Once more, he lowered his head to capture her

mouth with his. For long moments, he slowly explored her lips with his, and all she could feel was him. His mouth, the rasp of his beard brushing her delicate skin, until she moaned from the back of her throat. She started in surprise when she felt the tip of his tongue flick between her parted lips, then sighed in light-headed pleasure as he stole into her mouth to taste her.

Their tongues tangled together, her heart racing in her chest as she learned he tasted of tea and spice. Clenching her legs together to quiet the throbbing pulse that beat at her center, she curved her arms around his neck and leaned into his tall, hard body. His hands trailed blazing heat up and down her back, and she relinquished all thought in the pursuit of feeling. Feeling his powerful body against hers. Feeling her own delicate femininity. Accepting that this gentleman—this riveting man—intrigued her more than any she had ever met and sparked a fire in her.

After a moment, she found her courage and brought her fingers down over his broad chest to explore the indents before she lowered her hands to his flat torso which was fired with his body heat, with only a thin, single layer of fabric to separate his skin from her touch.

Barclay growled as her fingers slid over his body, releasing her lips to blaze a trail of torrid kisses along her jaw and down the slope of her neck while more sensation shot to her breasts ... and lower. She moaned in heady passion, desperate to feel more. Pressing forward, she delighted in the feel of his hard chest against her unbound breasts, with only her night rail and wrap and his shirt between them.

With a groan, his hands came up to her shoulders, and he gently set her back. As their mouths parted, Jane felt keen disappointment. Her eyes fluttered open in question.

"You are temptation itself. I must step back before I forget myself," he explained, as if she had voiced her thought out loud.

He backed up a couple of feet as their eyes made contact. "Jane, it is not my place to pursue this. Us. You are young, with a promising future. And I ... I am a bastard who is too old for you."

Jane was sure confusion marred her features as she tried to make sense of what he was saying over the pounding of her heart. "Are you saying you are a bastard because you are too old for me?"

"No. I am a bastard. And I am too old for you."

"Oh. I do not care that you are a by-blow." The comment about his age did not bear acknowledgment. He was still a young man.

Barclay huffed with a half chuckle. "You do not know the repercussions. You are too young to know."

Jane lifted her chin. "I am willing to find out."

He contemplated her. "What if I am not willing to put you through that?"

"It is your decision, but know that I am ... that is ... I would ... like to try."

He lifted one of his large hands, the hands that occupied her thoughts when she lay awake until the twilight of dawn, and ran his blunt, calloused fingertips gently down her cheek as if she were made of the finest china. "I must leave you now, before I do something I regret."

Barclay left her standing there, and Jane stood still for several moments while she caught her breath, wondering what would happen next.

* * *

BARCLAY WOKE UP, surprised how well he had slept after the interlude in the library. He examined the ceiling, recalling the taste of Jane on his tongue. She was sweet and soft, with a delightful constellation of freckles where her neck sloped down to meet her shoulder.

A constellation that he had licked with relish to confirm that her skin was infused with a trace of strawberries, as he'd wondered ever since Jane had shared her beauty ritual with Tatiana.

He was still uncertain what was right, but he felt compelled to see Jane again. To experience the invigoration of being interested in life and love once more, a sensation which had been missing since Natalya's departure. Perhaps his desire to spend time in Jane's company was overriding his good sense, but he could not think of a single reason why he should not seek her out. What harm could it possibly do?

Inhaling deeply, he assured himself that he was not too old for her by societal norms and they appeared to be well-matched intellectually, with perceptions and pursuits in common. And now that the earl had acknowledged him, surely the Thompsons' standing would be improved once society learned of it?

Saunton had even suggested he would host a dinner to introduce Aurora and Barclay to well-placed members of society, to assist them in making new connections, and the duke had pledged his support to the endeavor. A rise in status might mean no lowering of Jane's in the event that their relationship progressed to the desired outcome.

He pondered spending some time with Jane today, so they might get to know each other better. She was open to a courtship, so perhaps it was logical to somehow explore their compatibility?

Barclay stretched and rose, thinking of how he might discreetly arrange to be with her without revealing their attraction so they might explore the possibilities of their relationship without the interference of others' opinions.

Some activity that would not lead to firm expectations but would allow them to learn more about each other and to discover if theirs would be an advisable partnership.

He did not wish to participate in any of the activities arranged for the guests, so he would need to find something that they could do away from the eyes—and inquisitiveness—of others.

Would Tatiana be sufficient to act as a chaperone, considering that he and Jane were vaguely related and these matters were usually a little more relaxed in the country? Whom could he ask without revealing the inducement for his question?

* * *

JANE WOKE at her usual time. The kiss she had shared with Barclay had done nothing to restore her former ability to rest peacefully. She had lain restless until dawn, remembering the touch of his lips on hers and the feel of his hard body under that heated layer of linen.

She exhaled deeply and wondered what would happen now that he had revealed his attraction. Would he pretend it had not happened when she saw him next, retreating from their connection, or would he acknowledge their growing affinity?

It was unclear, based on his final words before departing the library.

Groaning, she rolled out of bed. The sooner she dressed, the sooner she could find her tray of coffee waiting for her in the library.

An hour later, she took a seat in the library, pouring her coffee while Ethan and Richard played an early game of chess. The earl's green eyes glinted in the sunlight from the window, mirroring his son's own emerald gaze as they both concentrated on the chessboard.

"Checkmate."

"No, Papa! How did you do it?"

Richard grinned. "I retreated to draw you in, and you followed, thinking I was defending myself."

Ethan focused on the pieces, clearly playing out the last few moves mentally. He lifted a hand to tug on his collar, a perfect imitation of what Jane had noticed the earl doing on occasions when he was under stress. Richard pointed out what he had done, moving the pieces back, and then demonstrated the final moves.

"Papa, Daisy told me we have a *gra-ta* in the woods?"

"You mean the grotto?"

"Yes. She said she heard it was very *boo-tee-fill*, but she does not know where it is. Could you take me there?"

The earl's face fell. "I wish I could, but I have meetings with my steward and tenants today."

"I could take him." Barclay's husky voice caused Jane to thrill in acute response. She had not noticed his entry, but he was at the door, dressed in his customary black and buckskins, and holding Tatiana by the hand.

Richard smiled hopefully. "Do you know where it is?"

"Of course. I have studied the plans for Saunton Park many times over the years. It was the project that made Tsar's reputation."

The earl nodded. "Then I would appreciate you accompanying my boy to the grotto. Jane, would you like to join them? Tsar outdid himself when he designed it, and it is especially lovely in the summer."

Jane could not help herself—she beamed. "I would be delighted to escort Ethan there." *And his uncle!*

Barclay approached to take a seat while Tatiana and Ethan chattered at the chessboard.

"Please, Jane. Take your time." He waved to the cup in her hand, his eyes warm as he studied her closely, and Jane smiled shyly in return as the earl excused himself. Spending time with Barclay was precisely what she wanted to do today. Had he reached a decision regarding a prospective courtship? He seemed more than amenable to her joining him.

She hurried with her coffee, loath to have any of the other guests happen upon them lest they be invited to accompany their party to the grotto. Clinking her cup down on the tray, she rose. "Shall we?"

She grabbed Ethan's hand, determined to leave on their unexpected outing. Glancing over her shoulder, she saw Barclay followed with Tatiana, and she could not deny her excitement to spend some time alone with people she liked so much.

Ethan chattered at her side, but Jane did not relax until they had exited the manor and were walking down a garden path that led to the woods.

"Jane, I cannot keep up with you!" Ethan complained. Jane realized her long, unladylike stride had been forcing him to trot beside her, and now he panted, his little face red from his exertions. "You are awfully eager to see the *gra-ta!*"

She paused, Barclay and Tatiana stopping along with them. Looking about, Jane realized she had succeeded in drawing them away from the house party. There should be no danger of Mr. Dunsford or Mrs. Gordon intruding on their privacy.

"Perhaps Jane is eager to spend time with you," suggested Barclay, his eyes twinkling with humor as he regarded her. Jane bit her lip, blushing as she accepted that the architect was not fooled. He must have noted her efforts to avoid the other guests. Then she cheered up when she worked out that he must have had similar notions if he knew what she was up to.

"Have you been to the grotto, Jane?" Tatiana's eyes sparkled, her enthusiasm reflected there while she took in the tall trees that they approached. Jane realized the child's silver-blonde hair was bare, lifting her own hand to confirm that she had left the manor without a bonnet in her zeal to spend time with Barclay. The gentleman repressed a smile at the gesture, himself bareheaded under the afternoon sun.

"I have not."

"Do you know anything about the grotto? About what is there?" Barclay asked, appearing so light-hearted—not at all the mourning widower who had arrived just days ago.

Jane shook her head. "It is the company that has me engrossed," she admitted in a low voice.

He flicked a smile in her direction. "It is a rather unusual folly. From all accounts, Tsar did magnificent work, and I am intrigued to see it for the first time."

"What is it, exactly?"

He shrugged, those wide shoulders drawing her gaze as she recollected the feel of his broad chest pressed against her breasts.

Remember to breathe, Jane!

"You will all have to see it for yourselves. I shall not ruin the surprise."

* * *

BARCLAY WAS PLEASED with the current turn of events. He had desired time with Jane far from curious eyes, and here he was entering the woods with only Tatiana and his nephew to witness their interlude. Lifting Ethan onto his shoulders after the boy had complained about Jane's energetic strides to leave the manor behind, he had been well aware of what enticed her. He shared her enthusiasm to spend time together and anticipated the delight of both Jane and the children when they reached the grotto.

Herding their little party along a path winding through the trees, Barclay led the way. Fortunately, the path was well-maintained, so there was no danger of Ethan colliding with any branches despite his exaggerated height perched on Barclay's shoulders.

The sound of birdcalls and a breeze rustling through the leaves above them were restful, and Barclay felt at peace. Reaching a fork in the path, he walked to the left. The woods were cooler, shading them from the midday sun, which was a relief considering both Jane's and Tatiana's faces had been bared to its relentless rays.

Soon they came upon the pond, Ethan gasping in delight as he looked across the water at the statue of Persephone gazing back at them from the entrance of a grand grotto. Traversing the perimeter of the green water, Barclay was careful to steer Tatiana away from the edge of the water, where the sides of the pond were covered in slippery green slime. They approached the statue, and he became transfixed by this unusual representation of the goddess of spring.

Her perfect features were turned longingly toward the entrance of the first cave. Rather than the customary depiction of her with a sheaf of grain, or as a mythical deity with a scepter and box, this version was scantily robed in draped fabric so thin it might have been made of gossamer. She stood on a bed of flowers to commemorate the spring she brought each year when she was reunited with Demeter, the tilt of her head evoking the sentiment of her joy to meet with her mother once more.

Jane stood at the base, her jaw agape, as Tatiana reached out her hand to brush it across the smooth marble. "It is beautiful," she whispered in reverence.

Indeed, Tsar had outdone himself. The roof of the grotto, entirely manmade, reached out over the water, adding to the magic of the quiet space, the goddess forever reaching to return above world. In the cavern, the sounds of the woods were muted and the sound of tinkling water could be heard. The water was piped to flow as a stream from the bed of flowers at the statue's feet to rejoin the pond. A water feature for which his grandfather was very proud, evoking the melting of the winter snow and the return of growth and renewal when Persephone rejoined her mother on the surface.

"Grandpapa designed this?"

He smiled at his daughter, wondering if the architectural blood that ran through their veins had just awakened in her. Perhaps she might be a great artist one day. Or work with the elder Thompsons in their business. Instinctively, he knew such a path would not offend Jane if she were to join their family.

"There is more," announced Barclay as he lowered Ethan to the ground. The roof dipped down, so it was no longer safe for the boy to ride so high. He led them to the back. Behind a wall extending halfway across the back, he found the hidden entrance to the second cave. They followed him, gazing about at the convincing shape of the cave and brushing their hands over the frieze depicting the underworld.

It was a revelation of design, but it did not escape Barclay's notice that his ... sire ... had commissioned the underworld—a strange choice unless one took the dead man's hedonistic ways into account. Of course, the Earl of Satan had bonded with this chapter of classic mythology. How fitting a subject for such a cruel and lecherous man. But today was for learning more about the woman who had been captivating Barclay since the first moment he had met her, and assessing their compatibility together with Tatiana, so he brushed his bitter thoughts aside.

Entering, Jane froze at the sight of the second statue. A hole had been cut through the roof above to highlight the installation with dappled light. Ethan and Tatiana gasped in amazement, and Barclay had to admit that his grandfather had orchestrated such drama that it fairly took one's breath away.

Hades himself towered above them, much larger than Persephone, with his long bident in one hand and the other gripping a leash which tethered the ferocious Cerberus, his three-headed guard dog. On Hades' head rested his helm, and his face was turned toward the first statue, hidden from view, with the same sense of longing. But this god longed for his wife rather than the above world, which Barclay could commiserate with.

Except, for the first time since Natalya had departed, she was not foremost on his mind this afternoon.

"Who is it?" Ethan breathed, his small face reflecting his awe as he stood at the base and gazed up at the dog. Cerberus stood taller than the boy, and Barclay had to confess his own awe at the scope and perfection of the statue. One could practically smell the fetid breath of the hellhound.

"It is Hades, the king of the underworld." He pointed up at the helm. "That is his cap of invisibility. It allows him to travel undetected by other gods, similar to a cloud of mist."

Jane walked around the massive statue, viewing it from every angle.

"The detail is so intricate. See his sandals?" She pointed at the feet, which were clasped in leather straps with every nuance depicted. Hades looked like he might step off his pedestal at any moment to search for Persephone.

Tatiana leaned in to inspect Cerberus, squinting at the

sharp teeth jutting from his snarling mouths. "It is ... magical," she sighed. "Like Ladin in his cave of treasures!"

Barclay beamed. He could not remember the last time he had enjoyed such a moment of union. Four special people together in this moment when he laid eyes on one of his grandfather's greatest works. A moment of pure and utter joy.

Eventually, they began their journey back to the manor. Tatiana and Ethan clamored along ahead of them on the path. Noting their distraction, Barclay discreetly reached out his hand to clasp Jane's. Her eyes remained on the path, but he did not miss the smile of bliss that crossed her face and he sighed his own pleasure at a perfect afternoon of happiness.

Soon they would return to reality, when they crossed the edge of the woods back into the garden, but no matter what happened after this walk, the wondrous visit to the grotto with Jane and the children would forever remain in his heart.

CHAPTER 9

*A*s they approached the manor, Barclay reluctantly let go to walk ahead and take Tatiana's hand. Jane came up behind him to walk with Ethan, and he sighed. Their glorious jaunt was over, guests coming into view on the terrace, and he longed to turn back to the woods where things had seemed so simple in the solitude of the grotto.

Climbing the sloping steps, Jane discreetly ventured over to where the countess, the Duchess of Halmesbury, and his mother sat drinking tea around a table. Barclay watched her departure with regret, not wanting their afternoon to end. On the other hand, he wanted to explore the unexpected unison he felt with the young lady without potentially censorious interjections from inquisitive onlookers.

The children hurried over to the refreshments nearby, Ethan clamoring to know what was on the tabletop, which he could not see from his diminutive height.

His reverie was interrupted when Mrs. Gordon appeared at his side, placing a hand on his forearm, and his heart sank. The widow was a lovely woman, and he had no wish to disappoint her. He tried to think if he had indicated he might pursue her. It would be uncomfortable to explore future possibilities with Jane while engaging in a flirtation with the widow.

"Mr. Thompson, I have missed you this afternoon. Were you taking a walk with the children?" The widow gestured to Jane with an arch of an elegant blonde eyebrow, causing a stirring of anxiety in his gut. Was that how people would view them? That he was courting a child?

"Miss Davis and I took Ethan and my daughter to visit the grotto." Barclay was aware his timbre was roughened a little from his disquiet.

"Oh! I have heard from the countess that it is wondrous. I was hoping to see it, but I have never learned the route to reach it. I am hopeless with directions." Mrs. Gordon gazed at him expectantly, and he realized she was prompting him to take her there. The thought of sharing it—their special place—with anyone but Jane made him clench his hands in agitation. No matter what happened in the future, whether Jane and he overcame their obstacles, he would always treasure introducing her to the magical caves. He could not impose on that memory by taking another to see it. Especially not the same afternoon.

"Perhaps one of the guests will accompany you. Mr. Ridley, I believe, is familiar with the way." Her face fell in disappointment, and Barclay felt guilt, but not enough guilt to intrude on his magical memory with Jane. "Shall we take a turn around the gardens?"

It was the least he could do after sidestepping her hints to visit the woods.

"That would be lovely." She looked about before lowering her voice. "I had a matter I would like to discuss in private."

He hesitated, then held out his arm and Mrs. Gordon

took hold of it, grasping him a little more tightly than was comfortable. Heading down the steps, they took the gravel walkway toward the formal gardens which could be over-seen from the terrace, and he admitted he was curious what the widow would have to say.

"Mr. Thompson, I do not wish to be forward." She spoke as soon as they were out of earshot of the other guests. "I would like to make my feelings clear."

"On what subject, Mrs. Gordon?"

"May I be frank, sir?"

He inclined his head in agreement, worry descending on him. What was this about? He was concerned he might have created expectations with the widow and this conversation implied he might have overstepped.

"I am aware of your family circumstances ... of your mother and the late Earl of Saunton."

Barclay halted to look down at the petite widow. She was several inches shorter than the willowy Jane. When he had kissed Jane in the library, it had been surprisingly easy to lean over and taste her skin, where the constellation of mischievous freckles marred her otherwise perfect flesh in the most delightful manner. He blinked to clear his thoughts, remembering that the widow had just raised the question of his bastardy, which was quite inappropriate.

Mrs. Gordon noticed the blink and, clearly misunder-standing the reason for it, hurried to put her words to him. "I wanted to assure you that as a good Christian woman, I would never blame the child for the behavior of the parents. I think it is lamentable that society treats upstanding men like you poorly for something that is beyond your control."

Barclay frowned as he digested what she had said. It was evident that Mrs. Gordon wanted to clarify that she would be receptive to courtship, but the way she had said it ...?

He cocked his head as he sought how to politely defend the implied censure of his mother. "I appreciate the support, Mrs. Gordon. Be assured that Aurora Thompson was but a child when she met the Earl of Saunton. He took advantage of a young girl who had not yet achieved her majority, and there was naught she or my grandfather could do to set it right. She has paid the price dearly while the late earl dealt with none of the consequences of their association."

The widow's face fell in alarm. "I did not wish to offend. It is ... admirable that Miss Thompson kept her child and raised him. Very commendable. Of course, as you say, she was merely a child herself when the incident happened."

A mere one or two years younger than Jane.

Barclay's discomfort rose. He folded his arms behind him to hide the tremble in his hands. "My mother is a fine woman, of quiet distinguishment."

"Of course she is. The whole situation is quite lamentable. It is deplorable how some members of the nobility behave, blithely aware of their own superiority. I shall ensure I make your mother's acquaintance forthwith. I am ... hoping that our own ... companionship will continue to blossom, and it is obvious that your mother is an important aspect of your life. I am certain that a connection with the widow of a respected vicar will assist her to claim ... an increased element of respectability."

"That would be appreciated, Mrs. Gordon." It did not escape his notice that she was making a case for courting her.

They completed their walk, and the feeling of contentment he had enjoyed in the woods, the first time feeling such since Natalya had died, scattered like so many ashes in the wind.

A knot persisted in his stomach as he tried to think how he could proceed with a courtship of Jane without becoming an irreparable cad in the eyes of decent society. The problem was that he himself would have such private thoughts if he saw an acquaintance of his courting a woman of such tender years. How much simpler it would all be if Mrs. Gordon were the one he could not stop thinking of!

Barclay accompanied the widow up the steep stairs to the terrace. They parted ways as Aurora made her way over to speak to him at the balustrade. Mrs. Gordon stopped to curtsy and gush at his mother, inviting her to enjoy breakfast with her in the morning while Aurora contemplated her with a serene expression.

"That would be lovely, Mrs. Gordon," she responded in her lightly accented voice. His mother's mother had been a lively Italian woman, and Aurora had never lost the slight intonations from when she had learned to speak from his grandmama.

His mother eventually made her way to him, appearing relieved to have pulled herself away from the interaction. "Barclay, I must admit, I am pleased that you are taking our discussion to court seriously."

Barclay inclined his head in assent.

"Son, there is no reason to hurry the process. Please assure me you will be certain before you offer to make a young woman your wife. What you had with Natalya was special, and our family enjoys ... a pleasant dynamic. It would be ill-advised to disrupt your grandfather's household with the wrong companion."

Barclay's lips curved into a smile at Aurora's transparent attempt to meddle. "Are you saying that Mrs. Gordon is a poor choice?"

"Not at all. Just ... be certain. There is no reversing that decision."

"Why did you never marry, Mother? You are a beautiful

woman, and I have to think there were some opportunities over the years?"

Aurora shook her head, her black hair gleaming in the shade of the terrace. "It is not a son's place to ask such a question."

He shrugged. "This has been an unusual trip we have taken. We have spoken on other matters we would not ordinarily broach in London, and I have always wondered."

Aurora put her hands out on the balustrade, leaning down to look at the lovely landscaped gardens spread out beneath them. "Marriage is irreversible, and I never met the right gentleman. One who could accept my situation ... you ... and make me feel like taking the risk was worthwhile. Watching you with Natalya over the years—you were exceptionally fortunate to find someone who was your perfect counterpart."

"It was difficult knowing that it had a time limit, but I would never erase my time with Natalya for all the riches in the world."

Aurora turned back, her eyes searching his. "I believe you are destined to find such a connection again, Barclay. You have always been fortunate, and it is my dearest hope to see you happy as you once were. Assure me you will not settle ... that you will be sure before you offer for a young woman?"

Barclay's eyes flickered over to where Jane sat talking to the countess, leaning in as Sophia whispered something in her ear. Jane lifted a hand to Sophia's face to carefully tuck an errant curl of distinctive red-blonde hair behind her ear. The countess laughed aloud that a Miss Toussaint would scold her for neglecting her hair if the lady's maid were present to observe her current state. Richard's wife was glowing with good health, her rounded belly a reminder of the child they would soon welcome into their family. Hopefully, the heir that the earl needed to protect his family holdings.

Barclay could not help imagining Jane with a babe. Her love of children was obvious from all the times he had seen her with Ethan and Tatiana. She would make a wonderful mother, and he could not help hoping that in that esteemed future, he would be the husband at her side. But would it be fair to expect her to mother a child of Tatiana's age?

"I shall endeavor to think the matter through thoroughly before making my decision."

How would Aurora react if and when he revealed that he might have found a true affinity with a young woman barely older than his mother had been when she had found herself in trouble?

Hell, if only Natalya were here to discuss the matter.

But his late wife had abandoned him since his first night at Saunton Park. Her spectral presence had departed, and he would have to find counsel elsewhere than in his memories and imaginings.

* * *

JANE WROTE FURIOUSLY, her quill racing across the page. She had to stop and sharpen it, dipping it in ink, and frustrated at the interruption. She needed to get the lines out of her head before her thoughts evaporated into the dimmed room.

Bending over her notebook, she scribbled the verse, her inspiration inking the page.

The afternoon had been an utter delight. The time with Barclay, having him show her the magic of the grotto, existing in a bubble of time and space far from any civilization, had been a revelation.

She was uncertain where matters stood. Barclay had

stated no intentions yet, but she hoped … she hoped their relationship would progress.

There had never been such an attraction with any gentleman of her acquaintance, and her heart was in jeopardy of falling head over heels before she knew what this was … where it might lead.

Could Barclay be her Darcy?

Jane could now understand the troubles Emma had faced during her strange courtship with Perry. She had encouraged her sister to pursue the relationship, but Emma had balked. Now that Jane's affections were engaged, she knew what it was to want a man, yearn for him, but yet be uncertain of her reception.

Barclay had raised issues with a potential courtship. Their difference in age, and his lamentable status within society as a by-blow. She wanted to brush them aside and leap into his arms, but Emma had pointed out that marriage was a commitment that could not be undone and advised her to be cautious.

Jane now acknowledged that Emma's advice was true. She could not simply race headfirst, not knowing the gentleman's thoughts on the matter.

As she finished the last line with a flourish, she heard footsteps behind her.

"Do you have new verses to read to me?" Barclay's husky voice was low, intimate, causing a shiver of desire to chase over the surface of her skin to settle low in her belly.

"These are private verses," she whispered back, surprised how coy she sounded in the silence of the library.

"This is a private moment," he responded. He had come up behind her, leaning over the back of her chair to whisper in response and placing a fleeting kiss to the shell of her ear that he had just warmed with his breath. Jane closed her eyes at the exquisite tension of their shared moment, disappointed when he withdrew to walk around and take the opposite seat. Her heart lifted once more at the warm affection reflected in his eyes.

"I admit I was quite inspired ... by our visit to the grotto." She hurried to add the last, biting her lip in a wave of shyness. In all the years that men had displayed their regard for her, gathering around her at social events, Jane had never met one who intrigued her as much as Barclay.

Perry certainly had his charms, but it was clear from the very first moment that Emma was the one he had desired, and Jane had experienced no envy over the matter. She and Perry did not enjoy the meeting of the minds that he did with her sister.

A slow smile spread across Barclay's face in response, the electricity between them sparking in the same manner as rubbing wool made one's hair crackle and stand on end. Even now, her hair fairly crackled from the heat of their shared gazes.

Barclay was ... different from other prospective suitors. He seemed more intrigued by her as a person than he was by her appearance. Jane knew she was considered lovely by other people—gentlemen had made no secret of it. She was tall and willowy. Her hair was a wave of silky, ebony curls, and she had high cheekbones and symmetrical features which one could easily compare with portraits of English beauties. She had a fashion sense and a way with colors—taking care of her physical form something of a pastime.

But with Barclay, she was aware of something else. Something new.

Jane had become aware of herself as a person. An individual. Barclay had listened to her verse with such intensity, and when he had spoken, Jane had for the first time seen herself as an intellectual. An artist. Someone who composed lines to communicate the marvel of what she saw in the world—in others—and she discovered that another person thought she had meaningful observations to impart.

She knew this was a meeting of the minds of which Emma had spoken before her departure from Saunton Park. An indefinable kinship that somehow their thoughts were synchronized, and that they found more joy in the world when sharing each other's company.

Or, at least, she hoped he was sharing the sentiment and it was not wishful or youthful infatuation on her side.

Yet … his presence in the library for the third night suggested he felt it, too.

"What do you compose tonight?" He glanced down at the quill in her hand. Jane realized she had been frozen in motion since she had heard his step behind her.

"I was inspired by the statue of Hades. That such a hard and intimidating god should be so obsessed with a beautiful woman that he abducts her to his dark lair. I like to think he tricked her into eating the pomegranate seeds because he could not … not do it. That perhaps he truly loved her so much that he could not bear the thought of a future without her so granted her freedom while ensuring he could remain a part of her life."

Barclay huffed slightly. "That is a romantic view of the story, and I admit there are aspects of him for which I have empathy. His world is dark, and he is surrounded by the dead. She must have represented the very light and life which he was no longer part of. But I admit I have a difficulty when I recollect that it is the late earl who commissioned the work, considering the misdeeds which must have inspired him for such an odd choice of subject … That, and the fact that Hades was Persephone's uncle."

Jane chuckled. "Yes, that he was her uncle engenders"— she sought for an appropriate word—"repulsion. I refrained from including that in my thoughts when I wrote these lines.

A story can be viewed from many angles by the emphasis one places, and I chose to emphasize the love for tonight."

"That is insightful to consider."

Again, she was struck by how Barclay talked to her with sincere interest in her thoughts. She felt mature in his presence—a woman with valuable thoughts and opinions.

Barclay brought his hands up on the table to stare down at them. Jane was riveted. She had been fascinated by those large palms and long blunt fingers since she had first seen them. She remembered the brush of his calloused fingertips the evening before and repressed the shiver of hot desire. The feel of his lips on hers still played through her mind at the oddest moments.

"I would …"

Jane leaned forward, but Barclay failed to continue. "Like to court me?"

He chuckled, still staring down at his hands. "When did young women become so direct?"

She drew her lips inward, not responding immediately. Eventually she released the breath she had been holding. "I am not usually so forward, but I find myself …"

Silence fell once more until Barclay cleared his throat. "I simply do not know how this new relationship with the earl will affect my social standing. And you are so young."

Jane lifted her hand to chew on a nail in agitation. "I would like to try. I have … met no one like you before."

His gaze rose to meet hers across the table. "Nor I you, Jane. If my wife were still alive … I am convinced you would have been the best of friends."

Jane tentatively smiled, but she found it difficult to breathe, thinking about that. It was at once both a deep honor and so depressing a thought. If his wife were here, and they were the best of friends, would Jane have been in the horrible position of coveting the woman's husband?

She hoped not. She hoped she would have the fortitude and honor to simply ignore him as a man who was unavailable. Fortunately, it was a theoretical situation she would never need to experience.

The gentleman's regard for his late wife was what first attracted you so!

Recollecting the conversation she had overheard here in the library that night when Barclay and Aurora discussed his situation was a consolation. Without that event, he would simply be an inordinately handsome gentleman attending the house party. Handsome in the same manner as his two brothers—Richard and Peregrine—to whom she had experienced no attraction.

"So what do we do?"

He hung his head to stare at his clasped hands on the table once more. "I do not know. I need to think on it. This whole situation is so unexpected. Just four days ago, I was still in deep mourning for my wife, and now ..." He swallowed hard.

Jane felt tears prickling her eyes in sympathy. The enigmatic gentleman had felt loss to such a great depth she could not comprehend it. She had only met him a few days earlier, yet already the idea of his death was too devastating to consider. Barclay carried a substantial burden, and she did not want to pressure him. He needed time to reach his conclusions about how to proceed with this unexpected affinity of theirs, and she would not hurry a man who even now still wore black to grieve the passing of his too-young wife.

"Take your time, Barclay."

He looked up at her, searching her face. "I appreciate your patience ... Jane."

She smiled, wishing she could reach out and grab him when he arose to leave the room. Pull him into an embrace

119

and press her mouth against his once more as she inhaled his scent of spice, leather, and ink.

But the widower needed time to reconcile the past and the future, so she listened to his footsteps recede as she held a hand over her pounding heart. Damn! He was so fascinating, she wanted to chase him down the hall and fling herself into his arms lest he get away.

CHAPTER 10

*B*arclay knocked on the earl's door early the next morning. From inside the study, he heard his brother calling for him to enter. Opening the door, he stood hesitantly, not sure what he wanted to say. He needed to talk to someone about his conundrum, and it was imperative he obtain a man's perspective on his minor crisis. This seemed as good a time as any to lean on their fraternity, considering Tsar was a minimum of two days away in London.

"Barclay, please come in. Would you like some coffee? I just had some delivered a few moments ago."

He nodded, shutting the door to walk over and join Richard in the seating area overlooking the park. The earl noted he had closed the door with a quirked eyebrow, his green eyes curious as Barclay took his seat.

"Did you have something to discuss?" The earl appeared slightly apprehensive, as if steeling himself for bad news.

"I need some advice. I find myself without a confidant."

Richard straightened with a keen expression, clearly flattered that Barclay had sought him out. It was rather endearing that his younger brother was working so hard to include him as a valued family member.

He dropped his gaze to study his hands clasped in his lap. This was bloody awkward, but without Tsar to talk to, he was at a loss. He supposed he could discuss it with Aurora, but he found he did not relish it. What he wanted—needed— was the perspective of a steady man. Someone who understood the responsibilities of being a husband, a father, and a protector within the context of their culture.

Moreover, perhaps this was an opportunity to bond with the earl. After all, the gentleman had revealed his vulnerability on the issues surrounding Ethan's future, so it seemed only fair to reciprocate.

Nevertheless, Barclay was pleased the duke was out riding, so he only had to reveal his thoughts to one newly acquired relative this morning.

"My mother impressed upon me the importance of moving on. It has been two years since ... my wife died. We were very close."

"I regret I shall never meet Tatiana's mother. She must have been an exceptional woman to have captured the heart of such an intelligent artiste."

Barclay nodded. "You would have liked her very much. And she was breathtaking."

Richard pulled a face of sympathy. "I cannot imagine how I would cope if anything ever happened to Sophia."

Grimacing, Barclay smoothed his hands over his breeches as he thought about how he would never wish such an event on another man.

"Tatiana has made a request. She wishes to have a new mother, something Natalya made me promise I would take care of once she was gone. Tatiana is to grow up loved by two parents, and I am afraid ... I allowed my grief to prevent my fulfillment of that promise."

Richard leaned forward, pouring a cup of coffee and handing it to Barclay before pouring his own. "It seems a topic that requires some fortitude," he offered in explanation when Barclay raised a quizzical eyebrow at the interruption.

Barclay sipped his coffee before leaning back in his chair to gaze at the ceiling while stretching his legs out. He had been doing this frequently since his arrival at Saunton Park —studying the ceiling and cornices—a habit he had developed when he felt under pressure. "I am attempting to move on. To notice the women in my surroundings and note if there are any who appear to be suitable. However, there are complications."

"Complications?"

"First, there is my parentage. As we discussed, it is difficult to be a man in my position. It is even more so for my mother and daughter. Natalya knew she only had a short time to spend with me, so she forwent such concerns to follow her heart, but a new wife ... she may have to deal with the same issues for decades, and I do not wish to inflict that on a respectable woman."

Richard cocked his head. "You do not think that matters will be improved ... because of us?"

"Perhaps. Only time will tell. Even if matters improved, there will still be certain doors that remain shut. Some people are ... self-righteous."

The earl laughed. "I find they are usually the ones up to no good themselves."

Barclay smiled, enjoying a moment of unity with his younger brother. Richard had made every effort to build a brotherly relationship between them, and for the first time, Barclay felt a flicker of genuine kinship. "Just so. The guilty seem to speak loudest in accusation."

"Agreed. When I acknowledged Ethan as my son, I had at least three peers snub me within the halls of Westminster.

Men I happen to know have fathered secret children the length and breadth of London. They dared to disdain me for taking the honorable path, while they failed to take full responsibility for their own progeny. It was all I could do not to ask after their sons and daughters with solicitous concern."

"What did you do?"

"I disdained them in return. If they have such little integrity, they are not worthwhile connections. They are riffraff, despite the blue blood flowing through their hypocritical veins. But, then, I have the advantage of more powerful connections than they. The duke alone makes for a powerful ally in most matters."

"What of Sophia? Were there consequences for her when you acknowledged Ethan?"

"Some. None that perturb her. She is an unusual woman who is not overly fond of polite society."

Barclay's eyes scrutinized the cornices while he mused on this. "There are two candidates who might lead somewhere interesting. One is eminently suitable ..."

"And the other?"

"The other ... I do not know that it would be appropriate. But we share something. An affinity that runs deep. Something I have only experienced one time before."

Richard sighed. "With Natalya?"

"With Natalya."

"I once thought to marry someone suitable. I spent several Seasons searching for the suitable choice. My plan was to have the type of marriage favored by the nobility, where we barely spent time together and I continued my pleasurable pursuits discreetly on the side. Then one night, I overheard a young lady lambasting my character to her cousin, and I ... Please, do not scorn me when I say this, but I simply lost my heart. It made little sense to pursue her, but I simply could not imagine an existence without her by my side to disparage my prior roguish pastimes with her cutting wit."

"The countess?"

"Indeed. Sometimes your heart knows what you need more than the brain does. I needed someone strong, opinionated, who would not accept things as others expect them to be. Someone who would confront me about my worthless behavior. My heart recognized the void she would fill in my immoral existence, and my mind caught up."

Barclay lifted a hand to smooth his beard as he thought about what the earl had revealed. "The second woman is ... a revelation. I just hope I would do right by her if I pursued the affinity we share."

"I cannot say, but I will say that it is easier to contend with life's challenges when one has the right partner at one's side."

That was something Barclay missed. A wife and partner who always had his best interests at heart. Who was always on his side, even when he erred.

Clearing his throat, Barclay broached the most awkward of questions. "As you are a man of experience ... if I were to pursue her ... how does one go about courting?"

The earl was suddenly assailed with a paroxysm of coughing, quickly setting down his coffee cup before fidgeting with his cravat. Barclay narrowed his eyes while his brother squirmed with apparent shame. "I do not really know all that well."

"I do not understand."

Richard stood up and walked over to the window to stare out over the park. "I am more familiar with the art of seduction than with courtship, I am afraid. Perry could recite every rule, every nuance of courtship, but I ... can merely give you a rough outline. Such as, two dances imply a sincere interest. A third is practically a public proposal. Hothouse flowers are an appropriate gift but not a piece of jewelry or something personal or expensive. I always thought I would gather the details when I actually found a young lady worth courting."

"I thought you hunted for a wife for several Seasons?"

"Yes, but I never went past a single dance. None of the young misses captured my interest, so I only knew what was expected in broad strokes. Or defensive strokes, to never be caught alone with a young lady if one did not want to be hung by the parson's noose … and to be careful about that dancing rule of two and three."

Barclay huffed. "Even I know that."

"I am mortified to reveal this to you of all men. I was so afraid of becoming like our father, I changed my entire life around when I realized how perilously close I was to following in his footsteps. Fortunately, my conscience is eased because the moment I learned of Ethan, I knew I would acknowledge him. After meeting my boy, I learned of your existence—it is incredible to me that my father did not marry your mother, or at least acknowledge you. He should have been proud to bestow his name on you or, minimally, to pledge his support of such a talented man."

Straightening up, Barclay rose and joined his brother at the window. It mitigated his guilt to discover his brother had struggled with similar thoughts about their mutual parent. "You are a good man, Richard. And I must confess, hearing that you considered similarities between you and the late earl is a bit of relief. I have been doing the same since I was told he was my father, and it has worried me to notice possible elements of him in me."

Richard turned his head from the window to frown at him. "You? You are a bastion of honor and integrity, who is still faithful to his wife two years after her death. What could you possibly have in common with our father?"

"I think anything on the subject of women leads one to recall the loins that fired our conception, does it not?"

The earl winced. "Well, that is a repugnant thought to consider. However, I feel compelled to tell you I have not noticed a single trait in you that reminds me of our father. He was the worst kind of hedonist. If you knew ..." Richard shuddered. "There are no words to describe the hell that my younger brother lived in under his roof. Suffice it to say that when I see how you are with your mother and your daughter, I can assure you that you have not inherited even the tiniest fraction of character from the Earl of Satan. He was an irredeemable monster."

Barclay remained quiet for several moments before making his admission. "I am constantly reminded since I arrived here that he seduced my mother when she was just seventeen years old somewhere in this house ... or the grounds. It does not bear thinking."

Richard leaned a hand against the window frame while they both gazed out the window. Barclay watched a group of gentlemen striding in the direction of the lake, all carrying fishing poles and hampers. On the horizon, he noticed two riders crossing a field and wondered if they were the Duke of Halmesbury and perhaps his duchess, the second rider being much smaller, but he could not quite see the clothing or if there was a sidesaddle. On the other hand, given the size of the duke, even a fully grown gentleman might look small in contrast.

"I wish I could do more for your mother. Sophia and the duchess have pledged to introduce Aurora to the very best of society—the worthwhile best, that is. Not the judgmental biddies beneath our notice."

"I appreciate that ... brother."

The earl's head came up at that, his face expressing his delight. "Brother?"

Barclay nodded. "Just assure me your door will remain open in case I decide to blunder through a courtship during my stay in your home?"

"You have my support always. You are my blood, Barclay."

Barclay hoped that the earl's sentiment extended to a potential courtship of Jane. Richard was protective of his family, and the young woman was his sister-in-law.

Bloody hell! Did you need to think of a further complication?

How had he failed to realize he was thinking of courting Perry's sister-in-law? Emma Davis's recent marriage to his new brother made the impediments even worse. Barclay wanted to hang his head in dismay. Instead, he continued to stare out the window while attempting to regain his composure before his brother noticed anything amiss.

This was an impossible situation. He could only be grateful that Richard had not pressed him for the identities of the women he was considering. How would he ever reveal to his new brother that Jane was the object of his desire if he pursued her?

Leaving his brother in the study a few minutes later, Barclay realized he had not yet seen his mother. If he were to consider this courtship of Jane, he would need to discuss it with Aurora first. She was usually participating in lively discussions with their hostess by this time in the morning, but he had yet to glimpse her among the guests wandering the manor.

Setting off to look for her, he soon confirmed she was nowhere to be found in the main house and the library was vacant.

Walking back to the family wing, his professional eye gauged the architectural details in appreciation of Tsar's work, while he searched through the public rooms.

He headed down the corridor of arching windows where Tatiana had come to find him the other night during the fog. It was a well-lit space offering grand views of the park, and he once more admired how Tsar had incorporated the endless views into the very design of the grand home.

However, he was quickly distracted when he reached the family wing and approached Aurora's door. It was ajar and from inside he could hear a woman weeping. Striding forward, he pushed the door open to confirm it was his mother who sat in a plump armchair by the window. But she did not overlook the view. Instead, her face was buried in the crook of her elbow, which was propped on the ledge, while her shoulders shuddered with the force of her emotion.

Barclay's heart almost stopped in his chest to see his mother in this state. Quickly, he entered her bedroom and shut the door behind him.

Aurora was always calm and even-tempered. She had taken many knocks in her life, and there was little that could penetrate her fortitude. Decades of barbs and slights, even outright insults, had caused her to master the art of quiet dignity in the face of adversity. Barclay's alarm to see his mother sobbing alone in her bedroom had no bounds.

"Mother?" He approached her carefully, taking the seat next to her and reaching over to lay a gentle hand on her shoulder. "What is it? What has happened? Is it Tsar?"

Her voice was muffled. "No! It is not anything of import. Please leave me and do not be distressed by my ridiculous behavior."

"Mother, I cannot. Please, tell me what has happened?"

"I do not wish to speak of it, Barclay."

"Mother, please. I cannot stand to see you so distressed."

Aurora held up her trembling hand to display a letter he had not seen from across the room. "I received a response from the London Virtuous Committee of Charitable Endeavors."

Barclay's heart sank as he pulled his mother up from her chair to embrace her, where she wept into his shoulder. He was heartbroken to see her so distraught, tugging the letter from her hand so he might read what was causing her such distress.

"I was so sure ... I allowed my hopes to become engaged, thinking that this new connection to the earl would sway the ladies to allow me entry ... Oh, Barclay!"

A fresh wave of sobbing tore him in two. One half was devastated to see his strong mother reduced in such a manner, while the other half was enraged at the bitter old shrews who would cause his mother such pain.

Holding up the letter behind his mother's head, he scanned the lines on the page while anger thickened in his gut, threatening his very self-control.

Dear Miss Thompson,

In respect to your recent application to join the London Virtuous Committee of Charitable Endeavors, in light of your connection to the Earl of Saunton, Lord Richard Balfour, I regret to inform you that the committee has rejected your request.

Corruption is the scourge of our age, and it cannot be discounted that there are members of the female sex who behave with the ornamentation of excellent social conduct, a mask of propriety, and affectations of virtue, yet harbor inappropriate passions. These women tempt our men to conduct themselves in base behaviors, contributing to the moral decline of our society.

Notwithstanding your unwedded status, you have shown no inclination to address your inherent moral turpitude. After these many years, you have yet to display piety, baring instead the ornament of lewdness in that you have remained unwed to signify your innate passions for men have not abated.

The committee has tasked me with notifying you that no further applications will be considered. This decision was unanimous and final, and there is naught to be done that will persuade the committee to change their position on this matter. Once again, we should like to direct you to take advantage of our charitable endeavors as a recipient, not a member.

Ever yours,

Mrs. Iona Campbell

Secretary to the London Virtuous Committee of Charitable Endeavors

Barclay did not like to display his emotions, but he was sorely tempted to rip the letter in two. Or perhaps tear the drapes from the fittings. Or throw something through the window. Anything to assuage his fury at the unkind and unmerited words.

When Aurora had told him she wished to reapply, he wanted to dissuade her, afraid she might be disappointed yet again. But she had been so confident that a connection to a powerful and wealthy earl might change the minds of the spiteful harpies, so he had not the heart to squash her dreams.

"These women are worthless, Mother! You must cast them from your mind and speak of them no more!"

Aurora's tears had subsided, but her face still rested on his shoulder. "I should have paid you heed when you said not to write, but I was so sure …" Her voice thickened once more, and he was afraid she would weep again. Carefully, he settled her back into her chair and sat down, resting his hand on hers while he tried to find words of comfort. Guilt coiled within his belly, leaving him breathless from the strength of it. Guilt that, like a narcotic, threatened to drag him into oblivion.

"This is my fault."

Aurora looked up at him, confusion on her tear-stained face. "Why?"

"If you had given me up, you would have been able to lead a full life, free of scorn and derision. No one would ever have been the wiser I even existed."

"Never, Barclay! That was never an option. I would receive a thousand cruel rejection letters and never for a moment regret that you are in my life. This is just a silly dream that has been dashed for the last time. I am disappointed, but I will dry my eyes and life will continue."

"I have never understood why this particular society was so important to you."

Aurora sighed, hanging her head to focus on the hands she was wringing in her lap.

CHAPTER 11

*W*hen Jane opened her eyes to the morning light, the elation of the evening before had not worn off. They had spent a magical afternoon together, and Barclay was considering a courtship. She wished she could have shared more kisses with him last night, but she had promised him patience.

She could not deny her optimism that it would all work out. Jane had known from the first that her sister and Perry belonged together, that Perry was to be Emma's Darcy. After some setbacks, it had turned out to be an accurate depiction, which meant that her intuition in such matters had been proven correct. Which meant Barclay could very well be her Darcy … No, that did not seem right. Barclay was not a Fitzwilliam Darcy in character. But he could be her … Colonel Brandon? Sort of, but no. Mr. Knightley? No, that was not right either.

He was her … her … Jane gave up. There was no one to compare him to. He was simply … Barclay. And after the promising events of yesterday, she felt sure that soon he would be *her* Barclay if she just gave him some time to navigate his way out of the past and into a new future with her at his side.

Weary from the continuing insomnia that plagued her, but excited to see the gentleman, she threw back the covers and prepared for the day. She found her cart outside the door and wheeled it in. Then she ate her breakfast in a hurry, before using the mortar and pestle to create the strawberry water once more. She would happily have forgone the new beauty routine this morning, but she could not forget how Barclay had breathed his delight that she tasted of strawberries and almonds, and if there were a possibility of stolen kisses this evening, she wanted to be prepared to bewitch him once more.

His own scent of ink, leather, and spices she could not quite place was intoxicating to her senses, and she wanted to be enchanting to the gentleman who made her heart sing and mind awaken to new possibilities.

She recalled how Tatiana had spoken of her life when her mother had still been with them. How they had traveled with Barclay to the various building sites, and Jane grew excited at the possibility of such a life. Perhaps she could compose poetry and spend time with Tatiana while he was engaged in work. She would have the opportunity to explore England and meet many new people.

It sounded idyllic, reminding her of Emma's words from the day she had departed Saunton Park. Her sister had reminded her that she had once spoken of traveling, that she liked to write, and that she would like her own children.

With Barclay, she would access all these activities, including gaining a lovely young daughter—a sweet girl whose company she enjoyed.

Was she mature enough to assume such a role? To be a mother to a nine-year-old?

Jane bit her lip, assuring herself she could muddle her

way through. Tatiana had announced her willingness for such a relationship, and there had been no indication when talking to the grandmother that it was a regular occurrence.

She and Barclay might be at different stages in the journey of life, but she would commit herself to catching up. Whatever it took, she would do it because for the first time she could envision spending her life with one specific man and she knew in her soul that he would be worth any troubles she might encounter. What relationship did not have troubles to overcome?

Jane hurried with the strawberries. She needed to find her morning coffee in the library and then find Barclay.

* * *

AURORA CONTINUED to twist her fingers in her lap while Barclay waited for his mother to speak. Eventually, she sighed as if accepting a dark fate and spoke.

"I told you that Grandmama—my mother—was a member of the committee, which is why I so desperately wanted to be accepted?"

"You did."

"I did not tell you about the day Grandmama was expelled from the society."

Barclay frowned. Indeed, that fact had never been mentioned. He had always assumed that she had remained part of the group. By the time he was old enough to be aware of his mother and grandmother as individuals with their own hopes and dreams, the topic of the committee had faded into the past.

"It was a few weeks after you were born. I had returned to London with Mama, and we were settling into life with a new babe in the house."

"What happened?"

"Word was slow to spread at first, but then overnight, it seemed everyone knew about that Thompson girl with the bastard."

Barclay sank back into his chair. His mother had never told him what it was like when he was born. She never complained about the situation, and all he knew were the accumulated observations since he had reached an age to be included in adult conversations.

His gaze found the ceiling, and he scowled harder than he ever had at the cornices to quell the disquiet he felt to hear Aurora's anguish as she recalled the past.

"One night, I was returning from your room. We had my old nanny to assist me, but I spent as much time as I could with you, and so I was passing the drawing room. The door had not latched properly when I had left them earlier, so I could overhear their conversation. I ... I had never heard ... my mother cry before that night."

Barclay's gut roiled in protest. He squeezed his eyes closed as Aurora continued to tell her story.

"Mama was crying and Tsar was comforting her. She wept because they had abruptly severed their ties with her. That night I learned how hard she had worked to be accepted when she arrived in England, how joining the committee had been one of her great triumphs, and how the day they had accepted her had been a victory for her in her new life. How she had worked diligently as a member of the society and was proud of the charitable work she had done as a member ... I could not believe it."

"Could not believe what?"

"That I had been so foolish with the earl. That I had allowed him to seduce me into hurting my family. She was such a good mama, and I caused her pain with my selfish, foolhardy choices."

Barclay himself was beating back the anguish that he was

the cause of four generations of Thompson pain. His grand-mother had always been so happy and steadfast. Thinking of her weeping as she lost control of her social status, how his mother had suffered, how Tatiana would suffer in the future, Barclay had never missed Natalya more than he did right at this moment.

He had fumbled with attempting to court young English women in his youth, only to have fathers slam their doors in his face. Meeting Natalya's father in St. Petersburg and being so warmly welcomed to stay in his home, then meeting Natalya later that night to experience the same warm welcome, had been one of the best days of his life.

That a beautiful young woman like her had willingly accepted his proposal, then waved a hand at the snubs she experienced when she arrived in England, had been such a compliment.

Natalya had brushed it aside to assure Barclay that the doors closed to her would have been closed no matter what his parentage had been. *"They would have snubbed me for being Russian regardless. There is no harm, Barclay,"* she would assure him.

Barclay returned to the present when Aurora continued talking. "I vowed no matter what it took, I would gain a place on the committee in order to honor my mother." Aurora gestured at the letter. "Obviously, that vow will never be fulfilled. I know it is inconsequential in the grand scope of life, but I feel I have let my mother down all over again."

Barclay felt his heart crack in his chest, for he had let his own mother down. This connection to the earl had been about opening doors for Aurora. For Tatiana. And this letter proved nothing had changed.

He imagined the impossible. That he might come home to find Jane weeping at the rejections of the day, with no hope of him being able to fix it for her. No advice to offer other than to ignore the people who behaved in such a cruel manner. A young woman at the prime of her life, with her entire future ahead of her, and he knew there was only one decision he could make.

But, his own troubles aside, first he needed to assist his mother.

It was some time later when he escorted his mother to the public rooms. Aurora was composed, evidence of her tears had subsided, and her good cheer restored once more. It would seem she had needed time to grieve her disappointment, but now she was leaving the charitable society behind. That chapter was well and truly closed.

Barclay deposited Aurora with the countess and duchess for tea in one of the drawing rooms. Then he steeled his nerve and went to search for Mrs. Gordon.

He donned his beaver, noticing her on the terrace. Striding over, he exited the manor. "Mrs. Gordon?"

The widow turned, her face lighting up when she saw him. "Mr. Thompson! I was hoping to invite you to play nine-pins!"

Barclay ignored the fissure of irritation. Here was a mature woman with a solid reputation who was well aware of the issues she would encounter by his side. A woman who knew the pain of losing her spouse. And as a woman of nearly thirty years of age, it was possible the widow did not want any children, which would be succor to his mind. He could not possibly afflict his bastardy on another child. It was possible that the widow could grant Tatiana increased respectability. So he would play nine-pins for the rest of his days if it protected his mother and his child from further derision.

Eventually he would grow to enjoy it, surely?

He proffered his arm, and the widow gratefully took hold of it. A little more tightly than he was accustomed to, but he was a man of strength and he would grow to like that, too.

Resolutely, he plastered an affable smile on his face and escorted the widow toward the gardens.

* * *

WHEN JANE REACHED the library to drink her coffee, she found Tatiana waiting for her.

One of the maids assigned to the nursery for the house party had recently confided to her that the servants taking care of the children had given up trying to keep track of the little girl. Apparently, Tatiana would occasionally visit the nursery to play with Ethan and the other children, but left without a trace when she grew bored. Radcliffe had informed the countess who had told them to leave the child to her own devices unless Barclay instructed otherwise because it did not seem to be causing any difficulties and Tatiana was clearly independent.

"Have you seen my papa?" the little girl queried as she waited for Jane to pour her coffee.

"I have not, but I just left my bedroom."

"Oh." The little girl twirled a silver-blonde lock of hair around her little forefinger, her face thoughtful. "Would you play chess with me? Ethan beat me again. It is quite embarrassing. I am five years older than him!"

Jane smiled. "Of course. I will drink my coffee and then we can play." The coffee was beckoning vigorously this morning.

Tatiana grinned, then skipped to the window to wait for her. Jane noticed the girl freeze, then press her face to the window as if she were trying to see something more clearly. When she turned around, her face was reddened.

"Are you all right, Tatiana?"

"Uh … I will have to play with you later. There is something I must do." With that, the little girl raced from the room, her skirts fluttering as her legs pumped across the distance. Jane stared after her, then walked over to the window to see who had distracted the child. Whoever it was, it appeared they had disappeared from view by the time Jane reached the window.

She bit her lip, feeling anxious for Tatiana. Should she follow the girl to find out what had upset her?

* * *

Barclay viewed the pins, which really were too close to make for a challenging game, but it was how the ladies played and so he must engineer some method of enjoying it. Perhaps he could practice knocking down specific pins to hone his skill. His skill in—*damnation*—nine-pins. He swallowed and assured himself there was a way to make it a passable pastime.

Lifting a ball from the table, he made a show of preparing to bowl. Reaching back, his arm swung forward—

"Papa!" It was practically a shriek. Barclay swung the ball around to knock against his chest. He composed himself for a moment before turning to find his daughter standing a few feet away, her expression outraged.

Turning back to Mrs. Gordon, he forced a smile. "Mrs. Gordon, if you would not mind, I need to speak to my daughter for a moment."

The widow was unhappy. She grabbed her parasol, opening it up to stroll away. Barclay joined Tatiana and, grabbing her hand, walked her over to the shade of the oak tree. He sat on the bench and lifted his daughter to sit next to him.

"What is it, little one?"

Tatiana fixated on her toes. When she raised her face, he saw tears shimmering on her lashes, her large blue eyes wet, while the feeling of culpability from earlier stabbed him in the chest like a thousand knives. Good Lord, he was bungling his family duties. First, he had failed to help Aurora fulfill her lifelong dream of joining that society of hers, and now Tatiana looked like her heart was breaking.

"Why are you with Mrs. Gordon, Papa?"

"Our situation is difficult, little one. Mrs. Gordon might help us."

"But I like Jane. I want her to be my mother."

Barclay braced himself. He could not have another woman in his care be broken by their association with him. Mrs. Gordon might help both Aurora and Tatiana overcome this … this … damned notoriety. He was not afraid of ruining the widow's life with his situation because she was rusticating in the country and was willing to contend with the issues. They enjoyed a companionable relationship, but no deep feelings were engaged on either side. A marriage to her would be … safe … and he must do what was right for his family, no matter how much he might wish for something different.

"Jane is a young girl. You need a proper mother. One who can help you grow up to be a great lady one day."

"Mrs. Gordon does not like children."

Barclay stiffened. "How can you know that? Did she say something to you?"

"No, but I can tell. And I know Jane makes you happy. You smile when you are with her. Please do not do this. You like her, too. I know it. It is not too late. I left Jane in the library, and we can go join her there."

Barclay relaxed at the news that Mrs. Gordon had not acted in an untoward manner to his child. Reaching out his hand, he clasped his daughter's gently. "You must trust me,

Tatiana. I am doing this for you. One day you will understand."

His daughter started sobbing in earnest, and for the second time that day, Barclay tried to comfort one of the females he was honor bound to protect while they wept. He tried to embrace her, but Tatiana pulled away from him to stand. There she stood glaring at him, her arms akimbo and her face set in anger like a little warrior princess.

"You know nothing." Her face was red with pent-up emotion. "I know Jane is the one, but you will not listen!"

With that, she ran away, Barclay watching as she disappeared.

He needed to set this right, and this was the only way he knew how. Tatiana would be upset at first, but he was sure it would all work out in the end because it had to. He could not be the cause of any more disappointment for their little family because it was breaking him in two. Tatiana would be disappointed for a little while, but she would eventually forget the young woman. *They* would forget her … in time.

He should never have encouraged Jane or Tatiana with foolish hopes.

* * *

JANE SPENT the afternoon searching for Tatiana and Barclay, but they were nowhere to be found. Eventually she had played chess with her cousin Ethan, before returning to her bedroom to prepare for dinner. Eagerly, she had ventured to where the guests were gathering, but Barclay was not to be seen.

At last he walked in, dressed in black trousers, black tail-coat, and snowy white linen, which fairly took Jane's breath away as it did each evening. Barclay was especially fine in evening finery. Caught in a conversation with Mr. Dunsford, she could not help staring across the room at his tall form making his way over to his brother. Before she could make her excuses to leave Mr. Dunsford's side, dinner was called, and she saw Barclay hold out an arm to the widow, Mrs. Gordon, to escort her to the dining room.

Once entering the lavish dining area, where crystal, silver, and fine china glinted in the candlelight and austere Balfour ancestors observed them from ornate gilt frames, Barclay took his seat with the widow while Jane was stuck with Mr. Dunsford. The gentleman was solicitous and charming in his self-deprecating manner, but Jane wanted to spend time with Barclay. Who had made these seating arrangements? She was customarily seated with the family at the other end of the table, near Barclay and Aurora, but not tonight. Tonight, Mrs. Gordon had somehow claimed her usual seat.

Jane focused on her soup, and on engaging in conversation with Mr. Dunsford, but she did not know what she was saying or what topics they discussed. Her mouth met her social commitments while her mind raced about this new seating.

I will ask Barclay about it when he comes to visit me in the library!

Feeling much better, Jane relaxed enough to notice that Mr. Dunsford could not take his eyes off her. This stirred worry in the region of her belly. She was not attempting to lead the gentleman on, and she hoped he would not make an attempt at courtship. Her hopes regarding the young man had been before. Before the visit to the grotto. Before the kiss in the library. Just … before.

She could not possibly consider accepting his courtship now. Her affections were engaged with the darkly handsome man sitting near the earl. Who even now was leaning over to say something to Mrs. Gordon, who laughed in response, her face lovely and golden hair shimmering in the candlelight.

He would never pursue the widow. You promised him time to reconcile his grief with the idea of courting you.

Assuring herself of this helped, but she still longed for dinner to end and the midnight hour to arrive when Barclay would visit her once more.

After dinner, she laughed and talked with the countess and Aurora in the drawing room over tea, but her eyes kept searching out the ormolu clock on the mantelpiece. Time seemed to tick by so slowly, it was practically a crawl.

Playing parlor games with Mr. Dunsford at her side a short while later was fun, and made time pass more quickly, but her eyes still wandered over to the clock at regular intervals while noting Barclay's continued absence.

It was with some haste that she undressed later that night to don her night rail and tie on her wrap. Picking up her journal and quill, she quietly opened and closed her door, then strode down the family hall to the main manor.

Entering the library, she took up her usual seat and found the inkstand that was stored there.

Checking the clock on the wall, she lowered her head, as the midnight hour began, to write the verses she had been composing mentally.

Thirty minutes later, she checked the time again. He always came near the end of the hour, so she had time to finish the verses that he had inspired.

Sharpening her quill to dip it in ink, she lowered her head once more to continue writing on the page. She imagined reading the lines to Barclay, excited to hear what he might say. It had been mortifying to reveal her inner thoughts when she had recited her poetry, but Barclay had listened with such aplomb. Her confidence in her poetry had been growing ever since he had assured her that she had something of import to impart.

She finished the lengthy poem she had composed, hoping

that enough time had now passed that he would arrive at any moment. Sprinkling pounce over the words to dry the ink, she blew, then raised her head to learn the time. Her heart sank. It was ten minutes past one o'clock. Barclay should have been there by now. Pushing her chair back, she walked out to look for him, but the hall was empty and she saw no one in the corridor linking the family wing to the main house.

Confused, she walked back into the library to pace up and down. Surely he would visit to explain his absence all day?

Another ten minutes passed, and Jane's heart beat like a drum in her chest while her belly knotted with anxiety.

After another twenty minutes of assuring herself that he was running late, or had not noticed the time, or had some correspondence to attend to, she walked over to slump into an armchair by the fireplace and accepted the truth she had been dreading since dinner.

He is not coming.

In all her years on this earth, Jane had never felt so despondent. Barclay was rejecting her. He had reached a decision and had not even bothered to visit to explain himself.

For the first time, true loneliness descended like a fog rolling in from the coast.

She did not want to pursue another gentleman. Barclay made her feel special. Not for her appearance, but for her mind and character. Perhaps when the house party was over, she would lift her spirits by visiting Emma at her new home.

This adventure to join the earl in his home for a Season, then this house party to introduce her to prospective suitors, had all seemed so exciting just a few weeks ago. Now Jane simply felt homesick. It was not turning out to be how she had hoped.

To make matters worse, it seemed even Tatiana was

avoiding her now. She had yet to see the girl since she had run off before their game earlier that day.

Jane recalled the trouble she had gone to with the strawberry water that morning. There was no denying that she was a fool. Fortunately, no one was aware of her attraction to Barclay, so her foolish hopes were private to her ... and the gentleman.

She chewed her lip while she tried to think of something to settle her despair. It would be even more foolish to grieve over a passion that had never truly begun.

Perhaps she should give Mr. Dunsford another try? Discover if he could accept the fact that she favored coffee? Learn what he thought of her poetry, even?

No, sharing her lines with another was too much to bear. It was a reminder of her magical evenings with Barclay, which made the tears she was holding back threaten to escape once more. If only Emma were here to talk to.

She would have to begin with revealing her coffee habit, then learn if Mr. Dunsford and she shared anything in common. Raising her hand, she wiped the tears from her lashes and rose to go to bed.

CHAPTER 12

*T*he following morning, Jane sat in the library with her cup in hand while she gazed out the window to the clouds banked in the sky. It was a perfect reflection of her current mood. Dark. Melancholy. Silent.

She had never needed her coffee as much as she had this morning. It was the only comfort she had found since Barclay had failed to appear the night before. Fortunately, she had a full pot to keep her company until she could rouse herself to leave the library. After tossing and turning all night, she had not yet eaten; her appetite had failed her.

No book had brought any solace.

Dawn had not brought the sleep it usually did since this insomnia had begun.

Perhaps she should return to her parents' home in Rose Ash? She had slept fine there.

Jane grimaced. She had hoped to start the next chapter of her life, yet now she contemplated returning to the comfort of home. Perhaps she was too young to know her own mind. Perhaps she should speak to the earl about returning for a Season next year and take some time to mature a little more.

Emma had returned home, and things had worked out beautifully for her older sister.

Except Jane held no hope that Barclay would follow her as Perry had followed Emma. Returning home would simply be a temporary retreat so she might lick her wounds, think about what she wanted from her future, and then return to the Balfour household for another attempt.

Lud, it all sounds a lot of effort.

She sipped her coffee again. If she could just get a full night's sleep, perhaps she could reach a decision about how she wanted to proceed. Trying to make a life decision when she had not slept a wink was probably ill-advised.

Perhaps it was time to visit a herbalist and tackle this insomnia. She had thought it was the excitement of the unexpected Season that had ruined her sleep, but last night had been the worst yet and she certainly could not blame that on excitement. She had never felt less enthusiasm than she had in the past twelve hours.

Jane finished her coffee, turning to pour another cup and flinching in surprise when she saw Tatiana had taken a seat in the chair across the table without her noticing. Seeing the little girl was cheering despite her weary body and heart. At least one Thompson was not avoiding her.

The little girl was staring down at her slippers, her shoulders slumped.

"Tatiana, are you all right?"

"I came to tell you I am sorry."

Jane tilted her head in dismay. "Whatever are you sorry for?"

"I am sorry that Papa is courting Mrs. Gordon." Jane's heart squeezed in her chest. It was true, then. Barclay had reached a decision regarding Jane. She had thought it was about his grieving, that he simply needed time, but it would seem he had decided she was not the right woman for him.

Jane poured her coffee with unsteady hands while she tried to compose herself. "I did tell you that your papa had to find his own wife. He is a good man, and whatever he decides, I am certain that you are an important part of his decision."

Tatiana's face was forlorn as she continued to study her slippers. "It is not right. I do not like that woman. I like you."

"Oh, sweet girl. I like you, too. Whatever happens in the future, we shall remain friends."

Tatiana turned to look at her, her deep blue eyes brimming with emotion. "The afternoon at the grotto, I thought …" She shook her head. "I was so … sure."

Jane smiled, fighting back the urge to weep so she could be strong for the little girl who had known far too much pain in her short life. "Every moment with you has been a gift. I am certain that everything will work out for the best for you. Your papa loves you—" Jane paused to prevent her voice from breaking, then continued once she was sure she could speak. "—and he will do what is best for you. I know it. Please do not worry about me. You should put your attention on getting to know Mrs. Gordon if Bar—your papa is courting her."

"Would you have courted him? If he had asked?"

Jane bit her lip. What was the right way to answer, so that she did not sound critical of Barclay? "It would be a great honor to be considered for the position of your new mother. I considered it a great honor the first time you asked me, and nothing will ever change how I feel about you."

Tatiana jumped off her chair, running over to wrap her little arms around Jane's neck, who had quickly set her cup down when she saw what the girl intended to do. She embraced Tatiana back, squeezing her little form to her bosom while she quietly released her dreams of becoming the mother the girl had sought.

"We are part of the same family now, Tatiana. We shall see each other often, and I can read you *Aladdin* anytime you like." Realizing she might be imposing on Barclay's wishes, Jane winced over the girl's shoulder and tried to retract the offer. "Although I am sure that Mrs. Gordon has read stories to her husband's parish and will make a fine storyteller in my place."

"Thank you, Jane."

"You are, and always will be, very welcome, Tatiana."

After their embrace, Tatiana ran off before Jane could offer a game of chess. Feeling slightly cheered to learn the little girl had not rejected her, Jane went to find some food to break her fast. Her appetite had awakened.

Entering the breakfast room, the one reserved for the Balfour family, she found Aurora reading over a plate of eggs and fruit. Jane went to fill her own plate and then sat down across from Barclay's mother.

"How are you this morning, Aurora?"

"I am quite enjoying this visit. It has been a long time since Barclay has taken any time for himself. He appears happier since we arrived, and I must admit that, as a mother, it gladdens my heart to see my boy smiling again."

Jane was silent, focusing on her plate as she digested this news. "I am ... happy to hear that. He seems a good man."

Aurora smiled. "The very best of men."

Yearning pierced her chest. Jane struggled to control her breathing as she looked away. "Indeed," she mumbled. Her appetite was deserting her once more. Perhaps she was a silly young chit who did not understand enough about life to make a suitable wife for a man like him. Barclay seemed to think that the widow was a far more qualified choice, and he was an intelligent professional. Certainly, he must have insight into matters such as marriage.

Pushing her plate aside, she rose to fetch a pot of coffee

from the sideboard. Returning to her seat, Jane poured out a cup with relish. She added her cream and sugar before sitting back to sip the cup. Food be damned today. She was going to drink coffee until Barclay faded from her thoughts. It was the only thing that seemed to lift her spirits.

Jane noticed Aurora was frowning at the cup in her hand. Blazes, was the woman going to judge her for drinking the gentlemen's beverage? She needed it right now. Jane prepared herself to be lectured like a young chit to complete her feelings of inadequacy.

"Jane, I know it is not my place …" Aurora looked around, evidently confirming there were no footmen about.

Here it comes.

"But I feel I must inform you of the troubles associated with drinking coffee."

Jane took a sip to fortify herself, then set the cup down to force a smile. "You refer to the fact that it is a gentlemen's beverage and not acceptable in social circles to drink it as a woman?"

"Well … no. That is too fine a point of etiquette for me to comment on with any knowledge. I was referring to the other issues."

Jane frowned.

Aurora sighed, putting her fork down. "It is just that Tatiana mentioned that you have trouble sleeping at night?"

"That is correct."

"Did the trouble start around the same time as …" Aurora gestured to the cup on the table. "Perhaps when you began to drink coffee?"

Jane folded her arms and settled back to think. "I arrived in London. Then I tried coffee the following morning for the first time." She narrowed her eyes as she tried to recollect the sequence of events. "Yes. That was the first night I could not sleep. Why?"

"When Barclay was a young man doing his studies, there would be nights he needed to … not sleep. To stay awake to study or complete a design overnight. When that happened, he would drink coffee. Pots of it. He told me that the coffee kept his mind and body alert and allowed him to work through the night."

Jane glared down at the cup while her thoughts raced. She recalled how she had begun having trouble sleeping. Then how she had developed a routine of drinking coffee in the afternoon because it helped her feel better when she had had too little sleep. Then how she started drinking it before dinner when she grew so weary her eyelids threatened to seal of their own accord during dinner.

"Damn!" She gasped, clapping a hand over her mouth as she realized she had just cursed in the presence of a lady. Her twin brothers, Oliver and Max, were little terrors with a large vocabulary of uncouth words they liked to use when their parents were out of earshot, so Jane knew many words that were not fit for polite company. She rarely used them, but her lack of sleep and gloomy mood …

Aurora shook her head, raising a hand to wave her lack of concern. "It is all right. We are all family here."

"I think you are right! The coffee is causing me to stay awake. I have never had trouble sleeping before. In fact, my family has always expressed their envy that I could sleep anytime and anywhere!"

"What do you plan to do?"

"What would you suggest?" Jane found she really did desire input from the older woman. She missed having Emma or her mother to talk to, and Aurora made her feel at ease. Then, too, she respected that this woman had survived years of censure to keep her family together. Aurora could so easily have done what other women would have done in her position—had her child raised by strangers to protect her reputation.

"I would recommend you stop drinking it if your sleep is so poor."

Jane bit her lip. It would seem the only method of confirming that the coffee was the cause of her insomnia would be to stop drinking it and observe if her sleep improved. "I shall do that, then. I thank you for advising me."

Aurora nodded. "I must warn you that when Barclay stopped drinking coffee, there was some trouble."

"What kind of trouble?" Jane was already agitated at the thought that she had to give up the dark brew, which was currently the only joy she had felt all day. Now there was to be more to the problem? She shuddered.

"Barclay complained of experiencing the worst cravings when he stopped drinking it. He also complained of headaches for several days, which only were improved with a small amount of coffee. To hear him speak of it … it put me in mind of the troubles that some people have with laudanum … to a lesser degree, of course. I feel it is worth mentioning in case you notice any effects."

Jane dropped her head into her hands. "What have I done?"

"Do not trouble yourself. My mother was from Florence, and she told me it was commonplace for young men there to become reliant on coffee."

"How long will it take to recover?"

"Only a few days after you stop drinking it. Just expect some headaches and perhaps a foul temperament as a result."

"Thank you."

"It is nothing. I felt I had to tell you about it."

Jane pushed the coffee away and then pulled her plate back. Resolutely, she forced herself to eat. "How has your stay been so far?"

Aurora beamed. "Excellent. The earl and the countess are so gracious. It has been wonderful to enjoy such exalted company."

"I am so happy to hear that. I do not wish to be indelicate, but I think it is quite unfair for a lovely lady such as yourself to …" Jane was not sure how to finish the sentence.

"To be cast out of good society because of a mistake I made once as a child?"

"Um … yes. I apologize. It is just that my cousin Kitty—Ethan's mother—was in your position. There are barely any consequences for the father, yet the mother is never allowed to forget she erred."

Aurora sighed. "I am fortunate that my family supported me as your family supported Ethan and his mother. It is difficult for me, but it is Barclay who has had to live under that cloud of shame his entire life. He is blameless, yet it still affects him and Tatiana. He has struggled with it, and I would do anything to ease his burden."

"He has struggled?"

"Very much so. He blames himself. I was overjoyed when the earl came to find him to acknowledge him as his brother. It will balance out over time—that he is a brother of a powerful earl cannot be ignored. My father is very pleased about the improvement in Barclay's situation."

"I am so happy to hear that."

"More than that, I want to see Barclay make a suitable match. My son relied on his late wife more than he cares to admit. It has been difficult for him, and this new connection to the earl will open up new possibilities of courtship."

Jane hesitated, repressing a sigh at the thought of Barclay with his new wife, then took a bite from her fork. She had not considered that once he made his match, she would continue to see him with the new Mrs. Thompson because they were relations now.

After swallowing, she responded, "He is a good man ... and he deserves any happiness he can find." She could hardly blame him for his disaffection. The gentleman had many responsibilities to oversee, and he had simply concluded that Jane was an inappropriate partner. Only, it would have been less embarrassing if he had explained his decision instead of leaving her waiting like a fool.

I suppose it should flatter me that he thought I would work it out for myself.

But she was not flattered. She was hurt, despite her best efforts to be understanding about his situation.

"Yes ... he is." Aurora tilted her head when she replied, a look of bemusement crossing her face. Jane hoped she had not given herself away to Barclay's mother. Was it not mortifying enough that both he and Tatiana were aware of his rejection? Now she was about to alert his mother to her unrequited feelings.

Jane quickly finished her breakfast, determined to find Mr. Dunsford so she might play a game of some sort with him. Anything to stop thinking about Barclay and remind herself there were other men. Other possibilities.

She might be young, but Mr. Dunsford seemed to appreciate her youth, so it was time to stop ruminating over her infatuation with an unattainable widower and explore her other options.

Perhaps it would ease this relentless ache in her chest.

* * *

BARCLAY HAD JUST RETURNED to the manor from the stables. He did not frequently have the pleasure of riding, so before he could be recruited into another game of nine-pins, or shuttlecock, or any other of the inane games favored by many of the female guests, he had taken the opportunity to ride with the earl. Jane was never to be seen at those frivolous games, and his prior observations suggested she was involved in more worthwhile activities, such as chess. Perhaps she had played bowls that day he had tried to persuade Mrs. Gordon to play. She certainly had not shown up for nine-pins.

He and his brother had toured the park, an impressive estate, and Barclay had had the opportunity to appreciate Tsar's brilliance in selecting the location of the manor. Of course, the then-lord of the manor, the late Earl of Saunton, would have agreed to the advice from his architect, but he knew Tsar was excellent at persuasion, so would have steered and cajoled the earl into making the right decision.

After the brisk ride, Barclay's inner thighs ached in the pleasurable manner of a man who had exerted himself. Days of idle revelry at a nobleman's house party were too far out of his usual daily activities, so it had indeed been an escape to enjoy the pleasures of riding with a powerful beast beneath him and a skilled rider ahead of him.

As he entered the hall, Jane appeared in the doorway of the family breakfast room. He could not help himself. His hungry eyes scoured her form. Barclay was laboring to do what was right for his daughter. For his mother. And for Jane herself. But not for him, for if he were to be selfish, then at this moment he would stride up to the lovely young woman and sweep her into an embrace before lowering his head to capture her mouth.

Jane's eyes brightened with joy at the sight of him, but a moment later, it was as if a heavy cloud passed before the sun to block its light from the earth beneath. Her eyes dulled, and she averted her face to walk down the hall away from him. He watched her go, every fiber of his being urging him to chase her. Talk to her. Explain.

But if he was alone with her, then all his best intentions

to do right by her would fly out the window like birds escaping a cage and making their desperate dash for freedom. He could not be in the same room alone with her without hauling her into his arms to sip on her strawberry lips.

When she turned a corner in the corridor, his fascination abated. He blinked slowly, before realizing that Aurora had taken Jane's place in the doorway. She was studying him, her forehead creased in inquisitive concern. Squaring his shoulders, he hoped his mother had not seen him mooning over Jane. "Mother."

"Barclay," she acknowledged, but her curious expression did not fade and Barclay was afraid he had given himself away.

He quickly strode away to find Mrs. Gordon before his mother could press any questions to him. It was time to play shuttlecock, or battledore, or *jeu de volant*, or whatever the silly game was called with the ball and the feathers designed to lure a hawk.

Zounds, it would be ever so much more entertaining if they were to take part in actual falconry with the strange device rather than the ridiculous game with the rackets, where one simply kept the ball in the air. It was a child's game at best.

As predicted, the day passed slowly once he found Mrs. Gordon. The ladies she played with chattered ceaselessly as they hit the ball into the air, tittering every time it fell to the ground. Once again, Lord Trafford was there pretending the dreary game was delightful, but Barclay could see he tired of it, too.

Lord Trafford would evidently go to some lengths to woo a widow, which appeared to be why he was enduring these mindless games. As was Barclay. The widow Trafford was pursuing was quite a bit older than the young lord, but

Barclay assumed it was not courtship Trafford had in mind but rather ... other more lurid activities.

The day continued to drag on, and then it was dinner-time. He once again sat with Mrs. Gordon, which he had asked his brother to arrange, feeling a tug of conscience that the new seating arrangement had pushed Jane farther down the table. Thankfully, she appeared to be enjoying herself with Mr. Dunsford because she laughed and talked with him throughout the meal.

At least, Barclay told himself, he was pleased she had found a man more equitable in age. The coiling jealousy in his gut whenever the young buck's eyes dropped to her bosom was—it just was not his place to be jealous. If he would not pursue her, the young woman had the right to find a new suitor.

Had she forgotten him so quickly?

When he eventually reached his bedroom, Barclay sat on the ledge of the window and sightlessly contemplated the night. Natalya would no longer visit. He could no longer run off to the library to visit Jane. The night was infinite in that he could not sleep once again.

He had been so hopeful that his ability to rest had returned the last few nights, but since he had paced his room the evening before until the early hours, he knew that yearning to join Jane in the library would bar him from falling into a slumber for a while yet.

When the first light appeared, long before the sun showed itself on the horizon, Barclay went to his bed. Staring at the cornices in his agitation, sleep took him as the bedroom faded into darkness.

He was in the library, but he did not know how he had arrived here. This was not to be! He was meant to stay in his bedroom, no matter how tempting it was to walk the corridor to the main manor to find Jane.

Before him, he saw the figure of a woman sitting at the table, writing on a page. She did not stir as he approached, despite him almost panting in his desire to reach her side. As he drew closer, he was able to confirm it was Jane, her ebony curls loose down her back. Reaching out, he took a silky lock between his fingers. Raising it, he breathed in the scent of strawberries and almonds.

Jane turned in her chair, her face lighting up when she saw it was him. "You came!" she exclaimed in a sultry voice.

"How could I stay away?"

Her lashes lowered as she blushed prettily, and Barclay was tempted to trace the progress of the color rising across her skin with his tongue. Offering her his hand, he drew her to her feet to pull her into a hard embrace.

"Jane," he groaned as he captured her sweet mouth with his own. She tasted of strawberries and coffee, and he could not help lifting his hand to trace the curve of her cheek with his fingertips. "You are so soft."

She pressed closer to him, her tongue melding with his as they kissed deeply, tasting each other with desperation as if this was their last night on this earth. Inexorably, his hand rose to the plump breast which he had been tempted to caress during their first kiss in this library, but out of respect for her inexperience, he had restrained his desires.

Now she moaned, her head falling back as he massaged the generous mound and passion fired in his loins while his lips fell to the curve of her creamy neck. Licking the strawberries from her satin skin, he breathed in the heady scent of almonds while his desire mounted to collect at the base of his spine. Raising his hand, he slid his fingers over her neck and under the night rail covering her form to find the turgid nipple with his longest finger encircling the bud. It puckered and rose beneath his fingertip, causing him to growl against her skin in victory.

Picking her up, he sat her on the table to take his place between her thighs. Pressing his hardness against her soft, heated center, he *reached down to slide his hand over her slender ankle. Lowering his head, he pressed a soft kiss to the pulse that beat like a drum beneath her delicate skin. Trailing kisses up her long, naked calf to find her knee, he took his time caressing and nipping until she panted with newly awakened passion.*

Slowly, very slowly, he raised the hem over her long leg, where he placed his lips to the tender part of her inner thigh, causing her to buck her hips up in invitation, revealing the moist petals of her sex.

He was hard for her. Harder than he had ever been. He wanted to free himself from his breeches and bury himself deep within her—

Barclay started awake to find morning had fully arrived. Evidence of his arousal tented the coverlet, and he was covered in a fine sheen of sweat as he panted in his surprise. This was an unexpected—and problematic—turn of events.

It is merely a reflection of your desires reawakening! It does not mean you are meant to be with Jane.

Barclay sat up in agitation. He finally caught some sleep only to have it ruined—*improved?*—by visions of Jane. This situation was so bloody awkward. Dropping his head into his hands, he tried to make sense of what was happening.

Was his mind unraveling from the strain of attempted courtship too soon? For ten years, he had not thought about any woman other than his Natalya, and now he was dreaming of a young woman who was eminently unsuitable. Could this house party grow any worse than it already had?

Brushing aside his thoughts, Barclay rose to wash and prepare for the day. It would not do to dwell on what could not be. He must press forward and decide whether he could tolerate Mrs. Gordon as a wife to aid their family respectability.

It would be better if he did not engage his heart in his second marriage. He had already found and lost the love of his life, and men did not get a second chance to love so deeply. He was a lucky man to have done so the once, and it would be greedy to think he could do so again. Deep down, he knew he could never survive a second loss of that magnitude.

CHAPTER 13

*B*y the time Jane went to bed that night, she knew Aurora had been right about the coffee.

She had skipped her afternoon cup, then her cup before dinner. It was midnight, and she was pacing her room, her mind fixated on the notion that she should find a servant and demand a pot of coffee be brought to her immediately.

Aurora's warning regarding the cravings had proved correct, which could only mean that this truly was the cause of her insomnia.

Her body was utterly worn out, but she could not relax. She had thought about going to the library to write her poetry, but it was inconceivable. For one, she could not patiently sharpen her quill and dip it in ink—the mere thought of the energy it would take was enough to make her want to scream in frustration. Second, it would remind her of how Barclay had snubbed her.

Suddenly a great wave of melancholy washed over her— the foul temperament, perhaps? She had expected it to be irritability, but perhaps the combination of Barclay's rejection and deprivation of the demon brew was causing this hitherto unknown symptom.

It was all she could do to drag herself to the bed and fall in.

To her surprise, she fell asleep only to jolt awake again. Checking the time, she estimated she had fallen asleep for a half hour. Returning to bed, she closed her eyes once more, and after a while she dozed in a half sleep, half waking state with strange almost feverish dreams which caused her to jolt awake once more.

She gazed at the ceiling in the darkness of the room, afraid to fall back to sleep after the last disturbing image of Barclay at the altar with Mrs. Gordon while Jane sat as his sister-in-law in the family pew, pretending to be joyful while carrying a burden of heavy lead in her chest.

Eventually, the fatigue in her limbs pulled her into sleep once more.

When she awoke next, it was to find that morning had arrived. Sitting up, she moaned in agony. Her head was pounding so loud, she could swear there was an orchestra tuning their instruments inside her skull. The sun sneaking in through the drapes was enough to make her howl.

Taking hold of the coverlet, she threw herself back into the bed with the fabric over her head to block the light until the pounding slowly receded to manageable volume. Was this what men felt like when they imbibed too much?

Realizing that drinking some tea and eating breakfast might assuage her physical torment, Jane slowly rose from bed.

Damn the strawberry water! There was no energy for beauty treatments. This morning she was doing the bare minimum. Walking over to the door, she found the cart waiting in the hall and pulled it into her room.

After sipping a small amount of tea and consuming some

eggs and fruit, her headache had abated to a tolerable level—tolerable in that she thought she might conduct a conversation without embarrassing herself.

However, when she heard a light tapping on the door, she realized she had overestimated her capabilities in this fragile state. She wanted to shriek at whomever was behind the door to leave. Raising a trembling hand to her temple, she massaged to calm herself.

"Who is it?"

"Tatiana. May I enter?"

Jane gritted her teeth. The little girl would require some diplomacy, and she was not sure she had any to offer this morning.

"Of course."

The door opened, and Tatiana came into the room. At least, Jane assumed she came in because she was too busy rubbing her temples to notice what was happening behind her.

"Are you all right?"

"Yes, yes. I am suffering from a megrim, is all."

"Oh. I was wondering if I could ask you to join me and Papa for a walk?"

Jane clenched her jaw in irritation, nearly biting her tongue. Moderating her voice, she tried to think how to respond. "Did your father agree to that?"

Tatiana hesitated. "I have not asked him yet, but I am sure I could convince him."

And Jane was sure it was futile. Not to mention mortifying. She was the silly chit he had rejected. Worse, Barclay was well aware of how she felt because she had not known how to react when she had encountered him in the hall the previous morning. She was certain she beamed like a little girl, before allowing her disconsolation to be revealed when she had a moment later recalled they were no longer … friends, she supposed.

Damnation, this was going to become even worse if he announced a betrothal. Traveling home to Rose Ash Manor was becoming ever more appealing.

"Then, no. I am afraid I already made plans for the day." She had not, but she would.

"Please, Jane. I … miss you. It felt like when Mama was alive and we would do things as a family. I want …"

"I am sorry, Tatiana. I cannot. I already promised my time to Mr. Dunsford, and I must hurry if I am to meet him."

The child's face fell. "What about Ladin? Could you read to me this evening?"

Jane pressed her eyes closed, nearly bursting into tears at the lovely memory. But if she were to read to her this evening, Barclay might be there as he had been the first time, and she could not bear it in her current state. She would need time to recover from this fiasco with the coffee before she could feign any pleasantries with the girl's father.

"Perhaps in a couple of days, Tatiana. There is no telling if this headache will recede by this evening."

Perhaps by then her battered spirits would have time to recover. Not to mention this blasted thudding in her skull.

"I am sorry you do not feel well."

Jane managed a small smile. The child was so sweet. It truly would have been an idyllic life to spend her days with Tatiana while traveling at Barclay's side. She quickly squashed the errant musing. That was not to be, and she needed to focus on her health through this ordeal with the cursed coffee.

"Thank you."

The little girl came forward to wrap her arms around Jane's neck. "Please do not give up," she whispered against Jane's hair.

"Give up?"

"On Papa. Promise me you will not give up. We can be a family, I know it! I will make him see, I swear it."

Before Jane could respond, Tatiana let go of her and ran from the room.

* * *

BARCLAY STRODE down the family hall to meet up with the earl for a spot of fishing when Tatiana stepped into the corridor unexpectedly from Jane's room.

Drawing to a halt, he rubbed his temples while trying to think why this did not sit right. He realized he needed to dissuade the connection between his daughter and the young woman in order to prevent Tatiana from developing further hopes.

Dropping his hand, he straightened up to glare at his daughter, but she narrowed her eyes and glared right back at him.

"Tatiana, are you bothering Miss Davis?"

She scowled. "Miss Davis? I thought you called her by her given name?"

He clenched his jaw. "That was before."

"Before what?"

"Before I started spending time with Mrs. Gordon."

"No. That is not true. You spent time with Mrs. Gordon playing nine-pins. Then we all went to the grotto, and you called her Jane several times. Jane is family, and she invited us to call her … Jane."

Barclay glared down from his not inconsiderable height, but his little girl folded her arms and glared right back at him. If he did not feel so bloody remorseful, he might have been proud of his little warrior. She would do well in life if she could continue to stand her ground as she did now.

But not on this subject. Reaching out a hand to clasp her arm lightly, he turned and escorted her to Aurora's bedroom. They needed privacy for this discussion.

"Tatiana, it is inappropriate to bother Jane. She has her own life to live, and you must allow her to do so."

"Jane enjoys spending time with me. She told me so. It is your fault that there is trouble, and I refuse to turn my back on her."

Barclay walked away, raking his hands through his long hair, to stand by the window while he tried to think how to explain this to his child. Good grief, when had he last had his hair trimmed? Tatiana was not wrong about his need for a wife, it would seem.

"It is not possible for me to court Jane, and it would be inappropriate to spend time in her company, little one."

"Why? She is family. Her sister is married to your brother, Uncle Perry. If I want to spend time with her, I can."

"Tatiana, perhaps in the future. But not now. We must allow Jane her time. She is seeking a husband, and she needs to be allowed to do so."

She growled, causing Barclay to blink. It sounded more like a mewling because she was such a little girl, but it was unprecedented. He spun back to face her, discovering that her face had turned red with anger.

"You are a selfish man! Jane was to be my new mother! Mama would have approved. Now you are ruining it! Not only that, now you are trying to ruin my time with her!"

Barclay shook his head. "There are things—adult matters —which you do not understand. I am doing this for you. And your grandmama, and I need you to trust me."

"Why? I see what Jane did, but you will not listen. You changed. You were smiling and happy like you were when Mama was still here. Now you are back to your sadness. I am worried about you, but you will not listen to me. I know Jane is the one!"

Barclay hung his head, too ashamed to look at her while he tried to find the words to explain once more. "It is not right, Tatiana. Jane could marry anyone. She is the sister-in-law to an earl, from a good family, and there will be problems for her if she were to marry me."

"We are a good family! We look after each other. We spend time together. We try to make each other happy. That is what Jane would do if she were part of our family."

Barclay drew a deep breath. Usually, he was so talented with negotiations, but there was something complicated about dealing with one's own child. He knew he was trying to do what was best for her, and for Jane, but how did he tell Tatiana without ruining her childhood? She did not need to know about the troubles surrounding his parentage. The troubles she would deal with in the future. Nay, that must wait until she was much older. It was his duty to protect her innocence and allow her this time of ignorance for as long as he possibly could.

"You must give Mrs. Gordon a chance, little one."

"She does not like children!"

"How do you know that?"

"I … just know. I can tell. Ethan agrees with me."

Barclay shook his head. He did not know why Tatiana was convinced the widow did not like children. There had been no evidence of that. "Ethan is four years old and not an expert on women. She is very pleasant, and she can teach you many things."

"Like what?"

He was not prepared for the question. Good Lord, he was quickly learning during this house party that his daughter might look like her mother, but she had inherited all the stubborn traits of the Thompson family. Tsar was going to howl with mirth about all of this when they returned to London in a week or so.

Barclay would laugh himself if this was not so terribly disheartening. Perhaps that was a good sign. A sign that his mourning truly was over, if he even considered laughing. He could not recall when he had last laughed about anything, not truly, without forcing it politely, but since arriving at this house party, it seemed he had recovered his sense of humor.

"She can teach you to behave like a proper young lady."

"Jane can teach me that."

"Yes, but …"

"But what?"

"Mrs. Gordon was the wife of a vicar. She can teach you all about …" Barclay sought for something to say. "Charity!" he announced, proud of himself for thinking of it.

Tatiana considered this, and Barclay realized neither of them knew enough about Jane to know if she was involved in charitable work. After a lengthy pause, her face lit up, and she responded, "Grandmama can teach me that."

That was true. Aurora involved herself in charity work with their church.

"Mrs. Gordon has a lovely voice, and she must know how to sing. She could teach you to sing lovely hymns."

His daughter narrowed her blue eyes in a menacing manner. "Are you saying I cannot sing?"

Barclay coughed into his hand. If Natalya were here, she would do a much better job of handling their daughter. But if Natalya were here, they would not be arguing over who would be her new mother, so that was a moot point.

"You have a lively singing voice, little one."

Thankfully, she appeared mollified. Barclay straightened his shoulders and endeavored to return to his original point before Tatiana had debated him into a corner.

"I need you to leave Jane alone and allow her to seek a

young man to marry. We cannot stand in her way, or cause complications."

She shook her head. "I do not agree to this. I have already asked Jane to read me Ladin, and she said when she is feeling better, she will do so."

Barclay frowned, worried despite his vow to steer clear of the young woman. "Is Jane unwell?"

"She said she has a headache."

He exhaled. "Then I need you to listen to me. I am the parent."

"I should listen to you, even if you are wrong?"

Scowling, Barclay tried to think how to respond to that. "I am the parent, and you must listen."

Tatiana drew herself up to her full height. It was not much, but she was as regal as a queen when she replied, "I shall not. Jane is my friend, and you cannot stop me from spending time with her."

Before he could respond, she turned and ran from the room in a blur of skirts and stockings before he even had time to think. Bloody hell! He should have stood between her and the door, knowing she might bolt. Now he would have to wait to find her and start this discussion all over again. Natalya had always been so talented at dealing with Tatiana. He was a brute compared to her finesse with the child.

Damn, if his nine-year-old daughter besting him in debate was not a sign of his advanced years! This was precisely why this age gap between him and Jane would not work. If he did not know better, he would swear he had aged a hundred years based on how he had felt since he had found Aurora crying in her room.

* * *

JANE LEFT her bedroom at about two in the afternoon, once the pounding in her head had receded sufficiently to paste a smile on her face and feign some social pleasantries.

While preparing for the day, she had reached a decision. It was time to seriously consider a match with Mr. Dunsford. With him, she would access a path to the familiar. As the daughter of a landowner, she would marry the heir to a similar situation. This was a world which she could understand and navigate. Her sister was the wife of a landowner. Her father was a landowner himself, and her mother was the wife of a landowner. It would be perfect because she would have plenty of help to make such a situation a success.

It had been the original plan she had had for this Season, before Emma had meddled with her ideas of a meeting of the minds. She had tried following Emma's advice, which had led to bitter disappointment. Her sister's success with bringing Perry up to scratch had been a fluke, a once- in-a-lifetime lucky occurrence not to be repeated.

All that remained was to confirm that she and Mr. Dunsford had enough in common to make a marriage work. Anything to leave this miserable situation in the past.

Jane stopped in the hall to rub her weary hands over her face. She was having trouble maintaining the appearance of conviviality. Fatigue was setting in once more, and she cursed the coffee that had put her in this infernal mood, while craving a cup of the demon brew, which would release her from this current agony.

Be strong! Aurora said this will only last a few days before it wears off.

Inhaling deeply, she pasted the jovial expression back on her face and continued her walk to the library. She would rest there for a moment while she regathered her wits, then set off to find Mr. Dunsford. Hopefully, his attentions had not wandered to another female guest while she had been occupied with Barclay.

When she reached the library, she scowled at the coffeepot with loathing. And longing. It was hard not to recall the blissful sense of tranquility after drinking a cup. Shaking her head, then groaning when it caused the thudding to echo against her skull, Jane squared her shoulders as if preparing for battle.

Resolutely, she headed down to the main level in search of the other guests. She soon found the countess drinking tea in one of the drawing rooms with an accompaniment of women of all ages. The Duchess of Halmesbury gestured for her to come join them, so Jane walked across to take a seat.

The moment she sat, the babe in the duchess's arms turned to watch her. Reaching up two chubby arms, Jasper mewled loudly. The duchess laughed. "Jane, my dear son has grown weary of his mother. Would you like to hold him?"

Jane immediately reached for the boy. As soon as he was in her arms, gazing up at her with enormous eyes, she leaned forward to sniff his sweet scent and was hit with a wave of yearning. If she could find a beau to marry, she could start her new life. Perhaps have her own babe by this time next year. She nearly wept with the sheer desire to begin on this path. This Season was turning out to be a bitter experience, and there was no need to prolong the agony.

Drat! These symptoms from the coffee are turning me into a dreary mess!

As Jasper grabbed one of her fingers with his tiny fist, Jane thought once again about how she might be betrothed before the house party ended. She was ready, and she did not want to meet more men who would lead to more disappointment. All she needed was one suitable gentleman to propose. Her impatience was not to do with her throbbing head, she assured herself, nor the architect she wished she had never met. This was about stepping into her future.

When Jasper grew weary, his little eyelids drooping, she handed him back to his mother, who summoned their nanny to take him for a rest. Then Jane left to find Mr. Dunsford. Exiting the manor, she found him engaged in a discussion with several young gentlemen and ladies. He grinned broadly when he spotted her. Completing the anecdote he was telling, he quickly excused himself to join her.

Bowing, with a tip of his hat, he straightened and held out an arm. "Miss Davis, would you do me the honor of taking a turn in the gardens? There are several guests here to maintain propriety." He gestured back to the table. Jane accepted his arm, and they descended the stairs to walk the pathways of the formal garden.

"Tell me about your home, Mr. Dunsford. Is it far from here?"

"Not at all. About two hours at most, to the northeast of Saunton."

"And do you have a large family?"

"Alas, no. There are my father and my little sister. My mother died a few years ago. What about you, Miss Davis?"

"I have three brothers, all younger than me. And two sisters. You might have met Emma the day you arrived?"

"Ah, yes. The young lady who married Mr. Peregrine Balfour. I was most surprised when he mentioned he plans to remain at Shepton Abbey throughout the year. I always thought the gentleman loved the sophistication of London too much to rusticate."

"Do you visit London?"

"As frequently as family obligations permit. Now that I hear you will be there with the earl's family for the rest of the Season, I am quite inspired to follow you!" Mr. Dunsford smiled, revealing pearly teeth. He was the epitome of the gentry. Fine-looking, charming, and modest for the most part—having made her smile many times with his dry and self-deprecating wit.

Jane smiled in acknowledgment, thinking about how she had enjoyed their interactions. There was every reason to believe that they would enjoy the companionship of a good marriage and to believe she would eventually forget the architect who had awakened her to passion.

CHAPTER 14

*B*arclay had not seen Jane except for dinner last evening, which was a small mercy. Instead, he had spent his time with Mrs. Gordon, even mildly enjoying their game of nine-pins under the afternoon sun. He had been regaling the widow with various anecdotes about his clients across the realm, and she had giggled and laughed in a gratifying manner for most of their game.

He had not been aware that he could be so amusing, but clearly he had unplumbed depths of humor to share with a new wife.

As the afternoon progressed, they completed their game and walked with the other players back to the terrace. There they found refreshments awaiting them and took a seat at one of the tables. In the distance, he noted Jane arm in arm with the young Mr. Dunsford, and for a moment, he was distracted, before dutifully pulling his attention away to laugh at an anecdote Mrs. Gordon now told him about visiting one of the tenants' homes at Saunton Park.

Apparently, the widow made a habit of visiting the

various homes, seeing it as her duty, since until recently there had been no mistress at Saunton Park in many years.

Swallowing a dainty biscuit, Barclay reflected on how much he had changed since his arrival there. Here he was laughing and enjoying pleasant conversation instead of pursuing his wife's ghost. Soon he might bring a new wife home with him. Tatiana would have a mother once more, who could sit with her and play the pianoforte on a Sunday afternoon, as Natalya had done.

He could well imagine this woman bending her head over his daughter, as they learned a new piece of music together and he watched from the comfort of his armchair. It was the small moments he missed the most. The joy of sharing a lazy afternoon with Aurora sewing, Tsar reading his news sheets, and him … just watching his wonderful family in a moment of quietude. He missed it like the blazes.

Mrs. Gordon was a mature woman who understood the implications of marrying someone like him. She believed her reputation would further improve his credibility, and her fascination with him had not flagged.

Aurora had confirmed that the widow had taken pains to join her for breakfast, so Mrs. Gordon was willing to do the work required to make their family whole.

Several times during their conversations, he had clarified that he lived with Tsar and Aurora in their family home, to ensure that the widow found this acceptable.

"Have you traveled much, Mrs. Gordon?"

"I have a little. I used to live in Canterbury, which is where I met Mr. Gordon. When he learned of his new post here in the village, he asked my father for my hand in marriage. So I am well familiar with Kent, as well as Surrey, where I attended a ladies' seminary."

Barclay blinked. "Surrey? So far from home? What age were you when you were sent away to school?"

"I first left home when I was seven years old. I personally think it was a little too young, but it all turned out for the best."

He hesitated briefly before replying. The thought of sending Tatiana away two years ago would have been inconceivable to him as her father. More so because she had just suffered the loss of her mother, but even so, he could not imagine sending his daughter away at such a young age. Tatiana suffered from night terrors, and he was sure there would be no one to comfort her in the dormitories of a ladies' seminary in a different county from their family home.

"You say it was for the best?" he ventured.

"Certainly. I learned all my accomplishments there. Sewing, watercolors, dancing. They had a talented French teacher, so I speak fluently. Not to mention, playing ninepins and shuttlecock with the other girls was a pleasant way to pass the time."

Barclay restrained himself from rolling his eyes. He hoped he could convince the widow to bowl in the future by offering her his personal tutelage in the game.

"You have had many opportunities to use your French, then?"

The widow frowned in an effort to recall. Finally, she admitted, "I cannot say that I have. There are few opportunities in such a small village, but it serves well when I attend events here at Saunton Park."

"Because you have met French people here?"

"Well, no. The earl did not entertain prior to his marriage. But now that he has, I am sure I will have an opportunity to use it more! Or if I were to move to London." The last was said in a beguiling tone as she laid a gloved hand over his for a fleeting moment of suggestive impropriety.

Barclay had not the heart to inform her that, outside of

his work, he never used any of his French. She seemed quite hopeful on the matter.

If Mrs. Gordon were to take a place as his wife, she would instruct Tatiana on all the skills she had learned at the ladies' seminary. He still had a difficult time understanding why the widow's father had sent her away so young, but he supposed all that learning would be helpful for his own daughter.

He smiled, lifting another dainty biscuit to his lips while he considered the situation. Was he confident that Mrs. Gordon would be a good wife? Should he seek advice from his mother or his brother, or simply propose to the woman? She had shown her eagerness on many occasions. With the amount of time they had spent together, if they were in London, he would be required to propose by this stage of their acquaintanceship. Fortunately, he could think on the matter a little longer because the rules at a house party were considerably less *de rigueur*. He did not wish to marry for love again, and Mrs. Gordon seemed eminently suitable as a choice.

He noticed Tatiana had arrived, peering through the windows of the terrace door at him.

Lifting his watch fob, he recalled that he had promised her a game of chess. He bade farewell to the widow, who appeared disappointed at his departure. Barclay admitted his own vanity when he realized it was pleasing to have such an attractive woman seeking his company. He missed the feminine influence in his life, and his sweaty dream in the early hours suggested he missed other aspects of the marital union.

Brushing those thoughts aside, he strode over to join Tatiana, grasping her small hand in his to make their way to the library. It took a few minutes to reach it, the manor being a very large home to traverse. When they reached the room, he heard Ethan calling out victoriously, "Checkmate!"

Tatiana grimaced. "He practices far too much. I shall never catch up with him. How can a child be beating me so?"

Barclay hid a smile. She was a child herself, but he could recall how much relative ages had mattered to him as a small boy. Even half a year was something to brag about to younger children.

They had entered the doorway when Barclay's smile was wiped from his face. Ethan's opponent was Jane.

* * *

ETHAN HAD EASILY OUTPLAYED HER. Her head was thudding something terrible, and the effort to concentrate was more than could be borne. It set off fresh thudding, and she had to prevent herself from groaning from the agony of it. She had left Mr. Dunsford's side earlier when the light had wreaked havoc, and she had been afraid she would reveal her discomposure so she had joined Ethan for a game of chess.

Her cousin was far more tolerable company when she was this set upon. She could be herself and not behave with rigid propriety. Considering she hoped to make a match with the gentleman, it would not do to show any temper in his vicinity.

"You seem poorly, Jane. Are you not sleeping still?" Her cousin was so sweet, his little face twisted with fret.

"My sleep is slowly improving," she admitted, "but I have a headache at the moment."

"I thought you played poorly. It seemed too easy to corner your king."

Jane smiled tremulously. Ethan had only begun playing within the past few months, after Emma had introduced him to the game, yet he sounded like a professional player now. He had really committed to learning the game and was maturing before her very eyes, a little virtuoso in the making.

When she sat back in her seat, she caught sight of Barclay and Tatiana standing hand in hand by the doorway. Her heart sank.

I shall consider that progress.

The last time she encountered the widower in the hall, she practically leapt into his arms with joy before recalling he had rejected her.

It was little consolation. She still felt bereft in his presence. It had appeared to be progressing so well, and she had been certain she had found her Darcy. All that was needed was her patience with the man's grieving, but then it suddenly all ended.

Now she knew there was no Darcy for her, and she needed to find whatever happiness she could. Fortunately, she no longer needed to reveal her coffee-drinking to Mr. Dunsford because she no longer drank the demon brew that was causing these megrims.

Jane slowly rose to her feet, while Ethan clamored to his feet and raced over to the pair at the door. "Uncle *Bar-clee*, I have not seen you since the grotto!" He held up his arms, and his uncle quickly raised him up.

She winced. The grotto was quickly becoming a painful memory, rather than the sheer joy it had been at the time. Picking up her shawl, she pulled it over her arms, jerky in her impatience to leave the library. Her fingers trembled as she hastily prepared the board for play, putting all the pieces in their place. She needed a moment to collect her wits and consider the best method to leave the library without revealing too much of her angst. One had to have some pride after such a rejection.

Jane had no ideas of how to feign any social graces in this moment. All she could think of was the need to escape as quickly as possible. If she was not battling with this coffee issue, she would collect herself and deal with all of … this.

But she was dealing with the coffee issue, and it was incredibly uncomfortable. Her only solace was that Aurora said it would be over within a few days. Two had passed thus far.

Determinedly, she put the pieces back, but her fingers hesitated as she recalled the magic of being in Barclay's arms.

Truly, she needed to get away from the Balfour homes. She was certain to see the architect regularly unless she married and moved on. Even if she returned home to Rose Ash Manor, her family would visit Ethan and she would have no excuses to not attend with them, and Barclay might attend, too.

She might be forced to attend his wedding to another woman, to watch his family grow, to remember her one kiss with him here in the library of Saunton Park when she thought that anything was possible. That love was possible.

Squaring her shoulders, she made for the door. When she reached the Thompsons, she paused for the briefest instant to acknowledge them for the sake of the children present. "Barclay. Tatiana." She bobbed, then quickly exited before the disappointment in the little girl's face could register on her already fragile state.

She knew not if Barclay had acknowledged her presence as she strode away as fast as her fatigued legs could carry her. Returning Ethan to his nanny was something she should do, but the gentleman was more than capable of doing so. She needed to get away.

JANE HAD APPEARED DEJECTED when she had brushed past them. Not only that, she was pale and drawn. Ethan had been talking to her about a headache. And Tatiana had mentioned Jane having a headache earlier that morning. Evidently it had not improved. Perhaps that was the reason she was disconsolate. That notion assuaged his conscience over disappointing the young woman.

Realizing that he now had possession of Ethan, he asked the boy where he was meant to be. Ethan told them he needed to be returned to the nursery, which was on the upper floor of the family wing. So Barclay and Tatiana accompanied him back.

When they came upon the nursery, Barclay was impressed. It was light and airy, unlike many noble houses. There was evidence of recent work. The drapes looked new, the walls were clad in rich colors, and the schoolroom was well stocked with toys and children's books.

Richard had only discovered his son's existence earlier that year, so he must have immediately ordered the changes in the nursery to have had them ready in time for this house party. Barclay now understood his brother's dismay when Barclay had expressed his feeling of insult that the butler had presumed to take Tatiana to the nursery on their arrival at Saunton Park.

He had pictured something … gloomier.

Tatiana and he returned to the library in silence to play their game. His daughter was obsessed with learning the game so she might beat her little cousin, and Barclay was amused at this hitherto unknown spirit of competition in her that had surfaced. With each year that passed, facets of his daughter's personality made themselves known, and he wished her mother could be present to witness her transformation.

Once they were alone in the room of shelves and books, Tatiana sat in her seat across the table with the chessboard between them, but she did not begin playing. Instead, she watched him for long moments, causing Barclay to want to squirm in his own chair like an errant child caught in the act of some wrongdoing.

He knew what she was thinking about. He had been trying to not think about the same issue—a struggle the entire walk to and from the nursery. She was thinking about how Jane had hurried from the room. As was he.

When she failed to say something, he got up his nerve. "What is it, little one?"

Tatiana sighed and turned her head to stare out the window, a disappointed look on her face. "I always thought you were brave. I am sad to know ... that you are not."

Startled, he straightened in his chair. "What do you mean?"

"I saw how you were with Jane and that is when I realized ... that you were afraid. Afraid of her. Afraid to love. Because of what happened to Mama."

"Tatiana, it is not that. There are things you do not understand. Adult ... things."

She shook her head. "I think that is why I have been losing these games with Ethan. I am afraid to take a risk. Then he swoops in and beats me. If I am to win, I shall have to ... be brave." With that, she leaned forward and moved a pawn. Startled by her perception of the weakness in her chess, Barclay did not know what to make of what she had said. Instead, he studied the board and made his own move, allowing her to drop the subject.

Tatiana stuck to her newfound conviction, attempting offensive moves on the board that earned Barclay's respect. He still won, but she had done much better and there was a possibility she might corner Ethan the next time they played.

After their match was over, Tatiana joined her grandmother, and Barclay entered the billiard room.

He was to have a reprieve from thought, from debate, from feeling guilty for not being enough. Not doing enough to bring happiness to the women in his life.

And he would play a game that required skill.

Thankfully, there were no women in sight in this masculine retreat of mahogany and green baize. Inspecting the billiard table, he ran his fingertips over the intricately carved strapwork and eyed the well-formed legs. It was such a fine piece, Thomas Chippendale himself could have carved it.

Nodding to the assembled gentlemen in the room, he stretched his neck. Tension eased from his shoulders as he walked over to find a cue.

Mr. Ridley was at the table, setting the balls in place, while Lord Trafford and Mr. Dunsford selected their own cues. They were engaged in a discussion, which Barclay barely noted until their words caught his attention.

"So you plan to propose to the Davis girl, Dunsford?"

Barclay felt the tension in his shoulders return. He wanted Jane to be happy, only in the deepest recesses of his soul it was *him* she was to be happy with. Quickly, he reminded himself that this gentleman was an eminently more suitable prospect for the young woman than he was.

"That is the plan," responded the young man with his mop of perfect curls on his head. There was no doubting the skill of the valet who attended him, to Barclay's annoyance. Barclay had never obtained a manservant, although Tsar had offered the privilege. It had seemed an extravagance, although they could afford it. Until Natalya's death, she had performed little tasks such as cutting his hair—an intimacy that he had quite enjoyed.

"So then you shall reside in the country at your father's estate forevermore, like my good friend, Peregrine Balfour, who has made the inexplicable decision to take up estate management and leave the delights of London behind him."

Dunsford chuckled in reproach. "I would not go so far as to say that. I have always enjoyed the … delights … of London."

Barclay narrowed his eyes, not appreciating the implication. Jane was to find a good husband who would do right by her. Speaking without turning to look at the young fop, he joined in the conversation. "There are no current ... delights ... awaiting you in London, I trust?"

"What if there were? Proposing to Miss Davis surely does not preclude such a relationship on the side?"

Ridley straightened up from the baize-covered table to frown across the room. "I would not recommend it, Dunsford. Saunton is protective of his family, especially his womenfolk, since his change of heart earlier this year. If he were to discover you were anything but loyal ..."

"There is no reason for him to learn of my private matters!" interjected Dunsford. "Miss Davis would never learn of it. She will be happy rusticating at my family home with a babe to dote on. If she is anything like my mother, she will barely notice my absence. Tell him, Trafford. It is how things are done in polite society."

Carefully, Barclay chalked the leather-tipped end of his cue. It was that or turn and break it over the young fop's head. He was so angry, his hands trembled with his repressed emotion. Under any circumstances, he would dislike the views the spoilt dandy aired, but the thought of it being Jane in the loveless, societal marriage Dunsford described was too much to comprehend. She deserved the love of a good man.

Trafford threw his hands up in surrender. "I am not the ally you seek. I love women, but when I settle down, I do not plan to continue playing the field. It is difficult and fraught with the threat of disease if one makes a misstep with the wrong paramour."

"What rot!" sputtered Dunsford. "It is practically our duty to sow our wild oats. If we do not, we would bother our wives with an excess of sexual desires. No gentlewoman could handle such lust."

For the first time, Barclay was grateful the late earl had

not married his mother. She might have lost her reputation, but at least she had held on to her independence in Tsar's household.

His mother was a loyal, kind woman, and she would not have fared well with a treacherous lech for a husband. From what Richard had described, their own father was much worse than this little upstart. Aurora might be relatively traditional in her feminine pursuits, but she was single-minded about issues that were important to her. The Earl of Satan might have broken her spirit.

Ridley took his time responding. "I have shared the bed of many fine women of the upper classes. My experience is that their appetites are the same as any other women."

"You never met my mother, then!" exclaimed Dunsford.

Ridley and Trafford shook their heads, Ridley pressing his earlier argument. "Be that as it may, heed my warning when I say that Saunton will not like it, and he is not a man you should rouse to anger."

Dunsford tensed, his next words demanding and cock-sure. "And how will he know? Are you going to tell him?" It would have been amusing because of his medium stature, if Barclay were not seething with restrained anger.

Ridley shrugged. "Saunton need not be informed of such things. He would know. I would wager money that he will see through your ploy and turn down your proposal. The man knows what true love is, after all."

"That is nonsense! This pretense that he is in love with the countess will last as long as it takes to confirm he has an heir before he reverts to his old ways. It is in his nature!"

Trafford frowned, considering this statement as he walked forward to take his place at the billiard table. "I am as cynical as any man who has sampled the delights of the flesh, but I do not believe that is the case. The earl has sought the women of his past to make amends. His actions are not ones of impermanence. I agree with Ridley. If it is your aim to dally, do not choose Miss Davis as your wife. You will invoke not only the earl's wrath, but that of his younger brother who wed Miss Davis's sister. The Balfour brothers are formidable alone, but paired up, they would wreak havoc on your existence for daring to toy with a relation under their protection."

"The connection to Saunton is the very rationale for making the offer."

Barclay wanted to thrust his cue through the man's chest to stake Dunsford's beating heart.

He restrained himself with an effort. Overreacting could start rumors about Jane, so he needed to temper his reaction lest he create a scandal for the young woman. Of all Jane's fine qualities, her connection to Saunton was the least important. If he could trust himself to speak without flying into a rage, he would set the arrogant little arse right. He assured himself the benefit of staying silent was that he had learned the man's true intentions, so he might take action.

Perhaps he must warn Jane? No, he did not have that right. He would inform Richard, who would refuse the match.

Ridley went to stand near Trafford, inspecting the shot Trafford had taken. "Then trust me, Dunsford. Do not make this decision lightly. If you wish to wed Miss Davis, you need to be fully committed when you approach the earl. Anything less and he will know. Saunton is not a fool."

Dunsford came to stand by the table to await his turn to play. "I shall think on what you have advised."

Barclay placed his cue down. "If you will excuse me, gentlemen, I find that I have an earlier engagement I forgot to attend to."

Straightening his tailcoat, Barclay departed the room. He

187

would not take a chance on this. Jane was too important. He must find the earl to discuss the matter right away.

When he found Richard, Barclay would demand to know more about the reparations to the women of the earl's past. Richard had failed to mention such, and it was not acceptable that Barclay learned of it in the presence of the sniveling ninny who planned to propose to his Jane—he grimaced—to Jane. Not *his* Jane. Just Jane.

Setting off to find the earl, he learned that both Richard and the duke had left Saunton Park for an undisclosed errand in Chatternwell and were expected back in the morning.

Barclay fumed in frustration, hoping that Dunsford would not approach Jane without the earl's prior approval. He could not allow her to be disappointed if the earl had to veto the match after she had already accepted the proposal. Yet the young cad could not be trusted to submit to propriety if he was so shallow about matters of faithfulness. Dunsford might approach her without the earl's approval.

CHAPTER 15

In the morning, Barclay quickly arose to await the earl's return. From the library windows, he frequently checked the drive for the ducal carriage that had taken his brother and cousin to the town of Chatternwell in Wiltshire.

It was essential that he inform the earl of Dunsford's intentions. He could not allow Jane to be tricked into the type of marriage the young dandy planned. She was to have a long and happy marriage, and many children to mother. What Dunsford planned was beyond the pale.

Pacing up and down the library, Barclay had to admit he was worried for the lady's future. Somehow she had come to mean so much to him in a short length of time, and he could not allow her to be manipulated into an unhappy union with the loathsome little cad.

By midmorning, Barclay decided he should go to eat his breakfast. At least it would occupy some of his time while he waited.

Having just taken a seat with a laden plate, Barclay forked baked eggs into his mouth.

"Barclay!" He started in surprise, dropping his fork with a loud clatter as it bounced off his plate, splattering egg across the table. Turning around, he found Aurora, who appeared disheveled and mildly distraught.

"What is it?" Barclay quickly rose to his feet, thoughts of breakfast forgotten.

"Have you seen Tatiana this morning?"

He shook his head. "Why?"

"She was not in her bed when I awoke. I cannot find her anywhere."

Barclay's stomach clenched in anxiety. "When did you last see her?"

"I put her to bed after her dinner, and she was sleeping when I returned to the room. At least …" Aurora's brow furrowed as she attempted to recall the evening before. "Yes. She was there when I came back because I saw her plait on the pillow." She looked back up. "What do we do?"

"What happened when you woke up?"

"Her bed was empty. We customarily come down to breakfast together at this time, but she must have risen much earlier. I have been searching for her, but this manor is so large, it took the longest time to check the public rooms!"

Barclay ran a hand through his hair. "I will look for her."

"I already checked the nursery, and the library, and all the rooms on this level. And the terrace."

He tried to think. With a sinking sensation, he realized there was one place he would have to check. "Did you look in Jane's room?"

"No … Jane has trouble sleeping, so she has been rising late. I did not want to disturb her too early. Do you think Tatiana could be with Jane?"

Barclay briefly closed his eyes. He could hardly ask his mother to go to Jane's room. Tatiana was his daughter. His responsibility. He was going to have to march himself down that corridor and force himself to knock on Jane's door.

He still felt regret over how he had handled the situation with the young woman. Had she waited for him the night he had stayed in his room? She deserved better, but he simply did not trust himself to be alone with her yet.

You do not have a choice.

Barclay grimaced. "I shall learn what I can."

Aurora frowned. "Barclay, what is happening between you and the young lady? I feel as if there is an undercurrent, and now … you appear quite reluctant to speak to her. Jane is a charming young woman and—"

"There is nothing happening between me and Jane!" He kept a straight face, but he knew his mother would not be fooled. Not after barking as he had just done.

"Barclay—"

He turned and walked to the door. "I must find Tatiana." *And prevent this conversation.* Aurora would likely blame herself if she knew his motive for ending his connection with Jane. He rushed off before Aurora could press the issue.

As he hurried through the grand hall, Barclay tried to prepare for his imminent conversation with Jane. Should he apologize? The young woman was clearly aware that he had snubbed her. She probably perceived it as a rejection, while he was merely attempting to navigate this awkward situation and ensure he did not take advantage of her passionate—and youthful—nature.

He exhaled deeply to settle his nerves, but the knot in his gut remained where it was. Blurting out a warning about that worm, Dunsford, was ill-advised, considering the circumstances. She was more likely to reject the caution from him than from his brother, and it was vital that she heed it, so he would not risk telling her himself.

Jane was to be happy, and his admonition would be

poorly received after his callous handling of her the past few days. If only he could explain that he was doing it to protect her from himself. Reaching the corridor leading to the family wing, he hesitated to compose himself before entering.

* * *

JANE'S SLEEP had improved a little, but she was afraid that it was mostly due to sheer exhaustion. She had been struggling with headaches and fatigue since … She tried to recall. Since a few hours after her last cup of coffee.

She cursed Perry for not warning her of the effects of drinking the devil's brew, which she likened to a marsh now that she was aware of what it did. Drawn in by the pretty scenery, only to find herself sinking into the swamp-water, unable to extricate herself from the pull of the mud. She could happily raise her head to howl like a trapped beast— her head ached so much, she felt like a wounded animal herself.

What a fool she had been to muddle with the so-called gentlemen's drink. Her only consolation was that Barclay had been through a similar suffering, so it was not her gender that was the basis of her problem.

Rubbing her temples, Jane attempted to think. Which set off a series of thudding echoes in her skull. She had woken with a headache, and it had only been intensifying through the past hour. Somewhere in the quagmire of pain and regrets, she recollected that Aurora had said something about relieving the symptoms.

There had been something she could do to reduce the intensity.

What had it been?

Hazily, the answer came to her. Aurora had mentioned a small amount of coffee could ease the transition. Jane rose.

Resolutely, she made for the library, where there should be a pot of coffee waiting for her. She had yet to cancel the request.

Making her way slowly down the hall of arching sash windows, she headed for the main house. As she reached the end of the corridor, she nearly jumped out of her skin when Barclay suddenly appeared in front of her. She considered turning around and heading back to her room, but she could not see if anyone accompanied him to witness her cowardice, so, squaring her shoulders in frustration, she defiantly forged ahead, intending to brush past him.

"Jane?"

She halted. This was not the time to engage her in conversation. She was in no mood to hear anything he had to say. Between contending with the coffee issues, and coping with her feeling of loss over the burgeoning relationship he had severed so abruptly, Jane had no patience for a discussion. She needed to reach that coffeepot.

With determination, she resumed her trajectory. If the gentleman was to force a conversation on her, he would do so while she continued on her quest to alleviate her suffering. Reaching Barclay, she sidestepped him and marched on toward the library.

Behind her, he sighed heavily before turning to fall in step with her.

"Jane, have you seen Tatiana?"

"I have not." Her head hurt too much for pleasantries. That he had not sought her out to apologize for his behavior was disappointing, but she only had thoughts for the coffeepot, so she kept walking.

"Did she attempt to visit you this morning?"

Jane carefully shook her head, noting that she was only steps away.

"Not at all? It is just ... She is missing, and Aurora thought she might have …" Barclay trailed off as Jane strode into and across the room. To her great relief, the tray with the coffee was waiting in the usual spot on the table near the chessboard.

"Mr. Thompson, I have not seen your daughter since yesterday. Now, if you do not mind, I wish to be alone."

Barclay had followed her, surprising her when he spoke behind her shoulder. "Jane, I know it is not what you wish to hear, but I assure you I am doing what is best."

"Best for whom, Mr. Thompson?" She could not help herself. Her frustration came rushing out in a tight, angry demand.

The architect blinked before responding. "For you."

"Am I not the best judge of what is best for me?"

"You are so …"

"Young?"

He nodded, devoid of words to say.

"Too young to know my own mind?"

Barclay bit his lip, visibly uncomfortable at the question.

"Tell me, Mr. Thompson, when you were my age—what were you doing?"

His gaze dropped to his boots, which he studied carefully. After a moment, he mumbled a reply. "I was training to be an architect."

"And what did that involve? In that specific year?"

He cocked his head to think. "That would have been the final year of designing and drawing plans."

"You were designing buildings?"

"Elevations, mostly."

"But you were so young. How could you possibly have known your own mind? How could you know you would be an architect? How could you design elevations for buildings? Surely you were too young?"

"It is more complicated than that! There is my social status and ..."

"And?"

"I cannot debate with you. My daughter is missing. Do you know where she might be?"

"Tatiana frequently wanders off on her own. Why are you so anxious?"

"She was gone before Aurora awoke. To our knowledge, she has not had her breakfast."

Jane paused, apprehension washing over her despite her physical discomfort. "How long has she been missing?"

"Since sometime between last night and this morning. Do you know of places she might go?"

Jane rubbed her aching temple. "I cannot think." She reached a trembling hand out to grasp the coffeepot. Aurora's advice to drink a small quantity was now an urgent matter.

"Miss Davis!"

Her heart sank, as did her hand back to her side before the newest arrival could see what she was about. "Mr. Dunsford."

She saw a grimace flash across Barclay's face as he politely turned toward the gentleman standing in the doorway. Mr. Dunsford was prepared for the outdoors, a beaver tucked under his arm. "I was hoping to talk to you, Miss Davis. Could we have a word alone?" He glanced at her companion, who was glowering at her side.

"That is hardly appropriate," growled Barclay.

Mr. Dunsford frowned slightly at the accusation. "Yet you are alone with Miss Davis?"

"We are related. Miss Davis is my sister-in-law, as you are well aware. I must insist I remain to chaperone if you wish to talk with the young lady."

Jane quelled her irritation. Sister-in-law? Chaperone? She could cheerfully punch Barclay in the face. Drawing a deep breath, she feigned a calm voice. "I shall think about your question and get back to you. Mr. Dunsford wishes to speak with me, and I am sure it will be acceptable if we keep the door ajar, so please allow me to have my conversation with the gentleman."

Barclay turned his narrowed eyes on her, and in their depths, she observed concern. What was he concerned about? Mr. Dunsford hardly presented a danger, and he was a gentleman. A guest of the earl.

"I shall wait outside."

Jane shook her head. "That is hardly necessary. You should find Tatiana."

Barclay bit his lip, clearly torn. Lowering his voice, he spoke to her privately. "Just do not agree to anything. Tell him you will think about it."

Jane wrinkled her nose, a question hovering on her lips as the architect left her side.

* * *

As Barclay left the library, he could not deny his fears on her behalf. Jane was a sensible young woman, and he hoped his warning was enough to delay her acceptance of Dunsford's proposal.

Realizing that Tatiana had been missing another thirty minutes in his delayed search, he swiftly returned to the main house to find Aurora and learn if she had subsequently found his daughter.

As he entered the main hall, he looked up to find that the Duke of Halmesbury and the earl had returned. They were headed toward the earl's study, and Barclay considered taking a moment to inform his brother of the trouble with Dunsford as he had intended to do that morning, but the length of time Tatiana had been missing was more than could be borne. If Aurora had not yet found her, Barclay needed to search the grounds.

Raking through his recollections of the past few days, he quickly cataloged places Tatiana had visited in the gardens and park so he might begin his search.

He did not wish to involve the rest of the household in searching for her yet, but if he did not find her soon, he would need to ask for help.

Aurora was in the breakfast room but had not yet seen Tatiana. Barclay strode down the hall, exiting the manor onto the terrace. He peered in every direction but saw no movement in the gardens except for a group of gentlemen heading to the lake for fishing.

Stepping up onto the balustrade, he used the higher vantage point to scan the park, but still no sign of his daughter. Hopping down, he ran down the steps to search the area around the majestic oak where the ladies played nine-pins, but Tatiana was nowhere in sight.

His distress mounted as he accepted that it was time to ask his brother to form a search party. There were several ponds around the property, and his fear increased at the thought of Tatiana slipping into one of the waterways.

Barclay jogged back to the manor. The idea of something happening to Tatiana was too much to bear. He must find her.

CHAPTER 16

*A*fter her conversation with Dunsford, Jane's head was pounding so hard she thought she might faint. Holding a hand to her temple in an attempt to push the pain back, she vaguely remembered her quest—Aurora had said a small amount of coffee could assist with the symptoms. Now that she was alone once more, she quickly headed to the coffee tray. With trembling hands, she poured out an ounce of the black brew, adding a few drops of cream before swirling it in the cup and downing it.

Dropping into a chair, she licked the coffee from her lips and leaned her head back while she waited for the coffee to follow its course.

After several minutes, the pain receded to a dull ache. Raising her head, Jane opened her eyes and gently stretched out her neck. As Aurora had promised, the symptoms had dulled to a tolerable level, and for the first time since she had stopped drinking the evil beverage, Jane recovered the ability to think.

Quietly, she contemplated the situation with Barclay. If

Emma were here, her sister would recommend she be honest about what she was feeling. Zounds. If their situations were reversed, she would recommend to Emma to confront her feelings. She *had* told her sister something to that effect during her strange courtship with Perry.

Staring sightlessly out the window, Jane admitted the truth she had been avoiding since the night Barclay had failed to come to the library. She had foolishly fallen in love with the man.

Yet … had it been foolish? Everything in her being yearned to spend more time with him. More time with Tatiana. They would have had a perfect life together. Her ideal life. But she could not force the gentleman to court her, and only he knew what was right for his little family.

Clearly, he had decided that she was not it. Mrs. Gordon had something to offer, which apparently Jane did not. Which was why she was now making plans for her future. She had no choice—she could hardly sit around in her room and the library lamenting what could have been with the brooding widower. What a pathetic situation.

Nay, she needed to make her future. She did not want to return home unwed.

Rather, she wanted to begin a new chapter in her life, which was why she had made the decision she had while talking to Mr. Dunsford. She did not know why Barclay had cautioned her to think about it, so she had decided on the spot. There was no need to delay her response. The time for hesitation was over because attempting to be thoughtful and procrastinating the other night had lost her a chance at a great love.

She should have demanded her right to be taken seriously then, rather than earlier when they had quarreled. Now Barclay was committed to a path with Mrs. Gordon. For all she knew, they had already come to an understanding and planned to wed.

It might be too late to turn back the clock, but Jane would proceed with more decisiveness so she did not miss out on any more opportunities.

With that, she was reminded that Tatiana was missing. She had grown to know Tatiana well over the past few days —having an inkling of how the little girl thought, Jane could help find her. Straightening up, she thought about places perhaps she could look, her qualms growing now that she had recovered her wits. Tatiana needed her, and Jane was going to find her.

* * *

WHEN BARCLAY RETURNED to the manor, he found several guests had congregated on the terrace. Waving to Mrs. Gordon, he headed over to talk to her. Perhaps she might have encountered Tatiana somewhere.

Drawing the widow away to the corner, he briefly thought of his intention to propose to her. That would have to wait until he located his child, but he admitted to himself he was experiencing a certain reluctance to take the next step with the woman.

Perhaps he was just tired. His sleeplessness had returned, and he was quite bored at night. Natalya never visited anymore, and he could not leave his rooms lest he encounter Jane in the middle of the night, so instead he had been pacing his bedroom in the moonlight.

Perhaps Mrs. Gordon's presence will ease my sleep?

It seemed probable.

The widow smiled up at him from beneath the brim of her bonnet, and Barclay was reminded of his quest. "Mrs.

Gordon, have you perchance seen Tatiana anywhere in the house or grounds?"

She looked confused for a moment, frowning slightly. "Tatiana?"

"My daughter."

Mrs. Gordon's face lit up. "Of course, the little imp with the silver hair."

Barclay suppressed a surge of irritation. He was certain this woman was contemplating taking her place as his wife, but she did not know his child's name? "Yes. Have you seen her this morning?"

The widow's expression did not change, but something about how she spoke next made her cheerful countenance seem feigned. "Is she not in the nursery with the other children?"

Barclay sighed. "Tatiana has not been staying in the nursery."

There was no mistaking it, the widow was appalled. "Why ever not?"

"My daughter is not accustomed with being parted from her family for excessive time, so she has been staying with her grandmother in her room."

"Well ... that is hardly the way to teach her independence."

"She is nine years old, and she lost her mother only two years ago. We are allowing her to grieve at her own pace."

"Two years is a long time. I would say it is high time the young lady attend a ladies' seminary to master her accomplishments."

It was Barclay's turn to look appalled. "I thought you were telling me how you were sent to school too young?"

"I was seven. Tiana is nine years old. She should have been sent off when she was eight."

"Eight! Her mother had just died."

Mrs. Gordon thought about it for a moment. "You are correct. If one factors in some time for mourning, then she is the perfect age to be sent off to school. Perhaps I could contact the headmistress of my school in Surrey?"

"Surrey!"

"Yes. It is quite lovely. And the weather is mild like here in Somerset."

As his mind tried to follow the shift of conversation, he became aware of the sound of birdcalls and the chattering of the guests behind them. He took it all in while he came to the realization that he had been wrong. Very, very wrong. And Tatiana had been right.

Barclay could not help himself. He raised his hands to rake them through his hair. If only he had listened to Tatiana. She had warned him that the widow did not like children, and now he knew his daughter's instincts had been correct. Who would send such a young child away? A young child who suffered from night terrors and missed her mother like the devil?

He opened his mouth to argue these points, then shut it. He knew, without a doubt, that Mrs. Gordon would brush those issues aside as so much distraction from the issue.

Composing his thoughts, he prepared to speak again. "Would you like to have children?"

The widow's face was aghast. "Goodness, no! I hoped that you would be done with all that since you already have a child."

"Tatiana."

"Of course, Tiana."

"Tatiana."

"That is what I said. Tiana."

Barclay accepted that he had made a grave error. Tatiana had said that Jane was the new mother she needed. The new wife he needed. He had brushed his daughter's assertions aside and pursued a woman utterly unsuitable while the perfect wife and mother had been before him. Jane had lovingly read *Aladdin* to his daughter. They had partaken in activities together. She had even taught his daughter how to play cricket. With a smile on her face and tireless patience in her heart.

And Barclay had cruelly rejected her affections. Admonished her for her age, for her lack of experience. Snubbed her.

Now his daughter was missing, and he knew it was because he would not heed her advice to pursue Jane.

If only the ground would open and swallow him up. His behavior had been horrible. As horrible as this charming but shallow woman who watched him with a quizzical expression on her face, attempting to make sense of the familial bond he shared with his child.

It had been a horrible mistake when he had walked away from Jane. He now knew he had fallen in love with her that night in the library and fear had driven him to run from her. All the rest had been excuses he could have overcome. But fear had driven him to run. He had been afraid to love, as Tatiana had observed. Afraid to love and lose again, as he had with Natalya.

Barclay could not fathom his behavior. He had uncovered a deep fondness for a woman for the second time in his life, and he had thrown it away, giving in to his fear.

Even now, Jane could be agreeing to marry a disloyal little worm because Barclay had hurt her by denying their closeness. Which was his own fault, and there was nothing he could do to address it until he found Tatiana.

"Mrs. Gordon, I am afraid I must leave you to find my daughter. Who will be staying at my side where she belongs for as long as she so desires."

Her face fell. "I ... see."

He brushed any feelings of culpability aside. Mrs. Gordon had a different vision of the future than himself, and there was nothing to be done about it. If there was any possibility of making matters right with Jane, he would, but the widow was not an option now that he knew her philosophy about the rearing of children. Considering he was a single father, he should have been more assiduous in his assessment of her as a prospective match.

Barclay bowed, having said everything he wanted to say, and turned to walk away. He had wasted enough time. He needed to find the earl to request his help in the search.

* * *

Jane raced through the family wing, checking the bedrooms before climbing the stairs at the end of the hall. Searching the nursery took some time as several children greeted her and clamored to tell her stories about their day. Ethan held up his arms to be lifted, and Jane walked about the nursery, holding him to her side in an embrace while noting how much her cousin had grown. Walking about with him was not as easy as it had been even a year earlier.

She was able to finally lower him to the floor when he became distracted by a game the other children had begun, but only after he extricated a promise to meet him later that afternoon for chess.

Jane left the family wing and headed up to the attic level. There were several rooms containing stored furniture, old clothes, and even toys, so she hurried through the accumulation of goods while calling for Tatiana, but to no avail.

It was now midday, which meant she had been missing for some hours, and Jane admitted that her anxiety to see the child safe was increasing.

Reaching the landing outside the library, Jane stopped and tried to think where else the girl might go. Her mind kept drifting back to their last conversation. Tatiana had wanted her to read *Aladdin* to her, and Jane had made a vague agreement to do so when she was well again. This thought was accompanied by a flash of shame, because Jane had had every intention of avoiding that situation since Barclay had snubbed her, but the little girl had been quite excited by the prospect.

Damn this ache in her head. It had improved, but it still dulled her thoughts. Tatiana had mentioned something about *Aladdin* before that, but Jane could not think what it was. Something that could be a clue to where the girl had gone, if only Jane could remember it.

* * *

BARCLAY HAD INFORMED Richard of the situation, who called on Radcliffe, his butler, to form a search party using the grooms and footmen. The duke himself had collected up two gentlemen they thought could be useful, Ridley and Trafford, and they had gone to saddle their horses to search farther afield while the earl remained at the house to supervise the search parties.

Still worried but feeling infinitesimally better that the men were to search all the waterways as a top priority, he found Aurora in a drawing room to apprise her of what was happening. His mother was drawn with worry, sipping on tea and attempting to still her shaking hands.

"This is my fault," she exclaimed.

"Why would you say that?" Barclay had taken a moment to sit with his mother while he tried to think of places to look. He had a nagging sensation that he knew where Tatiana would have gone based on something she had said. Realizing he had not eaten, he quickly downed some dainty biscuits and a cup of tea to help him collect his thoughts back together. Perhaps it would come to him if he got some food in his body.

"I should have woken up earlier."

"Tatiana has never done this before, so it would have made no sense for you to do so."

Aurora's gaze dropped to her hands, where she was twisting her fingers together in her agitation. "I sensed something was wrong."

"With Tatiana?"

His mother shot him a perplexed glance. "Yes, with Tatiana. Who else?"

Barclay cleared his throat, nervous he had revealed too much. "What about her?"

"She was gloomy last night, talking about her mother and how, if she were here, she would settle this muddle. I did my best to cheer her up, but she seemed fixated on something to do with you and Mrs. Gordon."

Barclay leaned back to stare at the cornices. The ornate cornices that Tsar had especially designed for this manor, as part of his commission from the late earl. Barclay's sire. Four generations of Thompsons had their lives entwined within the walls of this manor, this grand design, and it was time for Barclay to confess his sins.

"This is not your fault, Mother. It is mine."

"Why would you say that?" Aurora asked in an echo of his earlier question.

"I had planned to propose to the widow. Tatiana was adamant I was making a mistake, but I did not listen. She insisted the widow does not like children, and I informed her that was stuff and nonsense. So it is my fault she has run away. Or is hiding. Or is lying somewhere injured."

Barclay lowered his head into his hands, his fear of something happening to his child causing his breath to come out in pants. What was the thing Tatiana had said that nagged at him? If he could just recall …

"Was she correct?"

He hesitated before answering. "Mrs. Gordon thinks *Tiana* should be sent to a ladies' seminary in Surrey."

"Tiana?"

"That is what she repeatedly called her."

"But … Tatiana is only nine years old. I know there are families that do such things, but I could never send a child away that young."

"I informed the widow that I, too, would not consider it."

Aurora was silent. Then she cleared her throat and asked the inevitable question. "What did she think of that?"

"It does not signify. Any woman who asks me to send my child away while she still mourns her mother's death can … get hanged."

Aurora chuckled. "I presume you were not so eloquent with the widow?"

"I was not. I did make it clear that there was no future for us."

"Why were you pursuing her, Barclay? I sensed that there was something between you and Jane Davis. Why would you pursue another woman if your affection is engaged by someone else?"

"I thought … that given our situation, I should not inflict it on someone so young. Someone with such a promising future ahead of her."

"You mean my recent situation with the London Virtuous Committee of Charitable Endeavors?"

Barclay's shoulders slumped at the memory of his mother crying earlier that week. "I do."

"Jane Davis strikes me as a sensible young woman with a good head on her shoulders. And her cousin is a by-blow, so she is aware of the difficulties associated with our situation. What were her thoughts on making a match? Is that why she was avoiding you?"

"No. She avoided me because I severed our connection."

"Oh, Barclay." Aurora covered her mouth with her hand, crestfallen.

He straightened up in his chair to defend himself, his gaze averted. "I thought I was doing the right thing. That Mrs. Gordon was the logical choice, given her maturity and social standing."

When he glanced over at his mother, it surprised him to find pity on her face. "Barclay, it is not about the logic of the match. It is about the person in question. Their integrity, their loyalty. Your loyalty. Natalya was not a match that made sense, but she stood by your side every day of your marriage. She did not care about the scandal in our family, she cared about us. As a family, we are strong. We can face adversity together."

Barclay hesitated for several seconds before admitting the truth of it. "Jane would make a wonderful addition to our family."

"I agree."

"I think it is too late."

Aurora stayed silent, waiting for him to explain.

"I hurt her, and I believe Mr. Dunsford intended to propose to her earlier in the library. Given how things are between us ..."

Barclay let his words trail off. If Jane had accepted a proposal, it would cause a scandal for her to reverse her position.

Unburdening himself to Aurora had helped ease the tension in his mind. In doing so, he turned his attention back to Tatiana to run through their last few conversations so he might seek a clue to where she might be.

Inspiration hit. Jumping to his feet, Barclay hastened out the door for the one place he had not searched. This time he was certain he would find his child, but he hoped she would be safe, recalling the pond's slippery edges covered in green algae that lay nearby to his destination.

CHAPTER 17

*B*arclay darted from the terrace, jogging across the gardens toward the woods. He was aware of drawing curious looks from the other guests, but he did not give a damn. He needed to reach Tatiana and ensure she was safe. Approaching the woods, he stopped to scan for the path they had taken days before.

As he entered the woods, the call of birds and the singing of insects were his only companions as he strode down the path. When he left the manor, he had been certain he would find Tatiana, but doubts had crept in as he kept walking. What if Tatiana was not there? His breath caught at the thought. That would mean she was still unaccounted for.

Why did he agree to this damned house party? It had created nothing but chaos and hesitation. He had been perfectly satisfied in his prior life, working hard and mourning Natalya's absence. Now he was in love with a young girl whom he had wronged, and his daughter was missing.

It was all so … complicated.

It was with a huge sense of relief that he caught sight of

the pond through the trees. Picking up his pace, he jogged the last of the path and, navigating a final bend, the pond came into view. Across its expanse stood Persephone, gazing back at him over the water. Barclay steadied himself on his feet, giddy with joy when he noted the figure of his daughter scrunched near the feet of the statue.

Careful to avoid the banks of the pond, Barclay ran the last forty feet to join her. His fear was assuaged, but his anxiety returned when he saw how her head was bent against her knees, her slender arms wrapped around her shins.

"Tatiana!"

Her head lifted to reveal a tear-streaked face. "Papa?"

Reaching down, he grasped her under her arms and raised her to his chest in a hard embrace. "Oh, little one, I was so worried about you."

She lifted her reed-thin arms around his neck, lowering her face against his chest, to hug him tightly. "She did not come," she whispered into his coat.

"Who did not come?"

"Jane did not come. I left her a note, but she did not come." And, for the third time in as many days, Barclay held a sobbing female to his chest. He looked about, then walked over to a bench near the back of the cave to take a seat. Settling Tatiana on his knee, he pulled out a handkerchief to carefully wipe her cheeks and dry her eyes.

"I do not think that Jane received your note, little one."

Big, blue eyes found his as she leaned her head back from his chest to look up at him. "How do you know that?"

"I asked her if she knew where you were, and she did not."

"Oh." Tatiana hung her head, her expression devastated. "I failed."

"Failed at what? Why are you here?"

Tatiana turned her face away to stare at the cave wall

sweeping around the bench. "You will not believe me. You did not believe me when I tried to tell you before."

Barclay raked a hand through his hair while he tried to think. He was afraid he had not been on his best behavior these past few days. In an attempt to be responsible and do his duty, he had hurt Tatiana and Jane. He should have listened to his daughter—to his heart—and in not doing so, he had let both of them down.

"I will listen now. Tell me what this is all about, and I promise to pay attention."

Tatiana bit her lip, evidently considering his words. Eventually, she turned her Baltic-blue eyes back to him. "Mama told me Jane was the one."

Barclay blinked. "Mama?"

"She visited me. She came to visit me, and she told me it was time for her to leave and that Jane was to be my new mother."

Barclay shook his head and tried to make sense of what she was saying. "Do you … mean that Mama came to you in your dreams?"

Tatiana shrugged, clearly disinterested in the distinction. "I tried to tell you that Jane was the one, but you did not listen. Mama said I must insist."

He sighed. Tatiana had conjured her mother through her grief, as he had been doing these past two years. It was not the important part of what she said. He needed to listen and understand her needs. Then later hope there was still an opportunity to repair things with Jane and make all this right.

"Why are you here in the grotto?"

"Mama came last night, and she said it was very important that you and Jane come back to the grotto. She said I must arrange it so that she could leave because she had been here too long."

Tatiana must have observed that he and Jane had forged a special connection and that the grotto had been a place that exemplified their relationship.

"I appreciate that, little one, but you really scared me. You could have fallen in the pond without adults here to assist you."

"The pond?"

"Yes, see that green slime?"

"You mean the *vodorosli*?"

He straightened in surprise. "What did you say?"

"Mama told me that when I came to the grotto, I was to be very careful to stay away from the *vodorosli*." A chill ran down Barclay's spine. It was not possible that Natalya had truly visited her ... was it?

"Where did you learn that word?"

Tatiana shrugged. "Mama said it last night. She said she could not remember the English word for it."

Barclay rubbed his fingers over his forehead. His daughter must have heard her mother say it in the past, plucking it from an old memory. He might not be able to think of a situation in which Natalya would have been discussing *vodorosli*, but that did not mean she had not had an occasion to use the word with Tatiana. "Algae. The English word is algae."

"*Al-gee*. That is a funny word!"

Barclay smiled. Their conversation was bizarre but, in an instant, Tatiana was just a nine-year-old girl again, and her simple view of the world utterly charmed him.

Brushing a frond of silver-blonde hair away from her face, he acknowledged that Tatiana had been right. She needed a mother, and he needed a wife. Not just anyone, but someone who could help him navigate the complexities of emotional intimacy. Someone sensitive to the issues his daughter and his mother faced. Someone sensitive to his own needs. Someone like—

"Jane!"

Snapping his head up, Barclay found Tatiana beaming. She was looking over her shoulder at the entrance of the cave where Jane now stood, a hand resting against the cave entrance while she panted from exertion. Across the pond, Aurora came into view as she stepped out of the woods, evidently following Jane to find them. Both women had their hair bared, apparently having hurried to the grotto without taking a moment to fetch their bonnets.

"Thank … the … Lord!" exclaimed Jane between pants. "I … am so … happy to … see you … Tatiana!"

His daughter wriggled off his lap, landing on the cave floor to race over to Jane and throw her arms about Jane's waist. "You came!"

"Of course I came … I needed to ensure you were safe."

"Did you get my note?"

"Your note …? No, I … worked out … where you were. You talked … to me … about reading *Aladdin*, but it … took me an hour or two … to remember that you called … the grotto your cave of treasures. I would have … remembered earlier … but my head was aching … and I could not think properly, so I searched for you … in all the wrong places before it came to me. Where was the note?" Jane was still recovering her breath, endearing in her haste to find his child safe and well.

"With your strawberries on your breakfast tray. I asked you to meet me here."

"Oh. I was too tired to make my strawberry water this morning."

Barclay stood. If there was anything to clarify Jane's suitability for the role of Tatiana's mother, certainly her knowledge of the inner workings of his daughter's mind was a clear sign. Not that the young woman would still consider him eminently suitable after his cloddish avoidance of her.

Nevertheless, he could not help noticing that she was ravishing—if only he could sweep her up in his arms to plant a kiss on her soft mouth, irrespective of his daughter and his mother's presence.

You cannot—the young woman may have accepted a proposal this very morning.

Barclay's gaze found the roof of the cave to inspect the composition while Aurora walked up behind Jane, also panting while she released the skirts she had been holding up to speed her progress. The women must have jogged through the woods as he had done. "Ta … tiana! You … scared me … to death … child!" Indeed, his mother had a sheen of sweat across her overheated face, but she looked overjoyed to see her granddaughter.

"I know how to look after myself," protested the girl with an indignant squaring of her shoulders.

"Of course you do, child. But you cannot stop us from worrying after you. Thirty years from now, we shall still worry after you as if you were still a babe."

Tatiana groaned. "Adults are so fearful."

"It is true." Barclay spoke from the interior of the cave, pulling those ice-blue eyes of the woman he loved to rest on him. He could not read her thoughts, because those windows to her soul were shuttered, revealing nothing.

Was Jane aware he had dissuaded Tatiana from spending time with her—a further insult it embarrassed him to have committed. Fortunately, it did not seem to have affected the relationship between her and his daughter. He had not the right to have said what he had to the child—to interfere in their friendship, which had done nothing but bring Tatiana respite from her grieving.

Aurora looked between Barclay and Jane, her curiosity evident. "So, why are we here?"

Tatiana grabbed her hand to pull her into the cave. "It is a grotto, and it is magical. Come see the other statue."

"I have been here before," Aurora responded. "I have seen the statue. Is that why we are here?"

Jane and he both were silent. He raked his hair once more before responding. "Tatiana wanted me and Jane to speak." He flung his arm up to gesture at the interior of the cave. "She felt we might work out our differences here because … it is magic."

Aurora tilted her head and turned her eyes up to the roof, back at Persephone, and then toward the hidden entrance to the second cave. "I can understand that. Love has grown here before, for at least one party. The other party … he is dining at the devil's table in the halls of hell."

Barclay grimaced. He had done his best not to ponder the question of where at Saunton Park he might have been conceived, but he feared he could now guess the answer. He could imagine a young Aurora having her head turned in such a romantic spot, especially if the old earl had been as handsome in his youth as his younger sons, with their striking green eyes and sable hair.

"Shall I take Tatiana back to the manor?" His mother did not meet his eyes, aware she had offered something improper, her expression nothing short of mischievous.

He cleared his throat. "I would appreciate that. Jane and I should talk perhaps … before we return."

Tatiana clapped her hands. "First you must come see!"

Tugging on Aurora's hand, Tatiana led the way to the second cave. As they entered, Barclay was again struck by the eerie solitude of the second statue standing in its private cave, with dappled light stealing in from the opening above.

She led them to a bench in the back, where a hamper and

blanket rested. Taking hold of Jane's hand, Tatiana led her forward to sit on the bench. "We did not see it before, but look."

Jane sat, then turned her head in the direction that the girl pointed, gasping in surprise. "There is a verse etched on the wall of the cave." She bent from side to side. "It is lit by the sunlight, and it can only be viewed from this bench!"

"What does it say?" Barclay's curiosity got the better of him, the question spilling from his lips before he could stop himself.

Aurora gazed at the statue in the middle, not looking at the verse but speaking its lines from the recesses of her memory.

> "Doubt thou the stars are fire,
> Doubt that the sun doth move,
> Doubt truth to be a liar,
> But never doubt I love."

Barclay smiled. "Tsar."

His mother smiled in response. "Indeed. He certainly loves his Shakespeare. I would have done well to recall that this was Tsar's creation, not your sire's. I confused the two, but"—she turned shining eyes to his—"but the sentiment holds true from a mother to a son, which is why I shall never regret my time here."

He inclined his head, touched by his mother's support. She stepped forward, taking Tatiana's hand from Jane. "Come, little one. Your father and Jane should talk while we return to the manor."

"I got them here!"

"You did, child. Well done."

Aurora and his daughter headed for the cave exit, leaving Barclay to stand awkwardly in the subdued lighting. Staring at his boots, he rubbed the toe of one boot against the moss on the lit floor while he thought about what to say now that he had his chance. "I think I may owe you an apology."

He heard Jane exhale deeply. "Yes, I believe you do."

Drawing a deep breath, he walked forward to drop to one knee next to her. He was alone with Jane, and he could only pray she was not yet betrothed to that audacious little worm, Dunsford.

CHAPTER 18

*J*ane looked at him in surprise. "What are you doing?"

"I thought I might declare myself," Barclay answered, fascinated by her irises which were particularly vivid in the light playing in the cave. "I might be too late, but—"

"Too late?"

"I know Dunsford intended to propose."

"Oh … I confess I did not heed your advice to wait when he spoke to me earlier in the library."

Barclay's heart fell. He had missed his chance, and Jane had accepted a proposal from another man. Feeling foolish, bent on one knee as he was so he could be at eye-level with her. Now he was stuck here with nowhere to hide as she pondered him from inches away. "I … see."

He made to rise, but Jane shot out a hand to stay him. "I gave Mr. Dunsford my answer because I saw no reason to delay. I informed him that I was honored by his offer, but unfortunately my affections were otherwise engaged and I would not be doing him a justice if I were to agree to be his wife."

Barclay closed his eyes, his fears spent. This day had been exhausting in every way, but when he opened his eyes once more, he was invigorated with renewed energy. Jane gazed at him with curiosity as he attempted to gather his frayed wits and press forward. "I am so relieved to hear that. I would have been sorely disappointed."

She smiled tentatively. "What of you? Are there nuptials to be announced? Between you and Mrs. Gordon?"

"Good Lord, no!" He bit his lip. "I apologize. I just learned of the widow's philosophy on children, and I am not yet recovered."

Jane's brow furrowed in question.

"She advised me to send Tatiana away to a ladies' seminary in Surrey," he offered in explanation.

She blinked in surprise. "Why would you do that?"

"That was my question. It was in that moment that I confronted what a fool I had been. Tatiana had warned me, but I did not listen."

Jane's gaze dropped to her hands in her lap. "What happened, Barclay? One moment, we seemed to be on the road to ... something special. The next, you had disappeared."

Barclay sighed before standing up to take a seat next to her on the bench. "The morning after we spoke, my mother suffered a great disappointment because of me ... Because she is ..."

"Unwed?"

"Precisely. It was harrowing to see her so upset ... The thought of something similar happening to you was too much to bear. Tatiana says I gave in to fear."

"Ah ... That explains her earlier protest about adults being fearful."

Barclay glanced up at Hades before eventually replying,

"She was right. With Natalya, I loved deeply, and when she …
left us … it was devastating. I had no expectations of feeling
that depth of emotion for another woman, but then I met
you and the possibility of love became a reality. Which
forced me to think of all the many ways it would go wrong.
The ways I could lose you. Or hurt you."

He noticed she was blushing, her hands having stilled
while she gazed at them unblinkingly. "Love?"

Barclay swallowed hard before reaching out to clasp one
of her hands in his. "Jane, I thought my heart was dead. That
I would never feel anything again. And then I met you, and
life came rushing back. You have captured Tatiana's heart,
and the approval of my mother, but more than that, you have
captured … me … my heart."

She still stared at her hands, but a wide smile spread
across her face. "I … am …very pleased to hear that because I
must confess you have had my heart since your first night
here. I … I …" She hesitated, but when she spoke again, it was
in a rush, as if she wanted to get the words out as quickly as
possible. "I confess I heard you and Aurora discussing your
situation in the library and I was utterly ensnared. I never
considered what—who—my future husband would be until
that moment, but when I heard you talk of your love for
Natalya, I could not help falling in love with a man who held
his loved ones in such esteem. It was inexorable. Fated. I
could not imagine anyone by my side but you."

She stopped as abruptly as she had begun, catching her
breath in shallow heaves, and Barclay was perfectly captivated. Why had he ever thought she was immature? Jane was
loyal, intelligent, and exuberant about life. She cared about
other people and did her best to take care of them. What he
had seen as immaturity was truly a woman who embraced
life with her whole heart, and she could teach him a thing or
two about the pursuit of happiness.

Raising her hand to his lips, he pressed a gentle kiss to her knuckles. "That was magnificently said. Much better than my paltry attempt to express myself. But then, you are the poetess, and I am a humble artisan."

Jane chuckled. "That was reasonably well said."

Barclay laughed in return, a feeling of lightness stealing over him as he released the past and accepted the future. Turning toward her, he tugged lightly on the hand he clasped to pull her into his arms. Staring down into her eyes, he gently cupped her head and brought his mouth down to hers, seeking her silky softness.

* * *

IN THAT MOMENT, desire awakened, and Jane exhaled in elation. Barclay quickly slipped his tongue between her lips to tangle with hers, as he had done the other night. She was familiar with such kissing before Barclay had surprised her with it in the library because she had inadvertently witnessed Emma and Perry in a passionate embrace before she had discreetly reminded them of her presence with a determined snore a few weeks earlier. They had both seemed quite taken, so Jane had imagined they must find it pleasurable in some manner.

With the wrong man, the thought of entangling tongues seemed grotesque. But with the right man ... with the right man, all thought was lost as her blood heated in response. She was fascinated by Barclay, by his scent and his heated skin and his rough beard against her face.

With the right man, she could do this forever.

Barclay was at once both hard and gentle. Fragrant with tea, leather, and spice, while masculine with a hint of salt and ink. He was rough with beard and thick hair, her fingers having found their way to combing through his dark locks, while his skin was smooth and the fabric of his waistcoat felt fine to the touch.

He was everything she had imagined in a man, and so much more. Which was why she protested when his mouth left hers, but grew distracted when he pressed kisses along her jaw to nibble on her earlobe. The tingling sensation this engendered was as unexpected as it was intense, racing across the surface of her skin to shoot all the way down to her toes, and she moaned in ecstasy as she pressed against him in craving.

Barclay pulled away unexpectedly, panting as he shifted back several inches, his face flushed with the power of his own passions which Jane observed with great relish while she, too, panted for her breath. Her own skin was warmed from within, every part of her body awake and aware of his. She would have leapt right back in his arms, but he seemed to be attempting to speak, so she waited impatiently.

Slowly, his flush receded, and his breathing settled. "I should be clear about my intentions."

Jane quirked an eyebrow in amusement, but waited.

"Miss Jane Davis, will you do me the honor of accepting me as your future husband?"

She beamed. "As soon as possible. I am more than ready to assume the role of your new wife."

He grinned, flashing white teeth against tanned skin. Barclay was not a nobleman. He was a man who worked for his living and did it well. She looked forward to seeing his works as a partner who traveled at his side.

"And to be clear, you are accepting the role of my little one's mother? You will love her as your own?"

Jane felt tears springing into her eyes as she laughed in joy. "I would be honored to do so, if that is what Tatiana wants."

Barclay exhaled, shaking his head. Jane watched that long

length, and her fingers itched to take him back to the manor so she might trim that clean but unattended hair, as she had thought of the first time she had seen him descend from the carriage. "Tatiana wants that very much. She has campaigned for you every moment we are together. I suppose she recognized this bond between the three of us with far more intelligence than I."

"She is very bright," agreed Jane. "Will we be traveling with you?"

"Of course. If that is what you want, I would love to have you accompany me. I miss introducing Tatiana to my world, and I would certainly enjoy your company."

Jane rubbed her hands together, barely able to contain herself that so unexpectedly the world had righted itself and she was to have the future she had envisioned with Barclay at her side. "And when shall we marry?"

"As soon as we can gather our families together." His expression of contentment faded. "Which means I must now inform the earl that I have been bewitched by the young lady in his care who has not yet reached her majority."

* * *

TAKING some time to enjoy the grotto with Jane, while dreading the forthcoming meeting with Richard, it was all he could do to hold on to the magic of the moment as long as he could. While they were here, they were enwrapped in the magic of the caves with their silent witnesses carved from marble and stone. Once they left ... the troubles of the world would return.

So they sat together, holding hands and eating from the hamper that Tatiana had arranged. Neither of them had eaten much in their quest to find his daughter, and the cheeses and fruits were welcome refreshments. He dared not wonder how Tatiana had obtained the hamper, hoping she had not pilfered from the kitchen without permission. An irate cook might wait for him to add to his issues when he returned to the real world outside the woods.

Eventually, they both knew they could not delay any longer, so Jane tucked the handle of the hamper over her arm while he carried the blanket and they headed back to the manor. Once they reached the edge of the woods, Barclay realized they could not continue together. As relations, they might relax some proprieties, but once a betrothal was announced, their being observed alone together would be cast in a different light.

Taking the hamper from Jane, he bade her to return ahead of him so he might dally in the woods for a while to give her an opportunity to make her way inside alone.

When sufficient time had passed, he began his walk across the gardens. As predicted, reality set in as he approached the manor, and many thoughts clamored to be heard.

What if Richard was angry at this turn of events? The earl had no inkling of their relationship.

What if they were met with disgust or derision? Their age difference was not too extraordinary, but coupled with his status as a by-blow, there were going to be people with thoughts. Some would express them; others would display it in their attitudes.

What if their match horrified Jane's family? They had sent their daughter to have a Season in London. Surely they had hoped she would make a match with a member of the gentry, or perhaps a minor peer. Instead, they would have to settle for an architect for a son-in-law. A successful, renowned architect, but a working man all the same. The field had made great strides over the past couple of decades as a bona fide profession, but it being accepted as a proper profession was slow going and not everyone saw it that way yet.

As he strode past the ornamental hedges and the terrace came into view, Barclay firmly put these thoughts from his mind. As Aurora had advised, the best course was to be united as a family and handle adversity as it presented itself. Avoiding adversity could not be the goal of living. Love, family, and work well done were far better goals. Adversity was simply what one dealt with when and where it could not be avoided, but what truly mattered in life was one's accomplishments, which included the health and success of the family to whom he owed his loyalty and support.

Passing by the majestic oak tree, Barclay saw several guests playing nine-pins, including Mrs. Gordon. He nodded politely, but did not break his stride. It seemed a hundred years since he had played the silly game and had attempted to convince himself he could grow to like it over time. It seemed the height of obnoxious stupidity that he had tried to convince himself to make such an unsuitable match. If Natalya had been here, she would have shaken her head at his asinine behavior and accused him of cowardice.

She would have been right. He had been afraid that if he loved Jane as deeply as he had loved his late wife, he would never recover if he lost her, too. Or caused her unhappiness.

But one could not live one's life in fear. Having the courage to take a risk brought much reward. Loving Natalya had been a privilege he would choose many times over, and he would never regret the life they had shared. Natalya knew her time was more limited than most, but she had had the courage to live her life to the fullest while she had the chance and had appreciated every moment she had walked the earth.

Something he should have paid more mind to since she had slipped into the unknown beyond.

Reaching the terrace, Barclay placed the hamper and blanket by the table of refreshments before heading inside. By now Aurora would have informed the earl that Tatiana was safe, and he hoped he would find his brother in his study so he could press on and discuss the awkward situation they were in.

All too soon, he approached the door of the earl's study, which was ajar. Likely to catch a breeze, as the day was warm enough for the manor to be mildly stuffy.

As he reached the doorway, he heard the Duke of Halmesbury speaking. "I am afraid I will not be available to accompany you to Chatternwell in November because of prior engagements."

"Nor I. I will be too far along for such a journey." It was the countess, sitting near a window with her hand resting on her rounded belly.

Seizing the moment, Barclay rapped his knuckles on the door to announce his arrival. All three occupants in the study started, appearing distracted by something as they turned their heads to find him standing in the doorway.

Richard was the first to react, jumping to his feet to beckon Barclay to enter. "Barclay, Aurora informed us Tatiana is safe and sound. We are very relieved to hear. The duke and the other men just returned from their search not ten minutes ago."

Barclay nodded, entering the room. "I thank you for all you did. I apologize for any inconvenience we caused."

Richard shook his head adamantly. "Not at all. We are here to assist in such matters any time you need us."

Barclay took up a seat across from the duke, the earl resuming his own seat at an angle from where the duke was sitting. Silent for several moments, Barclay considered scheduling a time to talk to Richard later that day. His brother was occupied with something, based on the uncomfortable silence that had descended upon the room after his arrival.

The countess cleared her throat at the window, sitting up. "Barclay, I was wondering … My husband is to visit Chatternwell in November to … survey his local estate. Chatternwell House. We were considering having the manor renovated in preparation for Ethan."

Richard straightened in his chair, his interest piqued. "That is correct. The estate is unentailed, and I am planning to give it to Ethan when he reaches his majority. The manor is quite outdated, so it will need work. Could you accompany me in November to provide me with an estimate? I would be very pleased to have you do the design."

Barclay was mildly suspicious that there was more than had been said, but pulled a notebook from his coat pocket. "What are the dates, so I may consult my schedule?"

"The seventh?"

Barclay reviewed the pages. "I could manage the first week of November if I move another appointment. A few days should be sufficient to travel from London to see the place and make my next engagement the following week."

Richard's face lit up. "That would be wonderful. I am quite excited to learn what we might do with the manor. If it needs significant work, I would like to begin so that it would be ready for Ethan when the time is right."

Barclay nodded. "If the work is minor, it may only take a year or two, but significant building or renovations may take several years to complete. It is best to assess the situation early on."

"I would appreciate it. I want my boy to be well taken care of. The estate itself is prosperous, but the manor has not been occupied in many years. Once we assess the manor, I shall be able to meet with my solicitor to make arrangements for Ethan's future."

Barclay rubbed his palms over his buckskins during the ensuing silence. He was vaguely aware that the others had been interrupted by his arrival and must have been discussing something sensitive. His own needs would have to wait for a little while. "I had another matter to discuss, but I can see you later this afternoon if you could give me an appropriate time?"

Richard shook his head. "No, no. We can talk now. We have settled our other matter for now."

Barclay took a deep breath. "I wish to discuss Jane with you."

"Oh, is this about Dunsford?" Richard's question caught him by surprise—Barclay blinked.

Across from him, the duke smiled benignly, leaning forward to explain in a low voice. "Ridley informed us of the young prat's intentions toward Miss Davis ... and the implied delights of London. We concluded that he will no longer be included on future guest lists."

Barclay sat back in his chair to stare at the cornices. He had never realized it was a nervous trait he had until he arrived at Saunton Park and found himself doing it constantly. "That is ... good news. But no, it is not the topic I had in mind."

He swallowed hard. This was damned awkward, especially after he had been here while the two men had discussed the inquiry from the older lord in London. Lord Lawson, was it? Barclay felt like a green youth as he tried to find the words to declare himself. Not to mention, he had not expected an audience when he did this.

"I think Barclay wishes to discuss a different aspect." He looked over at the countess, who was smiling at him across the room. She kept her stormy blue gaze on Barclay as she addressed her husband, her red-blonde hair lit from behind to form a fiery crown. "I believe Barclay would like to announce his intentions regarding our Jane."

He frowned. How could Sophia know that?

The countess shrugged at the unspoken question. "It did not escape my attention that Jane has seemed quite taken with someone since we reached Saunton Park. I asked my lady's maid, Miss Toussaint, to find out from the servants who had captured her attentions to ensure I approved of the match." She smiled. "I do."

Barclay froze. From the corner of his eye, he noted that Richard's jaw had dropped. Flitting his eyes over to his cousin, he saw the Viking duke was suppressing a smile, pressing his lips together firmly.

"What?"

Sophia rolled her eyes at her husband. "I was just happy she was not besotted with that Adam Dunsford. He is charming, but he struck me as rather shallow from the outset. I needed to be sure she was becoming attached to someone worthwhile."

Richard turned to Barclay. "You and our Jane?"

Barclay grimaced while the countess turned her gaze back to the window, settling back into her seat. "I ... know ... you ... er ... were hoping she would make a match with a younger man, but ... we are quite taken with each other and I wish to offer for her."

Richard shook his head, causing Barclay's stomach to roil in anxiety. His brother was going to refuse his approval? Agitated, he fidgeted with the sleeves of his tailcoat. Then he would visit the Davises to offer for her directly.

"Why do you say I hoped for a younger man? You are hardly ancient."

Barclay released his breath. He had misread the earl's reaction.

"I believe Barclay is thinking of the discussion we had

about Lord Lawson a few days ago." The duke spoke in his baritone, adding solemnity to the moment.

"That? How is that relevant?" Richard appeared genuinely perplexed.

"We discussed Lawson's age and the fact that he had grown daughters." The duke gestured to Barclay. "I think your brother drew conclusions about their similarities."

"They are hardly in the same category. Tatiana is only nine years old, and Barclay is … He is Barclay. He is hardly … old. He is the same age as you, Halmesbury."

Exhaling in relief, Barclay decided he needed to be more his customary assertive self. This had been a hell of a week at Saunton Park, but now it was time to revert to his usual state of decisiveness, which had made him the success he was. "Then you find it acceptable if I offer for her? We have discussed it, and we wish to wed."

Richard stood up to extend his hand to Barclay, which he clasped. With that, his brother hauled him to his feet to embrace him hard. "I would be delighted for Jane to make such a magnificent match. Congratulations, brother!"

While the countess rose to her feet to join them, the duke also stood, leaning over to shake him by his hand. "Congratulations, Barclay. We shall help make arrangements right away."

Sophia came over to clasp him by the upper arms. Reaching up on tiptoe, she pressed a kiss to each of his cheeks. "I am so happy for our Jane. You are a good man, Barclay."

It was at that moment that Barclay realized what he had not yet accepted. His family had grown these past few weeks. It was not the four Thompsons versus the world any longer. He had gained brothers and cousins and in-laws. Adversity would present itself in the future, but he and Jane would have many warm relations to stand by their side as they began their new life together. If Natalya had lived to this day, she would have been overjoyed on his and Tatiana's behalf.

Now all that remained was to meet Jane's parents and ask her father for permission to wed. Barclay swallowed hard, tension forming in his gut at the realization that he still had one more obstacle to overcome.

How were her parents going to feel about Jane marrying a by-blow? Who worked for a living?

Bloody hell, he hoped Mr. Davis was not too close to him in age.

CHAPTER 19

*T*wo afternoons later, Barclay's carriage drew to a halt in front of Saunton Park. Aurora and Jane stretched their limbs across from him, to prepare for disembarking. They had left for Rose Ash Manor the morning after Jane had accepted his offer. There they had spent the day and evening with Jane's rambunctious family.

To be fair, it was her younger twin brothers who were the rambunctious ones. Her parents were convivial, and her youngest brother, Thaddeus, was a studious boy. And little Maddie was a sweet delight who had run through the gardens playing with Tatiana, excited to have a girl visiting who was close to her in age.

Beside him, Tatiana opened her sleepy eyes, having fallen asleep against his shoulder. "Are we back at Saunton Park?"

"Yes, little one. We should find something for you to eat."

She rubbed her flat stomach, which gurgled in response. "I am hungry."

Barclay smiled down at his daughter. It had been some time since she had been so happy and relaxed as she was during their visit to Rose Ash.

233

Mr. Davis had graciously given his approval for the match, and Mrs. Davis had helped Jane to pack up her things in trunks, which were now tied to the carriage. There had been tears of joy, nostalgia over the passage of time, and much laughter as her family had celebrated their impending union. Jane had played lively Irish arias on the pianoforte while her family sang and danced with the Thompsons.

Soon the Davises would arrive at Saunton Park for their second wedding this month. He had sent Tsar an invitation to join them while the duke and the earl had been conspiring to arrange a marriage license during the departure to Rose Ash the day before.

"I am glad Maddie is coming to the wedding. I want to show her the grotto," announced Tatiana.

"With an adult, Tatiana. Do not go down there on your own," warned Barclay.

"Because of the *vodorosli?*"

"Yes, little one. The algae is slippery, and the pond looks deep."

"Will you teach me to swim, Papa? Maddie says she swims at Rose Ash with her brothers, and it embarrassed me to admit I did not know how."

Barclay grinned down at her, chucking her chin as the footman opened the carriage door and lowered the steps. "You have been cooped up in Town for too long if I have not yet taught you to swim. Perhaps we should ask the earl about a suitable swimming hole while we wait for the house party to end and for all our wedding guests to arrive."

Tatiana's eyes shone brightly in the shadows of their vehicle at this news. "Truly?"

"If we are to be discreet, I will join you," Jane interjected.

Barclay smiled across at his betrothed, still in awe of her beauty. He was having trouble with his sleep, not because he was in mourning any longer, but because his dreams were plagued with desire. The desire to take Jane to his bed and lick every lingering trace of strawberry from her creamy skin.

He shook his head and stood to descend the steps before he could allow his imaginings to run wild. Turning around at the foot of the steps, he assisted Tatiana down, then Jane. His mother disembarked last, an expression of contentment relaxing her face.

"Mother?" He held out his hand.

She smiled as she took hold of his hand to climb down. "You have done well, Barclay. I am pleased to welcome the Davises into our lives. Mrs. Davis is a generous woman, to have taken Ethan and his mother in when they were all alone. They weathered scandal for a boy who was not their own. I can think of no better match, and Tatiana will have aunts and uncles and cousins to support her long after we are gone."

"We have certainly extended the size of our family considerably. I am delighted that Tatiana now has relations of her own age."

They turned to watch Jane and Tatiana walking up the steps hand in hand to enter the manor, while the stone sentinels on the roof peered down to guard their progress.

"Perhaps I should have attempted to marry. So you might have had brothers and sisters," Aurora said in a wistful tone.

"Mother, you have done more for me than most in your position. I regret nothing about our lives. As wonderful as it is to unite with the Balfours and the Davises, the Thompsons are a strong family in our own right."

Aurora took his arm and squeezed it gently to express her approval. Then they followed his betrothed and his daughter into the manor.

After parting ways to freshen up after their travels, Jane and Barclay reconvened in the library where Richard was playing his afternoon game of chess with Ethan, while Tatiana observed their play. The duke was sipping a cup of coffee while contemplating the park bathed in late afternoon light and shadows.

Barclay looked back to the door when Aurora entered, her face lit with joy. He shot her a quizzical look as the duchess and the countess arrived behind her. As theirs was a family gathering to discuss the details of the approaching nuptials, the countess shut the door to the hall so that other houseguests would not wander in to interrupt them.

"Oh, Barclay! I have the most tremendous news." His mother paused, tears springing into her eyes and her voice thick with emotion. Holding a hand over her mouth, she gestured to the duchess to speak on her behalf.

"I was telling your mother that the duke and I are involved in charitable endeavors in Halmesbury. A close friend of ours manages a foundling home, The Halmesbury Home for Beloved Children, for which His Grace is the primary patron. We provide a home and schooling. For older children, we facilitate vocational training with honest local businesses to help them explore their options. His Grace and I had discussed creating a similar home in London, and your mother has volunteered to direct it. As an architect, I am sure you possess valuable insight about where we might establish a safe haven."

Aurora was ready to speak. "The Thompson Home for Beloved Children, in honor of your grandmother."

Barclay's hand rose to rest over his heart, which chimed with sheer happiness. He had never thought to assist his mother in creating her own society, rather than suffer the continual rejection of judgmental biddies. It was perfect. His mother would realize her own dream on behalf of the parent who had stood by her side when she had erred. "I will help in any way I can. I know Tsar will be delighted to assist."

236

Sophia spoke up from the seat she had taken near Richard, addressing the duchess. "Annabel, you and the duke are being so formal. I think it is time to relax the formalities."

The duchess chuckled. "It is a force of habit, I am afraid. Please, call me by my Christian name," she said to Barclay.

Halmesbury addressed Aurora from where he stood at the window. "Your agreement to direct the new home is very good news. It was imperative to find a woman with the right character to lead the home. Lady Lewis has a heart of gold, and the skills to manage a household, which is why the home is a success. These days, she has a director to assist her, but she still oversees the home. Miss Tho—" Sophia shot him a look, and the duke corrected himself. "—Aurora, you have the sensitivity to understand the children's needs, which is precisely what we were searching for."

Barclay was very pleased. His mother would fulfill her dreams to make a meaningful contribution. Aurora assisted charitable causes in London but had never acquired sufficient status to be entrusted with the type of role she had yearned for.

With the patronage of the duchess, along with the Thompsons' collective knowledge, the home was sure to flourish. Aurora had been taking care of Tatiana these past two years, but now his daughter would rejoin him on his travels, which would leave his mother with little to do other than manage the Thompson household. A project of this magnitude was an excellent opportunity for her to pursue her passion.

He felt a light touch on his arm, looking down to find that Jane had joined him. "I will help, too, Aurora. Whenever we are in London." Barclay smiled down at her, lifting his other hand to rest it on hers.

Blazes! He needed to spend some time alone with his

betrothed. His loins were demanding it in response to the whiff of strawberries tantalizing his senses.

* * *

JANE HAD SEEN Barclay's passionate glance in the library. And later, when they sat together at dinner, she had observed it again. It caused a quiver in her belly and her blood to heat in response.

Which was why she was not surprised to hear a knock on her bedroom door around midnight. She raced across the room, her feet bare on the rug and wooden flooring, to let him in.

Barclay was exquisite in the low light, framed by the door. He had allowed her to trim his hair before they had left for Rose Ash, and his black waves were now tamed to reveal his tan skin and accentuate his lively brown eyes. He had removed his tailcoat and vest, his linen shirt hanging loose over his breeches and the column of his throat exposed. His feet were bare like hers.

Jane looked back up to find the corners of his eyes creased as he smiled down at her.

She considered herself fortunate to have fallen in love with a man who was several inches taller than her—she liked it because it highlighted their differences. He was tall and hard, while she was willowy and soft against his body.

Jane reached out her hand, which he took, his fingers roughened by work. Pulling him into the room, she shut the door before settling against his chest to laugh up at him while his arms snaked around her to hold her in a firm embrace. "I thought you would never come."

He chuckled. "I could no longer stay away. Unless you wish to wait?"

Jane shook her head. "We are days from being married,

and when we do, the house will be filled with relations under foot. I want my first time with you to be … quieter. More special. I would suggest we go to the grotto, but I do not think it would be very comfortable."

Barclay pulled a face. "For more than one reason, I am afraid. I prefer this. It has been difficult to steer my thoughts away from when I would finally have you to myself. Waiting for your father's acceptance and then sleeping alone in your family home while you were mere steps away …"

She blushed, leaning her forehead against his chest, which emanated heat through the thin white cotton. "I … have thought of you, too," she admitted hoarsely.

Taking her face between his rough palms, he tilted her head back and leaned down for a gentle kiss. Melting warmth spread over her to leave her breathless, her eyelids heavy as they slowly shut so she might revel in his closeness … in his masculinity. Her head bobbed as if she were weary, but it was the opposite. Her body was afire with ambient desire, and she moaned against his mouth. To her delight, he accepted this invitation to slide his tongue between her parted lips and explore her mouth slowly, as if to savor the taste of her.

Tea and mint blended together to awaken her appetite as she kissed him back, matching him move for move until he abruptly pulled away to lean his forehead against hers. Observing he was breathing hard, Jane grinned victoriously. Her man wanted her.

One of his arms came down around her waist, pulling her tightly against his body. Her lids flew open when she felt his hard length pressed against her mound and lower belly. "Oh," she breathed.

Barclay smiled as he tugged her night rail aside to reveal a shoulder and then lowered his head to nip and lick at her clavicle. "You taste like strawberries again."

She giggled. "I am sleeping enough to be making my strawberry water again."

"Then you should always sleep enough," he growled in response as he closed his mouth over her skin once more. Jane was hit with a wave of hot sensation—who knew that a shoulder held such potential? And then thought was impossible when all she could think of was the throbbing desire coursing to pool between her legs.

Jane found the hem of his shirt, sliding her hands beneath to caress his flat abdomen with her fingertips and setting Barclay to shiver and groan as her fingers worked up to explore the shape of his taut chest. "I want to see you," she whispered as his hands traveled down to cup her buttocks.

He inhaled deeply before raising his head to look down at her with hooded eyes. "Go ahead."

Raising his arms up for her, Jane grabbed the edge of the shirt to lift it up. She struggled slightly when she had lifted it up to his forearms, which he lowered so she could tug the garment off the rest of the way. Then she took a half step back to inspect him, hissing in amazement at his strong, lean form. She lifted a hand to trace the corded muscle of his forearm, grazed a hand over his hard chest which was a work of art worthy of a grand master, combed her fingers through the tight, curling hair before tracing down to where the pelt arrowed down, down, down toward the waist of his breeches. Barclay's large hand came up and caught hers when she reached his mid-belly.

"Too soon," was the only explanation he offered before he dropped her hand and lifted her over his shoulder, to her dismay. Crossing the room to her bed, while the side of her buttocks rested against his cheek ignominiously, he carefully laid her out on the sheet. Rising up, he gazed down at her with raw desire, devouring her shape which was covered only by a thin night rail she had sewn from a fashion plate.

His gaze riveted to her breasts, and she looked down to find what had him so fascinated.

Her nipples had puckered into tight buds, jutting against the cotton, and she could make out the color of her areolas through the thin fabric. Barclay bit his lip, and Jane appreciated the power she had as a woman to entice the man she loved to new heights of gratifying lust. He was such a composed individual, a gentleman through and through, so to see him so enthralled by her body was the epitome of validation.

She reached for him with a trembling hand, which Barclay raised to his lips to press a soft kiss to her knuckles, his beard scraping her skin. Lowering her hand, he dropped to his knees beside the bed. From his new vantage point, he ran his long, blunt fingers from her toes ever so slowly up to her ankle, where he took hold of the edge of her rail to gradually raise it. His fingertips continued to trail up the side of her leg, the night rail trapped by his index finger to slide up with his hand until he reached her knee, where he stopped to explore its contours. When his fingertips reached the hitherto unknown sensitive region at the back, she hissed, undulating restlessly on the bed as her center throbbed with longing.

Jane felt the folds of her sex swell, growing slick with her desire, and she moaned with restless energy as Barclay lowered his mouth to graze his teeth against her thigh. His fingertips brushed back up, taking hold of the night rail to continue his path up her leg once more, inch by inch. She was hot and very bothered when he traced over her upper thigh, pausing close to the crease between her thigh and … the … hot … melting … slit between her legs.

Her eyes flew open as he swept a thumb over her cleft, causing her to buck in thrilled surprise and her legs to quiver in enraptured tension. But Barclay's warm hand had already retreated to stroke up and down her inner thigh to tease her body to a melting point. In the light of the oil lamp, Jane's bosom heaved with her mounting passion, drawing Barclay's hooded gaze.

"I wish to see you ... all of you," he rasped in a low voice, which sent shivers down her spine. Jane scrambled to her knees, facing him, her night rail bunched at her thighs, which he took as the invitation it was. His large hands took hold of the hem and lifted, and lifted and lifted until suddenly the last of the garment whipped from her arms and she was before him without a stitch of clothing to veil her from his regard.

Barclay's breathing frayed with the strength of his lust while he drank her in from knee to breast, him on his knees on the floor in a pose of worship. He reached out a calloused hand to cup one of her rounded breasts, growling as he gently caressed the orb, which looked like ivory in contrast to his deeply tanned skin. Jane delighted in the feel of his roughness against her softness, mewling below her breath as he brought up a second hand to cup and lift the other breast. His mouth came down to cover her nipple in a wet, hot velvet lick. "Strawberries," he groaned.

Jane giggled. She knew of his fondness and had daubed it everywhere she could think of when she had freshened up for dinner earlier. He lifted his head in query before his lips curled in response. "You did it on purpose?"

She screwed her face and grinned.

"Everywhere?"

Jane blushed before nodding. "Everywhere."

He shut his lids as if to pray, then lowered his mouth once more to swirl her tight bud. Jane moaned, her head dropping back as he caressed and licked both breasts. Barclay lowered her back on the bed and continued to press kisses, moving down to her belly to make her core ache for him. His hand glided down until he cupped her mons. Her hips bucked in reaction to his touch, while his mouth came up to cover hers in a deep kiss.

Slowly, he parted her folds with a blunt fingertip to explore, and Jane was overtaken, her intimate muscles clenching with yearning as he brushed over the sensitive nub at the apex. All the while, Barclay kissed her, muffling her moans as sensation rocked through her. Rising, rising, rising until she keened at the fiery climactic event, hot sensation washing over her in waves.

Barclay lifted his head from the deep, drugging kiss. Rising to his feet, his hands went to the buttons of his falls. Jane watched in fascination, his body bronzed by the low light, as he slowly revealed the hard length he had pressed against her earlier.

A frisson of anxiety coiled in her belly when she saw the size of the appendage. She knew what to expect. Her mother had discussed it with her at Rose Ash the night before. Jane had not quite understood the physics of it then, and Barclay's proud shaft looked a little large to …

He returned to the bed, gently lowering his body over hers, nudging her legs apart with a knee and holding himself up with his forearms to peer down at her hungrily. Leaning down, he once more took her mouth in a kiss, while slowly brushing his length over her slick center. To her surprise, her desire mounted once more and her hips rolled up in invitation.

"I will be gentle, but this first time—"

"I know. Mama warned me."

Barclay groaned. "I do not wish to think of your parents at this moment, so I will pretend I did not hear that."

Jane chuckled before lifting her head to kiss him once more. With that, Barclay accepted her kiss, nudging his length against her slick opening. When he slid inside her,

Jane felt a sharp pain. Hearing her gasp, he stilled, waiting patiently. Slowly, she grew accustomed to his thickness, until carefully raising her hips to encourage him.

Barclay slid forward inch by inch until he was sheathed, his head thrust back in his effort to restrain his passion while he panted his lust. Jane rolled her hips once more, and Barclay understood her silent request. He gently withdrew to thrust back inside of her, and Jane grew ensnared by the glorious pulsating motion, losing all thought as she focused on feeling. Feeling him, feeling the heat of his body, the strength of his muscled limbs, the roughness of his legs, covered in short, coarse hairs, scraping against hers.

Then he reached between them to tease her nub once more, and light exploded in every direction as she was overtaken once more. Barclay followed her to the peak, groaning aloud as he thrummed, his warmth spreading inside her.

He collapsed onto his forearms, holding himself up but spent. After a few moments, he opened his blazing eyes to kiss her gently on the lips. "I … love you, Jane."

Jane beamed with sheer joy. "I love you, too."

* * *

BARCLAY CLEANED her and then himself, before returning to the bed to hold his soft Jane against his body, listening to her breathe as she fell asleep in his arms.

It was strange to be lying with a woman in bed once more. He had always been assiduous about whom he bedded. Apprehensive of consequences might explain it, but more than that, he preferred the act of lovemaking to be with someone special. Someone of deep affection. As such, this was the first time he had made love since Natalya's passing.

Then, too, he had always been exceedingly cautious because of Natalya's weak heart. It had been a necessity, both of them aware of the need to prolong her life as long as possible.

He was not sure if it was traitorous to be relieved that this was no longer a fear he would need to live with, Jane being a strong young woman with no health issues other than her recent bout of insomnia.

His time with Natalya would always be treasured, a part of who he was. But this new life with Jane would be different. He could plan on a future with her. They could grow old together, and it was such an intense joy to open this new chapter of his life.

Knowing he would not sleep, he closed his eyes to savor her presence before he left her for the night.

When Barclay opened his eyes, it was first light. His pulse quickened. He had slept for several hours and now he could be caught in Jane's bed!

He withdrew the arm wrapped around her, causing Jane to protest in her sleep. Gently rising from the bed, he quickly drew on his breeches and shirt. The servants could arrive at any moment, or even be in the hall. Quickly, he raced across the room. Leaning his head against the door, he listened for any sign of activity, before slowly opening the door. He looked from right to left, but the hall was empty, so he exited the room and quietly closed the door behind him.

"Papa?"

Barclay was certain he jumped ten feet in the air. Looking down, he found Tatiana sitting near his feet, leaning against the wall. There was no other word for it—he blushed. He blushed like a little girl to be caught departing the scene of carnal relations, mortified that his daughter had caught him.

Leaning down, he lifted her up and quickly made for the door of his own room, lest others come upon them and notice what he had been up to. Once he reached his room, he carried Tatiana over to the sofa to put her down. Taking up a seat next to her, he sought for something to explain what she had seen.

"What were you doing, little one?"

"I was waiting for you. Mama said if you were alone in a room with Jane, I must wait so I do not find you doing *zrelyy* things together."

Barclay shook his head, still waking up from the unexpected slumber. Again, Tatiana was using a word he did not think she knew. "*Zrelyy?*"

"That is what she said. What does *zrelyy* mean, Papa?"

Barclay lifted a hand to rake it through his hair. Could it be that Natalya had somehow spoken to their daughter? "Mature. It means adult. About your mother—"

"She came to say goodbye. Mama said that Jane is my mother now, so I must be a good girl and listen to her. I was happy for Mama but sad that she is gone. That is why I was looking for you. I ... I wanted a hug."

"Oh, little one." Barclay pulled Tatiana onto his lap to embrace her. "If I am alone with Jane, and you need me, you can knock on the door. I will always be here for you."

"Mama told me that if I leave you alone, I might get a brother or sister soon. She said she would like that very much, if I had brothers and sisters like she had in St. Petersburg."

These concepts were too *zrelyy* for a nine-year-old child. Barclay did not know what to say, so he held his daughter tight and wondered if all those nocturnal discussions with Natalya the past two years had been mere conjurings of his imagination. Or something else?

No, it was far more likely that Tatiana had dredged up memories during her vivid dreams due to all the excitement of the past week.

He supposed it did not signify, because he, Jane, and Tatiana were a family now. His sleep had returned, and they would live long and happy. If Natalya had been visiting in truth, she was now free to start the next chapter in her journey, no longer trapped here by her concern for them.

Barclay pressed a kiss to Tatiana's silver-blonde hair. "Are you happy, little one? About Jane and me?"

"Very," she mumbled against his chest. Soon she dozed off in his arms, and Barclay lifted her carefully and carried her to his bed to lay her down, pulling the coverlet over her before using a screen to block off the washstand from her view so he could start preparing for his day.

EPILOGUE

*T*he Thompson carriage passed through the gates of Chatternwell House, starting up the long tree-lined avenue bedecked with the colors of autumn.

Barclay folded up his designs for one of his current commissions, putting them away. Across from him, Jane scribbled with a pencil in her notebook. The duke had introduced her to a writer friend of his, Lord John Pettigrew. She was now compiling her first volume of poetry and regularly corresponded with Pettigrew who was mentoring her.

But, to his unapologetic satisfaction, Barclay was the first to hear any new poetry she composed. She was, after all, *his* bride.

Tatiana raised her head from the book she was buried in, noting that they were arriving at their destination. His daughter was learning some basic Russian along with Jane in preparation for a trip they planned the following year to St. Petersburg. It was high time Tatiana was reacquainted with

248

her Russian relations whom they had not visited since she was a babe.

The three of them conversed in Russian each evening over their supper, and he was pleased with her progress. Tatiana had an excellent ear for the pronunciation, and her maternal grandfather would be pleased because he spoke only a smattering of broken English.

Now that Barclay's daughter had rejoined him on his journeys around England, he schooled her once more. Jane gave her lessons in the mornings, but he was able to frequently take Tatiana to his building sites to educate her on architecture and art.

Jane closed her notebook. "Remind me where we are?"

"Chatternwell in Wiltshire. We are quite close to the town of Bath, which is northwest of here."

"How exciting! I have passed through Wiltshire, but never visited."

Barclay smiled. He was pleased with how much Jane and Tatiana loved to travel with him to see new places and meet new people. It was far more pleasurable to travel with his family than the solitary existence he had lived after Natalya had departed. He had commissioned a second carriage for when their family grew, and Tsar was in discussion with John Soane to hire gifted new architects from the Royal Academy to reduce Barclay's travel in future periods when Jane could not travel.

"I suspect Richard has a hidden agenda for this visit. However, the building commission itself is genuine."

Jane peered out the carriage window at the passing trees. "I wonder if it has something to do with his quest to make amends."

Barclay frowned. He had forgotten all about the strange conversation in the billiard room months earlier when Lord Trafford had mentioned something to that effect.

There had been so much occurring at the time, it had slipped his mind to question his brother about the oblique comment.

"Amends?"

The carriage drew to a halt in front of a small Tudor manor, and once again the subject was forgotten when the footman came to the door to lower the steps. As they descended, Barclay's new clerk of work joined them.

Marcus was an erudite young man who had a tendency to become queasy in carriages, so he preferred to ride with the coachman. This suited Barclay fine, because he could spend the time alone with his family.

The front doors opened, and Richard came bounding out to join them. "Barclay, Jane! And little Tatiana! Welcome to Chatternwell House." The earl swung his arms out to gesture at the building behind him.

Barclay looked up at the facade, assessing the age and condition before heading over to the front doors to crane his head back and forth to assess the condition of the walls, examining them with his hands. Marcus joined him, a flaxen curl falling into his eyes, which he flicked back with a slender hand. They debated what they thought while Richard conversed with Jane and Tatiana, lifting the little girl off her feet in an effusive embrace.

Barclay and Marcus entered the manor without invitation to inspect the building and foundations, all else forgotten as they explored while Marcus took notes.

A couple of hours later, Barclay found Richard drinking tea with Jane in a clean but worn drawing room. The room was drab, with old furnishings and faded drapes. Barclay imagined what it would look like with a lighter color palette and rich fabrics hanging in the windows, his professional eye engaged.

Jane smiled at his arrival. "Barclay, there you are. Tatiana went to take a nap after we arrived, so she is in her room upstairs. Have you had a chance to freshen up?"

He shook his head. Walking over, he lifted her hand to press a kiss to her knuckles. "I wanted to find you first. I ran off so abruptly."

She laughed, looking beautiful in the afternoon light bathing the room. "I am not offended. Richard was telling me about a local modiste who is holding an event tomorrow to celebrate the opening of her new shop."

Barclay took a seat, noticing that the earl was tugging at his cravat. His eyes narrowed in suspicion. He had long since noted that Richard fiddled with his knot when he was nervous. There was more to this visit than the condition of Chatternwell House.

An hour later, he cornered Richard in the manor library. "There is more to this visit than you have disclosed."

Richard's hand rose to loosen his cravat, confirming Barclay's accusation. "It is deuced awkward to speak to … you … about this particular matter."

Barclay cocked his head in question.

"Because of your history. Of what our father did to … your mother."

Remaining silent, Barclay waited.

"Very well. I used to be a glib arse. A rogue. Earlier this year, I realized the error of my ways. As a result, I sought the women from my past whom I had wronged … the ones I felt I had seduced into doing things beyond their experience. I needed to rectify any damage I may have done. It was how I learned of Ethan. Which led me to search out any brothers or sisters whom our father had abandoned to their fate."

"I see. I suppose I had an inkling, considering I am aware of Ethan."

Richard broke eye contact to stare at his boots, his legs stretched out in front of him despite the agitated movement of his hands while he explained. "I have made amends to all the women I felt culpable for. One of the young women has a situation that is more complex, so I am here to fulfill part of my obligations."

"The countess is aware, I assume. Considering it was her idea that I come to Chatternwell?"

"Sophia is aware of everything. She wanted to accompany me but, given her condition, it seemed unnecessarily trying for her to make the journey. Then, too, she is chaperoning Isabelle."

Barclay nodded. Their family had grown even larger when the earl had recently uncovered a young sister living in Saunton, whom he was now hosting. "Why is this situation complex?"

Richard jumped to his feet, walking over to the window to stare sightlessly into the gardens. "Are you aware I was once betrothed to Annabel?"

"The duchess?" Barclay exclaimed.

"Caroline Brown was a maid in her father's home whom I seduced."

"During the betrothal?"

The earl flushed, his ears reddened, and he did not deny Barclay's assumption. "Mrs. Brown was to receive a loan from Annabel, from her pin money once we were wed, to buy a shop ... which obviously went by the boards when the duchess caught us together."

Barclay choked, coughing as he sat up suddenly to soothe his throat. Fortunately, he had not been standing at this news, for he might have fallen over with the shock of it.

"And the duchess tolerates you after finding you *in flagrante delicto*?"

Richard blew a sharp breath. "Not at first. She eventually forgave my behavior once she heard of the amends I had made. To Mrs. Brown included. Which is why you are here.

Tomorrow Mrs. Brown is holding an event to celebrate the shop I loaned her the funds for, and I am to show my support to help launch her new business. During our house party, the duke advised I needed to attend in the role of a family man lest I raise suspicion regarding our former liaisons. I must be seen as a patron rather than a former paramour to protect Mrs. Brown from scandal."

"And is she ... a paramour?" Barclay hated to ask, but he needed to know the character of the woman before he exposed his wife and daughter to what might be an unsavory element.

Richard exhaled. "The young woman was rather innocent when I seduced her, so I would say she is a good woman who made a mistake by dallying with the wrong man. She deserves the assistance, and the duke accompanied me to Chatternwell to make the arrangements during the house party but was not available to return at this time. Instead of accepting charity, Mrs. Brown merely requested that I lend her the funds that Annabel would have done."

"Hmm ..." Barclay considered his options. "I would plant you a facer, but you have already borne the consequences of your misdeeds to correct the situation, so ..." Barclay raked a hand through his hair, before reaching a decision. "Jane and Tatiana will each be delighted to order a new gown. They have both recently complained that they needed a wardrobe more suitable for traveling, and we shall be here for a few days, so there should be sufficient time."

"I shall pay for the gowns."

"That is unnecessary."

"It is a gift. And I can escort them to the fittings while you assess the manor."

Barclay realized this was important to his brother, who had brought him together with his charming new bride.

Richard had also brought Aurora and the duchess together, to his mother's eternal happiness. So he relented.

"Agreed."

* * *

JANE ENTERED Mrs. Brown's Elegant Millinery and Dress-Rooms, on Market Street in Chatternwell, she and Tatiana excited to see a display of gloves and scarves by the window set out on walnut countertops.

Bolts of fabric were fitted into neat cubbies painted in ivory, alongside drawers that soared up the walls to the very ceiling. There was an explosion of colorful silks, velvets, cottons, and tulle to be seen in the morning light. Jane's eyes settled on the corner cabinet to marvel over an exquisite gown displayed within the walnut framework.

This was a very fine shop, and Jane was excited to leaf through fashion plates to find the newest in carriage dresses.

The proprietress was elegantly attired in a day gown of a rich mulberry which offset her wheat-colored hair and hazel eyes. Mrs. Brown left two older women to inspect silks, walking over to greet the earl and sinking into a deep curtsy. "My lord, I am honored to receive you."

Richard gave a small bow of acknowledgment. "Mrs. Brown, I wish to present Mr. Barclay Thompson." The earl had informed them during the drive to the shop that Mrs. Brown was yet unmarried but had earned the honorific when she was promoted to the role of housekeeper in a doctor's household the year before and had retained it to open her shop.

Barclay bowed, tall and dapper in his new burgundy tailcoat and buckskins, to greet the young woman. "A pleasure, Mrs. Brown," he said in that low, husky voice that still sent darting shivers of delight along the surface of Jane's skin.

The earl then turned to Jane, who was holding Tatiana by the hand. "Mrs. Thompson, Miss Tatiana, may I present Mrs. Brown? She is the owner of this fine establishment."

The young woman turned and curtsied once more to her and Tatiana.

Jane thrilled—she was still to grow accustomed to being introduced as Mrs. Thompson, but she loved the sound of it each time. She was married to Barclay Thompson, renowned architect, and she was pursuing her writing as Emma had recommended. They traveled together, seeing England, and she spent time with Tatiana, who was a child with intelligent thoughts and aspirations.

Beaming at the woman, Jane complimented her on the fine establishment and informed her that she and Tatiana were there to order carriage dresses. *Our first time ordering clothes together!*

Mrs. Brown cheerfully bid them to join her at a counter to view fashion plates. Jane was soon impressed with the shop owner's overall demeanor and knowledge of fashion this far from Town. The modiste had just returned from London and clearly made a study of the latest periodicals on the subject, and Jane admired the courage Mrs. Brown must possess to be running a business as a single woman in a new town.

Barclay and the earl wandered the shop, stopping to chat with the other patrons who were agog to be amidst such a noble visitation. Jane paid no mind, pointing to a velvet creation depicted on one of the plates, and Mrs. Brown agreed it would be quite becoming, suggesting a deep blue swath with a short, thick pile she had on a shelf nearby. Jane concurred and was delighted she would visit the shop for a fitting. Fashion plates were a pastime for Jane, who had sewn many gowns for herself, so she enjoyed conversing with someone who had pursued a trade in it.

The shop was a cave of treasures for the modiste residing in her heart.

Once Tatiana went to be measured, Jane turned to find Barclay gazing out the window at the quaint buildings clustered on the street, including a post office across the road. He cut a dashing figure in his buckskins and burgundy tailcoat, his Hessians shining with fresh polish.

"It is a beautiful town," she said, as she wove her arm through his.

Barclay turned his head, his warm eyes tracing over her face with affection. "Not as beautiful as you, my love."

Glancing about to ensure no one was paying them mind, Jane reached up to buss Barclay on the cheek, causing him to grin and pull her closer against his body with the arm she clung to. Leaning in, he whispered into her ear, "I am going to lick every drop of strawberry water from your skin the moment I get you alone."

Jane grinned in response. "There is a small hothouse at Chatternwell House, so I took the liberty of picking the strawberries."

His only reply was a low growl, his eyes vivid with affirming hunger.

Jane sighed in sheer happiness, leaning her head on his shoulder and scarcely able to believe that she was living the perfect life that Emma had suggested just months ago. She loved visiting towns such as this one with Barclay and seeing all their realm had to offer. But more than that, she loved traveling with him and Tatiana and wanted every young lady to find their perfect partner, including the pretty Mrs. Brown.

The modiste was obviously excited about her new shop, but she had an air of reserve about her that spoke to a possible mistrust of people. It made Jane's poetic heart ache on the woman's behalf, wishing she could share the happiness that Jane, Barclay, and Tatiana had found together.

"Are you looking forward to the holidays?" The low timbre of Barclay's voice caressed down her neck, interrupting her musings. Jane beamed, nodding.

She could not wait for all their families to unite at Saunton Park for a festive house party in a matter of weeks. Aurora and Tsar would journey with them to Somerset. Emma and Perry had confirmed their attendance, and the Davises would be coming, too, which meant Tatiana would have an opportunity to spend time with little Maddie.

It promised to be a joyous holiday season shared with many loved ones and her first as a married woman with a family of her own. "It is going to be a wonderful Christmas."

* * *

Learn if spending Christmas with William Jackson, the injured blacksmith from down the street, can help Caroline Brown toss her reservations away and seize her chance at true love, in _Caroline Saves the Blacksmith_.

AFTERWORD

While wrapping up *The Duke Wins a Bride* last year, I hit a patch of insomnia. When I say a patch, I mean three to four months of relentless nights of barely any sleep. Still working as the manager of a sales coaching team at the time, I pasted a smile on my exhausted face, and a cheerful inflection in my voice, to start a sales meeting every morning with a team of forty to fifty people looking at me with expectant eyes.

Part of that particular job was to be upbeat and inspire the team, but I will confess by the time I made it to my desk the smile would fall as I slumped into the only thing to provide relief—my morning coffee.

Right around the time I considered becoming an extra on the set of *The Walking Dead*, I learned I had developed a caffeine intolerance. Thus, my love affair with coffee spanning three decades came to an abrupt end.

I switched to decaf espresso and sleep slowly trickled back.

Later that year, when Mr. Jarrett and I discussed the idea for *Sleepless in Saunton*, you can figure out how I came up with the inspiration for why Jane was not sleeping.

But that is all coffee under the bridge, ha ha, and I now enjoy my Lavazza decaf espresso every morning without fail.

Aladdin was first published in 1710 and adapted into a play which was performed at Drury Lane in 1788.

The letter from the *London Virtuous Committee of Charitable Endeavors* rejecting Aurora's application paraphrases a passage from Fordyce's *Sermons to Young Women*.

Strawberry water is based on a Regency recipe from 1820, using well-ripened strawberries. It was used to soften and whiten the skin, and it had to be made fresh so it did not turn sour overnight (no refrigerators).

The dental elixir was created by a Parisian dentist, M. Leroy-de-la-Faudignières. He used the ingredients mentioned by Jane when Tatiana questions her about it. Sophia's lady's maid, being French, would have known of this excellent mixture to support oral hygiene.

Did women play cricket in the Regency?

The first recorded all-women's match was reported in the *Reading Mercury* in 1746, *"between eleven maids of Bramley and eleven maids of Hambledon, all dressed in white."*

The Hambledon team won.

In 1799, the Countess of Derby personally played in a match she organized at The Oaks, her home in Surrey.

Later, in 1811, *Sporting Magazine* reported on a match between Hampshire and Surrey women, which is mentioned by the earl in the library when he collects his son for their afternoon of bat and ball.

"The ground, which is spacious, was enlivened with marquees and booths, well supplied with gin, beer, and gingerbread. The performers in this contest were of all ages and sizes, from fourteen to sixty; the young had shawls, and the old, long cloaks. The Hampshire were distinguished by the colour of true blue, which was pinned in their bonnets in the shape of the Prince's plume. The

Surrey was equally as smart: their colours were blue, surmounted with orange. They consisted of eleven on each side."

Ethan's obsession with chess is an homage to my late (and favorite) uncle who started beating adults in matches at the age of four, being something of a genius. My father would tell me about it often, when he played chess with me as a young child.

Loyalty is very important to me personally, a trait I admire immensely. It takes strength and courage to demonstrate it, and I enjoyed writing about how Aurora and her parents forwent reputation and appearances in favor of family commitment.

In Barclay's attempts to do right by his family, he had to rediscover that genuine connections with genuine people are far more valuable than worrying about other people's opinions.

Jane had to find her direction and confidence in her own abilities so she might believe in herself to pursue her dreams.

Fortunately, Tatiana is a meddling little imp who helps bring them together when their inhibitions get in the way of what they really want.

Together, in times of trouble, a family standing together is stronger than an individual standing on his own. Family, old or new, is what brings the color and joy to life.

The *Inconvenient Brides* series continues when Caroline Brown, the maid who infamously dallied with the Earl of Saunton, reluctantly nurses the brooding blacksmith on Christmas Eve at the local doctor's request.

She may want to avoid men altogether now that she has the shop she always dreamed of, but fate has other ideas when she is forced to spend the holidays with the gruff tradesman from down the street.

Discover if the spirit of the festive season will help Caroline forgive herself for betraying a dear friend, while a haunted William Jackson struggles to overcome the demons of his past.

Can these two wounded souls help each other heal? Find out in *Caroline Saves the Blacksmith* if she will become the newest Inconvenient Bride.

DOWNLOAD TWO FREE BOOKS!

FREE GIFTS FOR SUBSCRIBERS:
Two captivating prequel novellas by Nina Jarrett full of
unrequited feelings and steamy romance.

**A writer for fighting for his muse. A captain returned
from war, searching for his wife.
Two delightful novellas about the power of true love.**

* * *

London, 1818. Dinah Honeyfield can't wait any longer. In
love with her family's long-term houseguest, she's
determined to get him to reveal his affections before her rich
industrialist father marries her off.
Lord John Pettigrew gave up his birthright to follow his
dreams. And with nothing to offer a potential wife, the
aspiring author despairs he'll never be able to win the hand
of the one who's been his muse.

Can they rewrite their future and plot a path to forever?

* * *

Mrs. Lydia Lewis has given up on broken promises.
Marrying her soulmate only to be attacked during his
heartbreaking absence, she finds refuge as an incognito ducal
housekeeper.
Captain Jacob Lewis is angry and hurt. Returning from
military service to discover his spouse has vanished into thin
air, he begins an almost hopeless search to bring her home.
Can this star-crossed pair reclaim newlywed bliss?

* * *

Interview With the Duke and *The Captain's Wife* are the
delightful prequels to the Inconvenient Brides Regency
romance series. If you like worthy heroes, fast-paced plots,
and enduring connections, then you'll adore Nina Jarrett's
charming collection.

**Subscribe for instant access to these twin tales of passion:
NinaJarrett.com/free**

ABOUT THE AUTHOR

Nina started writing her own stories in elementary school but got distracted when she finished school and moved on to non profit work with recovering drug addicts. There she worked with people from every walk of life from privileged neighborhoods to the shanty towns of urban and rural South Africa.

One day she met a real life romantic hero. She instantly married her fellow bibliophile and moved to the USA where she enjoys a career as a sales coaching executive at an Inc 500 company. She lives with her husband on the Florida Gulf Coast.

Nina believes in kindness and the indomitable power of the human spirit. She is fascinated by the amazing, funny people she has met across the world who dared to change their lives. She likes to tell mischievous tales of life-changing decisions and character transformations while drinking excellent coffee and avoiding cookies.

ALSO BY NINA JARRETT

INCONVENIENT BRIDES

Book 1: The Duke Wins a Bride

Book 2: To Redeem an Earl

Book 3: My Fair Bluestocking

Book 4: Sleepless in Saunton

Book 5: Caroline Saves the Blacksmith

INCONVENIENT SCANDALS

The Duke and Duchess of Halmesbury will return, along with the
Balfour family, in an all-new suspense romance series.

Book 1: Long Live the Baron

Book 2: Moonlight Encounter

Book 3: Lord Trafford's Folly

Book 4: Confessions of an Arrogant Lord

Book 5: The Replacement Heir

THE DUKE WINS A BRIDE: BOOK 1

**Her betrothed cheated on her. The duke offers to save her. Can a
marriage of convenience turn into true love?**

In this steamy historical romance, a sheltered baron's daughter and
a celebrated duke agree on a marriage of convenience, but he has a
secret that may ruin it all.

She is desperate to escape ...

When Miss Annabel Ridley learns her betrothed has been unfaithful, she knows she must cancel the wedding. The problem is no one else seems to agree with her, least of all her father. With her wedding day approaching, she must find a way to escape her doomed marriage. She seeks out the Duke of Halmesbury to request he intercede with her rakish betrothed to break it off before the wedding day.

He is ready to try again ...

Widower Philip Markham has decided it is time to search for a new wife. He hopes to find a bold bride to avoid the mistakes of his past. Fate seems to be favoring him when he finds a captivating young woman in his study begging for his help to disengage from a despised figure from his past. He astonishes her with a proposal of his own—a marriage of convenience to suit them both. If she accepts, he resolves to never reveal the truth of his past lest it ruin their chances of possibly finding love.

Buy *The Duke Wins a Bride* on Amazon or major bookstores.

* * *

TO REDEEM AN EARL: BOOK 2

A cynical debutante and a scandalous earl find themselves entangled in an undeniable attraction. Will they open their hearts to love or will his past destroy their future together?

She has vowed she will never marry...

Miss Sophia Hayward knows all about men and their immoral behavior. She has watched her father and older brother behave like reckless fools her entire life. All she wants is to avoid marriage to a lord until she reaches her majority because she has plans which do not include a husband. Until she meets the one peer who will not take a hint.

He must have her...

Lord Richard Balfour has engaged in many disgraceful activities with the women of his past. He had no regrets until he encounters a cheeky debutante who makes him want to be a better man. Only problem is, he has a lot of bad behavior to make amends for if he is ever going to persuade Sophia to take him seriously. Will he learn to be a better man before his mistakes catch up with him and ruin their chance at true love?

Buy To Redeem an Earl in the Amazon or major bookstores.

* * *

MY FAIR BLUESTOCKING: BOOK 3

A young woman who cares little about high society or its fashions. A spoilt lord who cares too much. Will they give in to their unexpected attraction to reveal a deep and enduring passion?

She thinks he is arrogant and vain ...

The Davis family has ascended to the gentry due to their unusual connection to the Earl of Saunton. Now the earl wants Emma Davis and her sister to come to London for the Season. Emma relishes refusing, but her sister is excited to meet eligible gentlemen. Now she can't tell the earl's arrogant brother to go to hell when he shows up with the invitation. She will cooperate for her beloved sibling, but she is not allowing the handsome Perry to sway her mind ... or her heart.

He thinks she is uncouth, but intriguing ...

Peregrine Balfour cannot believe the errands his brother is making him do. Fetching a country mouse. Preparing her for polite society. Dancing lessons. He should be stealing into the beds of welcoming widows, not delivering finishing lessons to an unstylish shrew. Pity he can't help noticing the ravishing young woman that is being revealed by his tuition until the only schooling he wants to deliver is in the language of love.

Will these two conflicting personalities find a way to reconcile their unexpected attraction before Perry makes a grave mistake?

My Fair Bluestocking is the delightful next chapter in the Inconvenient Brides Regency romance series. If you like worthy heroes, fast-paced plots, and enduring connections, then you'll adore Nina Jarrett's charming novel.

Buy My Fair Bluestocking on Amazon or major bookstores.

* * *

BOOK 5: CAROLINE SAVES THE BLACKSMITH

A fallen woman. A tortured blacksmith. When the holidays force them together, can they mend their broken hearts?

She has a dark past that she must keep a secret. He has a dark past he wishes to forget. The magic of the festive season might be the key to unlocking a fiery new passion.

She will not repeat her past mistakes ...

Caroline Brown once made an unforgivable mistake with a handsome earl, betraying a beloved friend in the process. Now she is rebuilding her life as the new owner of a dressmaker's shop in the busy town of Chatternwell. She is determined to guard her heart from all men, including the darkly handsome blacksmith, until the local doctor requests her help on the night before Christmas.

He can't stop thinking about her ...

William Jackson has avoided relationships since his battle wounds healed, but the new proprietress on his street is increasingly in his thoughts, which is why he is avoiding her at all costs. But an unexpected injury lays him up on Christmas Eve and now the chit is mothering him in the most irritating and delightful manner.

Can the magic of the holiday season help two broken souls overcome their dark pasts to form a blissful union?

Can be read as a standalone book or as part of the Inconvenient Brides series of Regency romance books. Order on Amazon or major bookstores.

Printed by Amazon Italia Logistica S.r.l.
Torrazza Piemonte (TO), Italy

54204704R00159